GUNSIGHT RANGE

(Allan) William Colt MacDonald was born in Detroit, Michigan in 1891. His formal education concluded after his first three months of high school when he went to work as a lathe operator for Dodge Brothers' Motor Company. His first commercial writing consisted of advertising copy and articles for trade publications. While working in the advertising industry, MacDonald began contributing stories of varying lengths to pulp magazines and his first novel, a Western story, was published by Clayton House in *Ace-high Magazine* in 1925. MacDonald later commented that when this first novel appeared in book form as *Restless Guns* in 1929, 'I quit my job cold.' From the time of that decision on, MacDonald's career became a long string of successes in pulp magazines, hardcover books, films, and eventually original and reprint paperback editions. The Three Mesquiteers, MacDonald's most famous characters, were introduced in 1933 in *Law of the Forty-fives*. His other most famous character creation was Gregory Quist, a railroad detective. Some of MacDonald's finest work occurs outside his series, especially the well researched *Stir Up The Dust* which was published first in a British edition in 1950 and *The Mad Marshal* in 1958. MacDonald's only son, Wallace, recalled how much fun his father had writing Western fiction. It is an apt observation since countless readers have enjoyed his stories now for nearly three quarters of a century.

GUNSIGHT RANGE

William Colt MacDonald

GUNSMOKE

First published in the UK by Hodder and Stoughton

This hardback edition 2010
by BBC Audiobooks Ltd
by arrangement with
Golden West Literary Agency

ISBN 978 1 408 46264 5

British L... ...able.

Printed and bound in Great Britain by
CPI Antony Rowe, Chippenham and Eastbourne

CONTENTS

Chapter I : POWDERSMOKE

The bottle, Nash Canfield realized rather abruptly, during one of his more lucid moments, was already more than two-thirds empty. He glanced suspiciously over his shoulder, half expecting to discover some thief who had been filching drinks on the sly, but there was no one else in the big shadowed room of the Terrapin Ranch house. Dusk light entered but faintly through long windows. The front entrance door was tightly closed; in the opposite wall of the room a door leading to an inner hall stood slightly ajar. Navajo rugs covered the floor. There were a few pictures; the furniture was comfortable.

Canfield twisted in his leather-upholstered chair, his blood-shot gaze returning to the bottle on the table at his elbow. What the devil! He'd had only a couple of drinks. Or had it been more? Whose business was it, anyway, how much he drank? Sudden anger surged through him as, with shaking hand, he managed to refill his glass. He downed the liquor at a gulp and slumped back in his chair, muttering "Whose business is it, anyway?" Not Tracy's certainly, Canfield told himself. Tracy was definitely through with him. She'd made matters very clear to him a long time ago. Anyway, the bottle hadn't been full when he started. Another thought penetrated his stupefied brain: just when had he started drinking, this time? Two days ago? Three? With an effort he pieced together the events of the present day. Scenes as viewed through a foggy haze followed one another in a slow and confusing manner. Taken all in all, Canfield told himself, it was damn' bewildering. He strove to concentrate. This morning—or was it this morning various things had started to happen? He glanced toward the nearest window. It was growing dark now. Yes, it must have been this morning when he'd been so rudely awakened. Oh, Lord! With a head on him the size of a rain barrel and a taste in his mouth like the hoof parings from a blacksmith shop. Canfield shuddered, and stretched a wavering hand for another drink.

Thought momentarily came clearer. It would be night before long. He'd better light the lamp. He groped on the table for the lamp but failed to locate it. Damn' funny how he could find that bottle every—*hic!*—time, but the lamp eluded him. To hell with the lamp—and with Tracy and the Terrapin. Where was Tracy? A cold, relentless woman, that's what Tracy was. Rousing him out of bed when his head was split wide open, with little imps carrying tongs running in and out of it and pounding with sledge hammers. Her and her nagging about the crew's pay being three days overdue, and her insistence they had to be paid today. And the look on her face like she hated the ground he walked on. Canfield cursed resentfully. By God, he'd show her a thing or two yet.

The scene shifted suddenly and he saw himself in the saddle, heading for town, with a thousand devils pounding at his skull at each jolt of the horse's hoofs and a thirst on him that only whisky could slake. And next he'd found himself in the El Toro Saloon, and pretty soon the headache had vanished and he began to feel good. And then there was another bar (he couldn't remember leaving the El Toro) and another and another. By God! if he hadn't made every bar, right through town, until he came to John Calydon's place. It was while John was trying to tell him he already had had enough to drink that Canfield had suddenly found Tom Jenkins at his shoulder, and Tom saying something about Mrs. Canfield sending him in to make sure Nash drew the crew's wages from the bank before it closed. S'funny, he couldn't even remember Tom coming into Calydon's place.

By God! Who did Tracy think she was, sending Tom to watch him? It wasn't even noon yet when Tom got there. Hours to go before the bank closed. A vague memory of entering the bank with Jenkins now seeped through Canfield's mind. He remembered Tom making out the withdrawal slip and Tom holding his hand while he signed it. And just as they left the bank, Tom carrying the money in a canvas sack, they'd met Rick Hamilton. Canfield swore an oath. There was another bustard he'd have a reckoning with some day soon. He remembered quarreling with Rick, before Jenkins broke it up, and then a lot of men standing around hooting and yelling. Canfield had no memory at all of getting into the saddle again, but sometime later he had opened his eyes to find himself on the trail to the Terrapin Ranch, with one hand clutching the saddlehorn and in the other a bottle of whisky he'd gotten some place, he didn't remember exactly where. Some friend must have given it to him. Jenkins was nowhere in sight. He'd probably rode on ahead with the money to pay the crew.

Something else clicked in Canfield's mind. It had been the drumming of hoofs that had roused him next, on the way home. He'd looked up to see a bunch of riders flashing past in the opposite direction. After they had passed, he'd realized they were his own men, Terrapin hands. Canfield swore bitterly as he remembered now the contemptuous looks on the faces of three or four of the punchers, that of Tom Jenkins among them. Just like a bunch of cowhands, Canfield sneered drunkenly, ready to spend their money the minute they got it. He remembered that someone had told him that a cowboy was a creature half horse, half man, with a strong back and a weak head. Hell! What did it matter? He was home and he had another bottle of liquor when this one was finished. Had he bought that bottle, or had someone given it to him? At least, he remembered putting it on the mantel when he came home.

Canfield squinted through the gathering gloom in the direction of the fireplace, his bleary gaze searching the form of a bottle that should be standing there, but it was getting too dark to see well. Goddammit! Ought to be a light in here. He raised his voice and called, "Tracy!" There was no reply. Must be Tracy wasn't home. Where in hell was she, then? Probably gone to visit her old man. Well, dammit, Canfield assured himself, he could light the lamp himself, by God! He struggled up from his chair, slumped against the table and braced himself there, while the fingers of one hand sought a match to scratch. A kerosene lamp stood in the center of the table, surrounded by some books and magazines, a box of cigars, a pair of silver-inlaid spurs and the nearly empty bottle of whisky. The match burned out in Canfield's hand, while he was reaching for the bottle. He took a long draught, then set down the empty bottle with a bang. It tipped over and rolled to the floor.

Canfield didn't even hear it drop, as he groped through the darkness for the lamp. His pawing hands knocked the spurs and a magazine to the floor and finally encountered the base of the lamp. He started to lift the chimney, felt it slipping from his hand and in the endeavour to save it, managed to send the lamp crashing to the floor, where oil from the cracked base oozed into the Navajo rug on which it had landed.

Frustrated, cursing in a drunken mutter, Canfield stooped and groped under the table. When the lamp wasn't at once located, the thought seeped into his mind it was probably broken anyway. So to hell with the lamp too. There was more than one way of skinning a calf. He started to rise, sprawled on his face, and with some effort once more stumbled to his feet and started in the direction of the fireplace of roughly hewn granite. The stumbling journey through darkness seemed endless and after the first couple of steps he lost his direction. He struck a chair, knocking it on its side. Finally, after almost completely encircling the room, Canfield's hand brushed against a small table which always stood near the fireplace. Now he knew where he was, he panted triumphantly. A foolish giggle escaped his loose lips. "Damn' if I ain't got me a nice lil'—*hic!*—jag, this time."

He braced his weight against the small table and that, too, went over, but he managed to stay erect. He swayed uncertainly in the darkness, then ventured a faltering step. A second step brought him to the granite face of the fireplace. Carefully he lowered himself to a stooping position before the fireplace opening. He knew there'd be a fire laid, ready for the touch of a match. Three matches were scratched on the hearth, each one breaking without bursting into flame, before Canfield managed to light a fourth. His shaking hand thrust the flame into the crumpled newspaper and shavings beneath the wood, and after a moment the fire caught. There was a huge backlog of live oak; stacked over and around it was a good supply of well-dried mesquite roots.

The flames spread rapidly. A bright glow filled the room. Canfield staggered up and back, his features dripping with perspiration. "Whew!" he panted. "Thash hot." His mind returned to the whisky bottle that should have been on the mantel. It was there! Just where he had placed it. "Beau'iful sight," he mumbled maudlinly. "Mos' beau'iful sight . . . ever saw. More beau'iful than—than Tracy, even. Not—*hic!*—cold like Tracy, either. Bourbon—*hic!*—man's besh frien'."

At the third effort he managed to coordinate his hand with his bleary gaze. The bottle retrieved and he retreated two steps from the fireplace, lifting the bottle to his lips. A bitter wail left his mouth. Cork in bottle. Got to get a corkscrew. Where in hellsh corkscrew? Break neck off bottle, thash what he'd do. The fingers of one hand curled uncertainly around the neck of the bottle. It became gradually borne in on Canfield's mind that the cork protruded slightly. Utter relief swept through him as he realized the cork had already been pulled.

That was something else he couldn't remember having done —opening the bottle. His feeling of relief was replaced by one of utmost dejection: maybe the bottle was empty. His hopes revived when, upon being shaken, the bottle gave forth an encouraging gurgle. He held it before the light from the fireplace and saw that he held a full bottle. Canfield grinned vacantly. 'Shomebody—damn' good frien'. *Hic!* Give bottle and pull cork. Tracy can't shay no more I—*hic!*—haven't any frien's. I wonder who give me thish?"

After a moment he gave up thinking about it. The important thing was not the donor, but the fact that he had a full bottle at hand. On weaving, stumbling legs he returned to his chair near the big table, worked the cork from the bottle, and then, throwing back his head, tilted the bottle straight up and swallowed a long draught of its contents. He finally lowered the bottle and sank into his chair with a weary sigh of relief. This was better. He fumbled for his handkerchief and mopped at his face. After a minute or so, he took another long drink, then placed the bottle on the table with a bang.

Gradually some of his alcoholic fog was dissipated. Canfield's mind momentarily cleared. He sat watching the flames leap in the fireplace. He'd have just one more drink, he decided then go to bed. What was it Doc Sturven had said about going easy on whisky? Oh well, those old medics didn't know everything. Still, he could use a good night's sleep. And tomorrow, by God, he'd have it out with Tracy. There was a lot to be settled in that direction. Again anger surged through him. He'd taken just about enough from Tracy. Minutes drifted by.

Steps crossed the gallery fronting the house. A moment later Canfield heard the knock that sounded on the front door. With an effort he swiveled around in his chair and growled, "Come on in." The door opened and a tall, blond young cowpuncher, with good features, entered the room, carefully closing the door behind him. For a moment he just stood there, looking about the room lighted only by the dancing flames in the fireplace. Shadows made grotesque patterns on the opposite wall.

"You, eh, Rick?" Canfield grunted, peering across the room.

Rick Hamilton didn't reply at once. He cast a disgusted glance at the man in the chair, then his eyes went around the room, taking in the overturned furniture, and the lamp with its spilled oil seeping into the Navajo rug.

"Well, what in hell do you want?" Canfied snarled.

"I was hoping you'd be sobered up by this time——" Hamilton commenced.

"I'm sober—sober enough to talk to you." Canfield repeated, "What in hell do you want?" And added, "Where's Tracy?"

"I don't know where Tracy is, but I'm glad to learn she's not here. That's one thing I came out to learn——"

"If you don't keep your young snoot out of my business—" Canfield commenced on a rising note of fury, then paused. His heart had commenced to pound; he was finding breathing difficult. Beads of perspiration stood out on his face. After a moment the feeling passed and he breathed easier.

Hamilton came a few steps farther into the room. "I figure anything that concerns Tracy is my business, Nash. You made certain remarks in town today. Those have to be retracted or I'm going to kill you. Tomorrow, after you've slept off this jag, you'll go to town and do a hell of a lot of apologizing——"

"I haven't the least idea what you're talking about," Canfield started, then stopped and commenced to rub the back of his neck.

"That's something I'm aiming to tell you, if your drunken stupor has knocked the memory out of you," Hamilton snapped. "If you don't care about yourself, you might have some consideration for Tracy. I'm damned if I know how you can ignore Doc Sturven's warning. He told you if you didn't cut out the liquor you were hell-bent for an early grave."

"T'hell with you and Doc Sturven too," Canfield said thickly. "Look, why don't you get to hell out of here before I throw you out? I'm sick and tired of listening to you and——" He paused, making strangling sounds in his throat, then started up from his chair, eyes bulging, arms thrown wide. He lurched convulsively toward Hamilton who had started back, ready to defend himself, but there was a blindness in Canfield's eyes now. His face had grown livid, his mouth was twisted to one side. One hand tore at his throat. Quite suddenly his body was seized by violent spasms and he took two stiff-legged steps before crashing to the floor where the convulsions continued. After a minute the spasms ceased and only a series of quivers ran through Canfield's exhausted frame.

Rick Hamilton swore and knelt by the side of the sick man. "Can I get you something, Nash?" he asked. "What did Doc Sturven say to do when this happened——?"

"Get Doc—get Sturven—right away," Canfield gasped. "This—this is—dammit, go get the doc."

"Let me help you to bed——"

"Don't touch me," Canfield moaned. "Get Doc—quick."

"Quick as possible," Hamilton nodded. Rising to his feet, he hurried toward the front door, closed it behind him, crossed the gallery and leaped into the saddle of his waiting horse. He didn't see the shadowy figure that was slowly approaching the house as he departed, but a minute later, as his pony turned toward the road that led to Hyperion, he heard the sound of a gun explosion, or thought he did.

Instantly, Hamilton pulled his pony to a halt, listening. Had it been a gun explosion? It sure sounded that way. "I reckon I ought to go back," he told himself uncertainly. "Maybe Nash has got a gun and killed himself. Not that that wouldn't solve a lot of difficulties——" He broke off. "I reckon I'd best go back. Maybe I shouldn't have left him that way in the first place. I might have been able to do something for the man."

Still a trifle uncertain, he turned the pony and reined it back in the direction of the house. He saw at once, as he dismounted, that the front door stood open, and the thought ran through his mind that he had closed it when leaving. Mounting to the gallery, Hamilton quickly pushed past the open door, then came to an abrupt halt.

A tall, blond girl stood in the center of the room, her back to Hamilton, and a few feet from Nash Canfield who was threshing about on the floor, his face purple, eyes starting from their sockets. In one hand, held loosely at her side, the girl clutched a six-shooter; the other was raised to her eyes as though to shut out sight of the horrible spectacle on the floor. There was a definite odor of powder smoke in the room. Hamilton's gaze went quickly from the gun in the girl's hand to the writhing, jerking figure on the floor and saw crimson seeping through Nash Canfield's shirt.

Rick Hamilton exclaimed, "Tracy! My God! Did you have to do that?" And then, in lower, hopeless tones, "Yes, I reckon you did," as he saw the dark purple bruise at one side of her forehead.

The girl turned slowly toward him, eyes wide and vacant. For a moment she just stared at Rick without speaking, though her lips moved as if she were trying to say something. Running steps were heard at the rear of the house, then Wagner, the Terrapin Ranch cook, came bursting in, to stop short at the sight that met his eyes. "What in tarnation hell——?" he commenced, then shouted, "Catch her!"

The gun dropped from the girl's listless fingers. Hamilton leaped to break her fall as she swayed back, and lowered her gently to the floor. From his kneeling position at the prone girl's side he spoke over his shoulder, "Get a lamp in here, cookie, so's I can see what I'm doing. And some water."

The cook turned and hurried toward the back of the house, his eyes narrowing as he stepped across the now still figure of Nash Canfield, sprawled awkwardly on the floor. In a few moments he had returned with a lighted lamp and glass of water. Hamilton forced a little of the water between the girl's lips. After a minute her eyelids moved slightly and a long tired sigh welled up from her breast. Meanwhile, Wagner had been inspecting the room and Canfield's body. He came slowly back to Hamilton and the girl. "Just exactly what happened here?"

"I'm not just sure," Hamilton replied shortly. "We'll have to ask Tracy. She'll be all right in a little, I reckon. She just fainted. Coming out of it now."

"That's more'n he'll do," Wagner said in flat, level tones.

Hamilton's head jerked up. "What do you mean?"

"Canfield's dead, Rick." His eyes went to the six-shooter on the floor. "Tracy did the job complete with one slug."

Hamilton frowned. When he finally spoke, he said, "I don't think she did it, cookie."

"What! Hell's bells! She was still holding the gun when I come in here."

Hamilton said again, coldly, "I don't think she did it."

His glance locked with Wagner's for a long minute before Wagner said thoughtfully, "Anything you say, Rick, anything you say."

Chapter II : DANGEROUS INVESTIGATING

El Paso, Rick Hamilton considered, as he stepped from the lobby of the Grand Central Hotel to the sun-bathed plaza of bright morning, had certainly boomed during the past few years. A boyhood memory of scattered adobe buildings was now replaced by a view of many brick and timber structures. The town had grown in population, no doubt of that. Cowhands and men in miners' togs strode along the street. Saloons had multiplied; real estate offices seemed to keep pace with the bars. Horse-drawn vehicles and riders moved around the plaza. Hamilton tugged uncomfortably at the white collar about his neck, thinking, damn this having to put on city clothes. It was going to be warm before the day was finished too. Anyway, he'd retained his riding boots, and the wide-brimmed sombrero, though new, felt comfortable. A scowl crossed his bronzed features. Hell! He hadn't come to El Paso to enjoy himself.

Following the directions given by the hotel clerk the previous evening, he crossed the plaza diagonally and set out along San Francisco Street, his high-heeled boots clumping along the sidewalk. A mule-drawn streetcar jangled past and Hamilton eyed it with some curiosity. Ten minutes' walk brought him to the offices of the Texas Northern & Arizona Southern Railroad offices where an inquiry brought forth the information from a clerk that Mr. Gregory Quist wasn't in, but that he might be found at his room at the Pierson Hotel, as Mr. Quist wasn't expected in that day. The clerk added the necessary directions for finding the Pierson Hotel—a new brick building at the corner of St. Louis and Kansas Streets. Hamilton thanked him and started to turn away, but the clerk felt talkative:

"Stranger in town, aren't you?" Hamilton conceded that he was. The clerk went on, "You're the second stranger been in

here inquiring for Greg Quist in the past two days." Hamilton
nodded politely, anxious to get away, but the clerk continued,
"Something queer about that jasper. He hung around here
yesterday afternoon waiting for Greg to come in and when he
arrived and went into his office, at the back there, I go up to
the stranger and tell him to just go knock at Mr. Quist's door.
And he says, 'Was that Quist just come in?' and when I tell
him it was, this stranger says, 'That's not the man I want to see.
I must have been mistaken.' And with that he ups and takes
out from here like a bat out of hell."

"Funny way to act," Hamilton said, not particularly interested. "What did Mr. Quist have to say to that?"

"Never did get to tell him," the clerk said. "I was called
home early"—expanding pridefully—"because of the eight-
pound, ten-ounce baby that arrived at my house." Hamilton
interjected the proper congratulations and in a few minutes
more managed to leave.

Another twenty minute walk brought him to the entrance
of the Pierson Hotel. Inside the lobby, the man in charge of
the desk told Hamilton he wasn't sure if Mr. Quist were in, or
not. He could go up and find out for himself; proper directions
were furnished. Hamilton mounted the carpeted stairway to
the second floor and made his way along a corridor until he'd
reached a door at the rear of the building. Here he paused to
knock. Instantly, a voice bade him to "Come on in."

Hamilton "came on in," closing the door behind him, and
found himself in a room twice the size of an ordinary hotel
chamber. There were the usual hostelry furnishings—carpet
on the floor, bed, dresser, two straight-backed chairs and a
rocker; a washstand held a bowl and pitcher and a couple of
clean glasses; towels hung on a rack, and a small table held an
oil lamp. At the other side of the room, placed near one of the
two open rear wall windows, were a roll-top desk and swivel
armchair, and seated at the desk was Gregory Quist.

"Mr. Quist?" Hamilton asked. Quist nodded. Hamilton said,
"I've a letter of introduction to you." He held forth an envel-
ope. Quist glanced at it, tossed it on the desk. "I'm Rick
Hamilton." He liked the firm grip Quist gave him.

"If you'll have a chair for a few minutes until I finish this
letter I'm writing," Quist said, "I'll be ready to talk to you."
His voice was low and resonant, with a sort of musical quality
as though the tones welled deep from his thick chest. Rick
Hamilton couldn't decide just then what color Quist's eyes
were, but finally concluded they were nearer a topaz color
than anything else. Quist had thick tawny hair; in a country
where most men wore beards and mustaches he was clean

shaven, with a wide, thin-lipped mouth and rather bony features.

Hamilton took a chair by the other open window and found himself gazing out in a northeasterly direction toward Franklin Mountain. Nearer the hotel were unpaved streets lined with adobe structures with here and there a newer brick or frame house. Not much farther on the houses became more scattered followed by the gradual undulations of wasteland—gray alkali soil, mesquite, sage and cactus; a brilliant sun formed black shadows.

After a time, Quist rose from his desk with half-lazy, cat-like movements. Hamilton ventured, "Nice room you have here."

Quist nodded. "I like it. When the hotel was built I arranged for this. They knocked out a partition for me. Most people like to be at the front of the building. I find the afternoons cooler back here. Where you staying?"

"Grand Central. I got in last night, late. This morning I inquired at the Texas Northern & Arizona Southern offices, and they directed me here."

"I stay away from the railroad offices as much as possible. I find more privacy here, and then I'm away from El Paso much of the time." Quist moved to his coat hanging on a rack and placed some papers in an inner pocket. He returned to his desk. "Pull up your chair and tell me what I can do for you."

Hamilton did as directed, hesitated, then said bluntly, "I'm hoping you can find a murderer for me."

"So?" There was something quizzical, slightly sardonic in the look Quist gave Hamilton, and his smile had nothing to do with the topaz eyes. "If that's all you want I could probably fill the requirement in five minutes or less on any of El Paso's streets."

"I've heard that El Paso was wild."

Quist shook his head. "Nothing like it used to be. Marshal Stoudenmire and then Jim Gillett gentled it down considerably. Nowadays we've quite a progressive little town. Business is booming—but you're not interested in business. You said something about a murderer."

"Didn't Mr. Fletcher's letter explain anything?" Hamilton asked.

"Jay Fletcher," Quist stated with some amusement, "is a damn' good division superintendent, but he never does say much in letters unless it pertains to railroad business. This letter he gave you merely acts an an introduction and suggests that I help you. Inasmuch as he doesn't mention the T.N. & A.S. being concerned, I somehow doubt it."

"You're a detective, aren't you?"

"Sometimes I doubt that, too," Quist said whimsically. "I'm down on the pay roll as a special investigator." He added, "In railroad business. Unless your business has to do with the railroad, I doubt I'd be available to help you. I'm under contract——"

Hamilton interrupted, "Mr. Fletcher—he's an old friend of my father's, by the way,—thought I might run into something like this. He had the foresight to also get me a letter from the president of the T.N. & A.S." This Hamilton now presented to Quist.

"Apparently, you came well fortified," Quist said dryly. He opened this second letter, perused it swiftly, then dropped it on the desk. "President Traxton's letter merely asks me to help, if I can see my way clear, Mr. Hamilton. I'm not sure I can. Traxton does mention that your sister is a heavy holder of T.N. & A.S. stock, and he thinks all possible should be done to aid the company's stockholders. At the same time he points out I'm under no obligation to help you—as he damn' well knows; according to my contract I have a free hand——"

"You'll at least listen to what I have to say, won't you?" Hamilton pleaded. "Jay Fletcher warned me I might have trouble interesting you——"

"Apparently, you've had quite a lot of correspondence with Jay. Exactly what did he tell you about me?"

"He said, frankly, that if anyone could help us, you're the man. He wrote what you'd done when you were with the Cattle Association and how you'd cleaned up the cattle rustling rings. Then you joined up with the railroad companies——"

"Hired out my gun is, perhaps, a quicker way to put it," Quist said wryly.

"It was more than gunwork, as I get it," Hamilton said earnestly. "There were those train robbers up in Wyoming— that was for the Union Pacific, if I remember correctly. Another big robbery was cleaned up for a Kansas road. Wasn't it in Oklahoma you captured that gang of freight thieves? In Utah, for the Denver & Salt Lake Railroad, you were responsible for the arrest of those train wreckers——"

"Enough, enough——" Quist interposed impatiently.

"There was that business on Jay Fletcher's division, near the town of Cenotaph. Jay called it the Thunderbird murder mystery.[1] He even had you entangled in a romance over there——"

"Romance!" Quist laughed harshly. "Apparently, Jay Fletcher has been running off at the head. Because I like a

[1] See *Thunderbird Trail*, Doubleday & Co., Inc., N.Y., 1946.

girl is no sign—hell's bells! Romance has no place in the life
of a man with my kind of job. I couldn't ask any woman
to——" Quist broke off, then, "That's neither here nor there.
All the jobs you've mentioned, since I've been working for
railroads, had to do with railroads. I take it your problem has
nothing to do with the T.N. & A.S. so I'm afraid I can't help
you."

"You'll at least hear me out," Hamilton persisted, his color
rising.

"I'd do that for any man, Mr. Hamilton," Quist said courte-
ously. He rolled a brown paper cigarette, after proffering the
"makin's" to his visitor, scratched a match and inhaled deeply.
"You mentioned a murder. When did it take place? Who was
killed and why? I'm listening."

"We own—at least my father does," Hamilton commenced,
"the Circle-H ranch, near the town of Hyperion——"

"Hyperion? That's over in the Gunsight country, isn't it?"
Hamilton nodded. "You know where it is?"

"I know a lot of places in Texas," Quist said evasively.
"Sorry I interrupted you."

"Nearly four years ago," Hamilton continued, "a man named
Nash Canfield arrived in Hyperion and stayed at the hotel. He
said he had come west for his health." Rick Hamilton frowned.
"Eventually, we learned there was nothing wrong with his
health that staying out of bars wouldn't cure. But at that time
he was on the water wagon. He had money. He met my sister
who was eighteen at the time. I'll admit Canfield was likable in
many ways. I wasn't too put out when my sister—Tracy—
married him." He looked at the floor. "I guess it wasn't long
before Tracy realized she'd made a mistake, but we didn't
know it for a long time. Canfield bought some ranch country
and had a big house erected—finer than anything else we had
in the Gunsight country. He bought paintings for the walls and
nice furniture. He purchased a herd outright and announced
widely that he was now a cattle raiser, branding the Terrapin
iron." Hamilton swore softly. "Nash Canfield just didn't fit
into the West—though it took a long spell for him to realize
he didn't, in spite of his money. Eventually Canfield slumped
back into the ways he'd followed in the East—drinking and
women."

"A bad combination," Quist said softly, "when overdone."

"You don't realize how bad. Canfield just let everything go.
Tracy had to take over the management of the ranch. Occa-
sionally the constant drinking made Canfield very ill and he'd
slow up for a time. I remember once when a protracted bout
turned him into a wild man and it took four of us to manage

him. I was there when he was undergoing an attack of delirium tremens on another occasion, and I tell you it was a pretty nasty sight. The doctor warned him against such drinking, several times, insisting he'd kill himself. But Doc was proved wrong. Somebody else did the killing, with a slug of lead."

Quist said shortly, "Good riddance, I'd say." He added, "If it's Canfield's murderer you want me to find, I think you're wrong. Why seek a murderer who is, undoubtedly, a benefactor of humanity?"

Hamilton eyed Quist curiously. "Jay Fletcher warned me you could be pretty hard, but he also said you were just."

"Damn nice of Jay," Quist commented sardonically.

Hamilton continued, "I'm making a long story of this, I'm afraid, but I wanted you to understand the sort of man Canfield was. I'll skip details and get to what happened about a year ago. Canfield had been on one of his prolonged drinking sprees, and the Terrapin crew was overdue for its wages. Tracy routed him out of bed one morning and insisted that he go in to the bank and draw the money due the men. She got him started, then later sent the Terrapin foreman, Tom Jenkins, after him, to make certain he went to the bank. In Hyperion, Jenkins found Canfield had got no farther than the bars. After some persuasion, Tom got him to the bank. As they left the bank, Canfield saw me on the street and started a quarrel. We finally got that business hushed up and——"

"What was the quarrel about?" Quist cut in.

"It doesn't matter greatly," Rick Hamilton evaded. "Things he said about Tracy. He didn't like me and was liable to say anything to rile me. Eventually Jenkins got him on his horse and they started for the Terrapin, though a few miles out of town Jenkins took the money and rode ahead. He got to the ranch, paid the crew and they all started for Hyperion, leaving only Wagner, the cook, at the ranch. On their way to town, the men passed Canfield, half-asleep in the saddle."

"Did Canfield get home without further trouble?"

"As far as we know. No one, except Wagner, was at the Terrapin when he arrived. He practically fell off his pony at the corral, then staggered back into the house. Wagner unsaddled the horse and beyond noticing that Canfield was drunk again, gave it no further thought."

"That was natural under the circumstances, I suppose."

Hamilton nodded. "None of the crew ever paid any attention to his drunkenness. I rode out to the Terrapin in the evening and found him still drunk. The room was a mess. He'd knocked over the lamp and some furniture. Somehow he'd got a fire started in the fireplace. With that spilled oil and all, it's a wonder he didn't burn down the house. I tried to talk to him, but he flew into a rage and about that time one of his attacks hit him. After Doc Sturven's warnings about overdrinking you'd think he—— Well, that's neither here nor there. I left to go for the doctor and when just a short way from the house, I heard a shot. I returned and found Tracy standing not far from Canfield, who was writhing on the floor. She had a gun in her hand. Later, it came out that one ca'tridge had been fired."

"So your sister shot him, I'd say," Quist commented flatly.

Hamilton frowned. "I just can't believe it. Tracy can't remember shooting him——"

"Can't remember?" Quist asked quickly.

"Don't jump to conclusions, Mr. Quist. Tracy doesn't even remember arriving at the Terrapin. I'll explain. That morning, after getting Canfield started to town she had gone to our place to see my father, at the Circle-H. She'd promised to ride with a message from him to Gabe Bedell, of the Rocking-B outfit. Tracy remembers that much. Somewhere along the trip, her horse had gone spooky over something or other and bolted with her, through a stand of cottonwood trees. A low-hanging limb had swept her from the saddle, we figure. We don't know exactly what happened. There was a bad bruise at one side of her head. It's likely she was unconscious for a time. At any rate, she managed to make her way on foot to the Terrapin. Beyond that, and that's only vague, she's not sure what happened, herself, though she does have a sort of confused recollection of seeing Canfield on the floor and of hearing a shot fired. She was out of her head for a time and quite ill for a couple of months."

"The killing was reported at once, of course."

"Naturally. I was arrested, brought to trial and found not guilty——"

"*You* were arrested——?"

Hamilton flushed. "I wanted to keep Tracy out of it. I pleaded not guilty, but we cooked up a story that I had arrived at the Terrapin simultaneously with Tracy and we had found Canfield dead."

Quist smiled thinly. "Have you ever heard there's a severe penalty for perjury?"

"I know all about that," Hamilton said shortly. "What does it matter? I didn't kill Canfield. I'm sure Tracy didn't. Canfield was very much disliked around Hyperion. Everybody knew the sort of dog he was. I doubt anybody believed my story, and Tracy was too sick to appear at the trial or give any sort of testimony. Half the people in the Gunsight country believe

Tracy killed him in self-defense, or that I killed him to protect Tracy. The condition of the room made it look as though a struggle had taken place. Most people, including the authorities, were satisfied that Canfield was gone. We've got a lot of friends around Hyperion."

"I can well believe that," Quist observed in dry tones. "But what about the testimony of this cook, Wagner——?"

"We've got a lot of friends," Hamilton said meaningly. He and Quist exchanged a long look before Hamilton continued, "And now we'd like you to find out who the murderer is."

"Good God," Quist said impatiently, "why dig up old bones? The matter is settled as I see it."

"It's not settled in my mind, nor in the minds of the people in the Gunsight country. Everyone feels that either Tracy or I killed Nash Canfield. It's ruining Tracy's life. She seems to have lost all interest in things—the things that matter, anyway. As for me"—Hamilton paused awkwardly—"well, there's a girl I like, and until I'm cleared—well, you see how it is."

Quist said, his voice still impatient, "Bosh! Forget the whole business, as everyone else will before long. Lord! Hamilton, do you realize what you're asking me to do? That killing took place a year ago. Any evidence there might have been could be taken care of by this time. Hell! I'm no miracle man."

"Jay Fletcher thinks you are."

"Fletcher is crazy——" Quist broke off. "You're asking for trouble, maybe, Hamilton, when you want me to dig into this old business. Suppose I did, which I'm not going to, I might uncover something you wouldn't like. It might prove to be damn' dangerous investigating."

"I tell you I'm practically certain Tracy didn't do it," Hamilton said doggedly. "Maybe you think I've lied and that I did it. Would I be coming here, asking you to investigate?"

"That's possible too," Quist said, and his voice sounded hard. "Leaving you and your sister out of it, if Canfield was the skunk you claim, perhaps somebody else did it. Your father might have been angry enough to protect——"

"Impossible," Hamilton said swiftly. "My father's an invalid —paralyzed. A horse went over a cut bank with him a couple of years ago. He's not been able to ride or walk since."

"Well, there might be someone else who didn't like Canfield."

Hamilton gave a short mirthless chuckle. "It'd be difficult to find anybody who liked him. He'd antagonized practically everybody in the country."

Quist shook his head angrily. "Damn you, Hamilton, you come in here and get my curiosity aroused, but I'm not going to do it, see? You go on back home and take up your life and forget this whole business. Things will work out. Your sister will get over it——"

"You positively refuse to help us then? We can pay well——"

"T'hell with your money. A man can use only so much and I've got all I need now. The T.N. & A.S. takes care of that and my first loyalty is to the railroad. So I'll just have to say——"

What he had intended to say, Rick Hamilton never knew. There was a high-pitched, whining sound entering the open window, followed an instant later by the sharp crack of a rifle from some distance off, and a sudden *thud* as the bullet entered the side of the roll-top desk. Objects rattled on the desk and then there was silence. Before he realized what was happening, Hamilton felt himself swept from his chair and to one side, as Quist, moving cat-like, jerked his visitor out of harm's way.

Chapter III : WINCHESTER WARNING

The two men stood silent, tense, in the room, well away from the two open windows. Quist exhaled a long breath. "Well," he said softly, and again, "Well! That's right interesting." He moved lithely to the open window near the desk and peered around the edge of the jamb. Rick Hamilton looked cautiously from the other window. He saw, across the roofs of various buildings, men moving along a nearby street. Beyond were scattered adobe shacks with nothing suspicious in that vicinity either. Farther on was an undulating stretch of range with no movement visible save that caused by the hot wind stirring the tips of the semi-desert plant growth.

Boldly, Quist leaned from the window opening and studied the country beyond. Seeing nothing to rouse his suspicions, he turned to the roll-top desk and inspected the bullet hole at the outer end. He studied the angle at which the slug had entered, then rummaged on his desk until he'd found the battered leaden missile. He straightened up and spoke to Hamilton, "This may have been fired from one of those buildings at the edge of town, or whoever fired it could still be hidden behind a rise of land still farther out. There's one or two clumps of mesquite high enough to hide a horse. What type gun would you say had been used?"

"Winchester rifle probably," Hamilton said promptly.

"That's my idea." Quist exhibited the slug in his hand. "Some battered, but I'd say it was a .38-55. If it hadn't struck that metal brace on the opposite end of the desk, it would likely have gone clear through." He frowned puzzledly. "What was the idea, I wonder?"

"Aren't you going out to see what you can learn? You might catch the fellow who fired that slug and——"

"He'd be gone by the time I could search those adobes, or scout the open country beyond." Quist shook his head. "This bullet has come from some distance—around three hundred yards, I'd say. If anybody else heard the shot, they probably paid no attention. Shooting on the outskirts of town isn't unusual—nor in town either."

"Look," Hamilton suggested. "Maybe you weren't shot at, at all. That might have been an accident. Perhaps some rabbit-hunter, or——"

"Think that over a minute." Quist smiled coldly. "Any hunter would be aiming at something on the ground, unless he was after duck in which case he'd be down on the river. No, the barrel this slug was shook out of was elevated toward my second story window. It wasn't an accident."

Rick Hamilton's eyes widened. "You think somebody tried to kill you?"

"No, I don't. That's what makes things look queer. I was seated at my desk, but well back from it. I wasn't in view in the window——"

"I was in line with the window——"

"Don't get foolish ideas, son. Sure, you were in line with the window, but seated so far back nobody who fired that rifle would know you were here. Unless you know of somebody who'd want to kill you."

Hamilton pondered a moment. "I can't think of anybody who'd want to kill me."

"You weren't in view. Neither was I. But the shot came through my window," Quist mused half aloud. "I can only figure it was a warning."

"Against what?" Hamilton asked quickly.

"That's something I intend to find out. Oh, sure, there're plenty hombres around El Paso who wouldn't grieve any if I were killed, but I can't think of anybody, right now, impetuous enough to——" He broke off, tossed the leaden slug on his desk. "Good thing that didn't hit my ink bottle, or it sure as hell would have messed things up." He reached to the watch pocket of his corduroy trousers, consulted his timepiece. "What say we go down and catch a bait? It's dinnertime."

"I'll be damned!" Rick Hamilton burst out. "Aren't you going to try and learn who fired that shot?"

"Sure I am," Quist replied lazily, "but I'm not going to get myself in a sweat dashing around that open country, or searching through those shacks." He adjusted a blue four-in-hand tie at his throat, slipped a coat on over his woolen shirt. One pant leg was caught at the top of his riding boot and he shook it out to fall even with its mate at his ankles. "Come on, let's go eat."

In the lobby below, Quist stopped at the desk. "Did you hear a shot a spell ago, Mr. Crosby?"

The clerk looked startled. "No, can't say I did."

"Probably wouldn't have paid it any heed if you had," Quist said. "The bullet ventilated one end of my desk."

"You don't say! Do you think——?"

"I've not given it much thought. Likely an accident."

The clerk looked dubious. "In your position I wouldn't be too sure, Mr. Quist. How will it be if I report it to the marshal?"

Quist shook his head. "The marshal's got enough to do. Forget it. I'll take care of any trouble that comes my way." He and Hamilton had turned away from the desk, when the clerk spoke again:

"Mr. Quist, that reminds me. There was a man in here inquiring for you this morning. No"—indicating Hamilton—"I don't mean this gentleman. Another fellow. He said he'd heard you had a nice room with us, and wondered if he could get one like it for a while. Asked exactly where your room was located. I explained you had the two rear windows on the left side of the building and how we'd knocked out a partition, and so on. You were out to breakfast at the time, but I told him if he came back later you'd likely let him have a look at your room. I'd forgotten all about him until now. Sorry. You didn't see him? Do you suppose he'd have had anything to do with that shooting——?"

"I couldn't say," Quist answered. "What sort of looking fellow was he?"

The clerk shrugged. "I didn't pay too much attention. The mail had been brought and I was busy sorting it. Frankly, he didn't look like he could afford a room like yours. He appeared to be just an ordinary cowhand. He wore a mustache——"

"That helps a lot," Quist observed dryly. 'A cowhand with a mustache. How old was he? Light or dark?"

The clerk was apologetic. "I can't remember exactly. He was sort of dark complected, as I remembered. Not young, but not an old man, either. I couldn't say for certain if he was tall or short."

Quist nodded and rejoined Hamilton. Hamilton commenced, "I wonder——" then paused. Quist asked him what he wondered. Hamilton continued, "This morning when I was at the T.N. & A.S. office one of the clerks mentioned I was the second man who'd been inquiring for you in the past two days. It seems some fellow came in yesterday afternoon and——" From that point on Hamilton related the clerk's story.

Quist heard him through in silence while they left the hotel and proceeded west on St. Louis Street, threading their way between passing pedestrians. When Hamilton had finished, Quist said, "Maybe that clears things up a mite. I'll make a guess. This hombre that was looking for me didn't know what I looked like, nor where to find me. All he knew was that I was connected with the railroad. So he went to the T.N. & A.S. office, waited until I came in, then got a line on my make up. After leaving the office he followed me, learned that I lived at the Pierson Hotel. This morning he hung around the hotel until he saw me go out to breakfast, then he went in and talked to the hotel clerk to get a line on the location of my room. Later he saw me return. Still later, from some point of vantage, he loosed a Winchester slug through my window. Does that sound plausible?"

"Reasonable enough," Hamilton conceded, frowning, "but why did he do it?"

"That question," Quist smiled thinly, "sort of interests me, too."

The two men turned south on El Paso Street, Quist pointing out various new buildings in process of erection. "This town is sure growing. If you've any spare cash, put it in real estate here. You can't lose." Hamilton pointed out, somewhat moodily, that real estate investments weren't what had brought him to El Paso. Quist laughed softly. "I rather gathered that from something you said this morning," he observed.

A momentary flash of irritation passed through Hamilton. Apparently, Quist hadn't taken his request too seriously. He realized now, glancing at Quist, that the man's thick chest and broad shoulders made him appear shorter than his actual six feet. Quist's black, flat-topped sombrero rested at a slant on his thick tawny hair, giving him a sort of careless, devil-may-care appearance that was instantly belied by the manner in which Quist's restless topaz eyes glinted alertly at everyone who passed. Hamilton wondered how old he was; it was difficult to say. Probably thirty, maybe thirty-five, though he looked younger.

At San Antonio Street they turned again and Quist slowed step. He stopped suddenly in front of an adobe one-story building bearing a sign which proclaimed it to be the Rio Grande Bar. A loose-jointed, unshaven individual in shabby clothing lounged in the shadow of the front wall of the saloon. The instant he saw Quist he directed his gaze to some distant point on the far side of the street. Quist stood looking at him, without speaking. Finally, reluctantly, the man's gaze came around to meet Quist's. He straightened suddenly. "Hell, Greg, I didn't see you comin'———"

Quist said softly. "Don't be a liar, Bailey. You know damn' well you saw me."

"Yessir, Mr. Quist, if you say so. How's tricks?" There was a hang-dog look on the man's face.

"A certain trick has me puzzled at present. Somebody fired a lead slug through my window this morning."

"The hell you say! I'm regrettin' to hear that———"

"I told you once not to lie, Bailey," Quist said sharply.

"Yes, sir. . . . I don't know anythin' about any shootin'."

"I didn't say you did. Tell Tolliver I want to know who did it. Leave word at the Pierson. Now, get going."

The man nodded, jerked at his tattered sombrero and hurried off.

Quist turned to Hamilton. "Come on, we can go eat now. There's a Chinese restaurant just around the corner that cooks a steak to the king's taste———"

"Wait!" Hamilton exclaimed "Do you mean to say that's all you have to do to learn who shot you? Ask that run-down———"

"Tug Bailey? No, Bailey will just sort of start the wheels moving. There's no heart left in the man. Right now he should be serving a term for horse stealing———"

"What's he doing on the streets, then?" Hamilton sounded a trifle indignant.

"I'll give it to you briefly while we eat."

A short time later, when they were seated at a table with a white cloth on it and with steaming platters of food sending an appetizing aroma toward the ceiling, Quist said, "El Paso seems to be a sort of gathering point for rough characters from other parts of the country. I've been around a lot and I recognize many who come here. I generally know what they're wanted for, or I learn eventually. I'm not a state or county officer, so I leave to the state and county officers the apprehension of such criminals as are wanted. I follow a hands-off policy, so long as such men don't harm the T.N. & A.S. railroad in any way."

Hamilton forked a juicy bit of steak into his mouth, chewed

silently a few moments. "You don't figure you're abetting the
lawbreakers by that attitude?"

Quist smiled. "To some extent, perhaps. But look at it this
way. I have my own job to do. I don't interfere with sheriffs
or marshals. What is more, so long as law-busters stay in El
Paso I can keep a line on them. Once they leave, they may be
planning to rob or wreck trains, or steal freight—God knows
what."

"But surely some of those men must hate you."

"Probably all of them do, knowing I have evidence that will
convict any time I feel like talking. But they know they're
partially safe as long as I keep my mouth shut. Consequently,
I can get favors now and then when I want to know something.
If you think my system doesn't work, talk to some of the inves-
tigators for the other railroads running into El Paso. They're
having plenty of trouble from time to time. But so long as the
law-busters keep their hands off the T.N. & A.S., I've nothing
to worry me."

Hamilton said. "You mentioned a man named Tolliver."

Quist nodded. "Redwood Tolliver. He runs what he calls
his hotel and bar a few miles out, beyond the city limits.
Sooner or later, every law-buster that hits El Paso, gravitates
out to Tolliver's place. It's become a sort of hide-out for criminals from other parts of the country—men who've had to
leave swift and sudden——"

"But surely," Hamilton protested this state of affairs, "the
sheriff knows about Tolliver's place. The marshal must be
dumb if he doesn't know what goes on."

'Of course they know," Quist smiled, "though they don't let
on. Again, there's a hands-off policy. Tolliver and his gang are
safe just so long as they don't pull anything crooked in El Paso
or in the county. What happens outside the county is none of
our business, and the local peace-officers have all they can
handle without digging up trouble. Now and then, of course,
somebody from Tolliver's comes into El Paso and steps out of
line. At that point he is immediately stepped on. And he knows
he'll get no help from Tolliver."

Hamilton looked thoughtful. "And all you had to do was
speak to that Tug Bailey——?"

"I'm hoping it will bring results," Quist said quietly. "Bailey
will spread the news among his pals. When he sees Tolliver
there'll be certain questions asked. Eventually, something
may come of it."

Hamilton shook his head. "You've already mentioned that
some of these men at Tolliver's hate you enough to kill you.
Perhaps one of them fired that shot."

"That's what I'm trying to learn," Quist said patiently.

"But suppose he'd killed you."

"He'd get no help from Tolliver, though I imagine there'd be a lot of secret rejoicing."

"But you'd be dead."

Quist shrugged his thick shoulders. "That's a risk I take."

"It doesn't seem to bother you a great deal."

Quist shrugged. "When my time comes, it comes, and there's nothing I, nor anybody else can do to stop it. But until it comes, I'm safe. So why should it bother me? . . . By the way, I can recommend the pie here too."

Strange man, this Quist, was the thought that ran through Rick Hamilton's mind. He didn't seem to have any nerves; at least if he did, they weren't readily exposed. He occupied himself with his food, mulling over the things Quist had told him.

Nothing more was said about Tolliver as the two sauntered about El Paso, Quist pointing out various scenes of interest. Now and then he discussed details of the business that had brought Hamilton to town, but each time Rick urged him to take the case, he shook his head.

"It's not for me, Rick," Quist said. "You can get somebody else to find your murderer—probably somebody better than I'd be on a case like that. If you're wise, you'll catch the next train back to Hyperion. I should have told you that right after we finished dinner, but I was thinking about that shot that was fired——"

"Cripes!" Rick said. "I'm disappointed that you can't see things my way. At the same time, I'm interested in that shot too. I want to see what you learn. The way you work with Tolliver and his gang has roused my interest. I'm just dubious enough about that phase of the matter to stay a while and see if you're proved right."

The topaz eyes twinkled. "I think I'll be able to show you —though I'll promise nothing."

It was nearly three in the afternoon when they returned to the Pierson Hotel after having passed some of the time in a place of Quist's choosing where certain things were pleasantly done with bourbon and mint, sugar and ice. Hamilton was engulfed in a pleasant glow, no more, when they stepped into the hotel lobby. Quist went at once to the desk:

"Has any word come in for me?"

"Nothing, Mr. Quist."

"Not even a note of any sort?"

"Not a thing, Mr. Quist. Were you expecting a message?"

Something like a chuckle escaped Hamilton's lips. Quist turned, met his eyes a moment, then swung back to the desk clerk. "No—no," he said ruefully, "I guess I wasn't—not yet. What newspapers have come in today?" He glanced at the papers spread at one end of the desk, selected sheets from San Antonio, Tucson, Denver and San Francisco, then turned and started for the stairway, Rick Hamilton at his heels. Reaching his door he unlocked it and stepped aside for Hamilton to enter, followed him inside and closed the door again.

Hamilton was grinning widely. "Now, this man Tolliver you mentioned——" he commenced.

Quist threw him a quick glance. "Don't say it, son. The day's not over yet." He tossed the newspapers on the bed. "There's some reading matter to pass the time. Make yourself comfortable. I don't think I'll be gone too long."

Hamilton stared. "Where you heading?"

"I figure to have a word with Redwood Tolliver."

Rick said, "Oh," and sat down on the bed. In a moment he was up again. "Any reason why I shouldn't go with you?"

"Any reason you should risk your neck?" Quist snapped

"You mean there might be some trouble?"

Quist swore under his breath. "I've described Tolliver and the men who hang out at his place. They don't like me. Does that answer your question?"

Rick nodded, his young face serious. "I'd still like to go with you. Maybe you could use some help."

Quist studied him with hard yellow eyes. "I don't like to be under obligation to people," he stated bluntly.

"Obligation?" Rick looked puzzled. Suddenly the color left his cheeks. "Oh, you mean I was putting you under obligation so you'd come back to Hyperion with me——." He broke off, cheeks suddenly flaming with anger, as he started toward the door. "You, Mr. Greg Quist, can go plumb to hell," he half-snarled.

"Wait!" Quist crossed the floor in quick, cat-like strides, caught Rick by the shoulder and whirled him around. His other hand dropped on Rick's shoulder and he looked steadily into the younger man's eyes for a long moment. He smiled and there was something humble in his voice when he spoke, "Rick, I can be such an awful bustard at times. Forget it, will you? I'll be glad to have you with me, if you feel that way."

"It's forgotten already," Rick said, flushing.

"Thanks. . . . I suppose you've got a gun with you?"

"It's in my satchel, over to the Grand Central."

"We'd lose time while you went for it. Forty-five, I suppose." Rick nodded. Irritation crept into Quist's voice. "Damned if I could ever understand why so many men tote .45s. I'll do some missionary work and loan you one of my .44s. With a .44 you can use the same cartridge for six-shooter or rifle. It seems to take a hell of a long while for folks to realize that, though. . . . We can pick up some spurs for you at the livery when we get you a horse."

He strode to a dresser drawer and withdrew a .44 six-shooter which he handed to Hamilton. "Here, stick that in your waist-band, under your coat. I hope you won't have to use it. If you do, take good care of it. It's one of a matched pair"—displaying his second gun.

Rick examined his weapon. He liked the feel of the gun and its balance. A quick inspection showed him the short-barreled weapon was loaded in five chambers with the hammer resting on an empty shell. "Look here, Mr. Quist——"

"Greg, to you. I don't want anybody that's siding me doing any mistering."

"Greg, then." This Quist had a way of getting under a man's skin. "What I mean—well, I'd hate to have anything happen to this gun. Maybe I'd best drift over and get my own hawg-leg."

"Bosh! You won't hurt it. If you have to use it, all you have to do is draw back the hammer and touch the trigger. You'll find the pull is right gentle."

While he talked, Quist had slipped off his coat and gotten into an underarm-gun harness into which he thrust the mate to the gun Rick was holding.

"That's quite a rig," Rick said.

"A very convenient rig if a man wants to jerk his iron in a hurry," Quist replied. "With this sort of holster, you just pull the gun straight out, instead of up and out as is usually done. A flat steel spring, incased within the leather, holds the gun in place until needed. It's a heap more comfortable to wear than a hip gun—and a fraction of a second faster on the draw. Sometimes that fraction counts." He again donned his coat, thrust a handful of extra cartridges into a side pocket, and handed Rick a supply of loads.

Rick glanced at the wide, nickel-plated-buckle belt that held up Quist's corduroys. "Don't you wear a ca'tridge belt?"

"Why should I tote all that extra weight? Any man that can't do his job with what's in the gun and an extra fistful, hasn't any business carrying a gun, or taking on a job where a gun's needed. . . . You ready to go?"

"Just waiting for you to say the word, Greg."

Quist drew the room door shut behind them and they made their way to the street.

Chapter IV : TOLLIVER'S PLACE

Mounted on horses procured from the livery next door to the Pierson Hotel, the two men headed south on Kansas Street, the ponies' hoofs kicking up dust along the thoroughfare, unpaved except for flat blocks of rock laid at street crossings. Arriving at the corner of San Antonio Street, they turned east, passing between a double row of adobe houses with here and there a brick or wood building breaking the monotony. Vacant lots commenced to appear and then after a time there were no more buildings to be seen, and all that remained to show there'd been a street were the deep wheel ruts running across hoof-chopped, sandy soil spotted with yucca, catclaw, creosote bush, and sparse grass. Here and there a mesquite tree rose above its surrounding growth.

After a time Quist led the way toward the river and before long Hamilton caught sight of the wide, muddy Rio Grande flowing sluggishly along several courses made by broad sand bars. Their course paralleled the river for another five minutes, then topping a slight hump of earth Rick saw a good-sized two-story building of adobe and timber just ahead. Two great cottonwoods stood before the building, and below them, ranged at a long hitchrack, were a number of saddled ponies. Other horses stood in a corral at the rear, and beyond the corral was a small mountain of rusted tin cans and other rubbish.

Quist drew his pony to a walk and Rick followed suit. Quist said, "There it is. What do you think?"

Rick frowned. "I don't know whether I've been influenced by what you said or not, but there's something damn' sinister-looking about the place. Or should I call it a dive?"

"You named it. Want to turn back?"

Rick eyed Quist steadily a moment. "I thought you aimed to convert me to using a .44."

Quist said, laughing, "On your own head be it. Come on."

They dismounted before the hitchrack, squeezed their ponies in between other horses and dropped reins over the bar. Rick looked the place over. There were four dust-encrusted windows in the lower front of the building, spaced on either side of a pair of wide swinging doors. A railed gallery ran across the upper story. Another door and windows up there, with above them, in sun-faded letters, a sign that read "TOLLIVER'S HOTEL." A man who had stood looking out above the swinging

31

doors when Quist and Hamilton dismounted had now disappeared, and a sudden silence replaced the babel of voices that had been issuing from the place a minute before.

Involuntarily, Rick's hand crept under his coat and felt of the gun thrust in the waistband of his trousers as he followed Quist through the batwing doors. Just within, Quist paused to give his eyes an opportunity to become accustomed to the light —or lack of light—after the sun-brilliance of outdoors. The scene became clearer after a time: Rick saw a long room with a rough, scarred bar at one side. Scattered about the remainder of the room were wooden tables. A number of men were playing cards; others just sat and drank. The bar was lined from end to end and presided over by a veritable giant of a man with a lined face and bushy red hair. Rick guessed correctly that this was Redwood Tolliver.

Rick noticed next that there was nothing of friendliness in the looks directed at Quist and himself. If Quist noticed the greeting—or lack of greeting—there was nothing in his manner to show it. He strode lithely toward the bar, spurs clanking across the rough board floor, tossing careless salutations toward those he recognized: "Hi, there, Hoot Owl! . . . Scratchy, you dog, when did they let you out? . . . Ringbone Janes, by all that's holy! Understand they're still looking for you over in Nevada, Ringbone. . . . Shuckhead! When did you pull in? . . . Damn! This is just like old home week, seeing all my old friends. . . . Tiger-Eye Morse! You old bustard! I'm bettin' a plugged peso · you've just run some posse to death. . . ." There were other similar remarks, but no one replied, except with scowls. Rick noticed, however, that everyone kept his hand well away from his gun. The concerted hate of the room seemed to swell, silent, ominous, and direct itself on Gregory Quist.

Roughly, Quist elbowed a couple of men away from the bar to stand in front of Redwood Tolliver. "Make some room for me and my pal, boys. This is Trigger Hamilton. You've all heard how he run Billy the Kid out of Tutumcari, several years back. It was Trigger that sotfened the Kid up for Pat Garrett." Now a low buzz of conversation ran through the room and momentarily all eyes were directed in Rick's direction. Rick suppressed a gasp. Trigger Hamilton! Was there no limit to what this man Quist would do? Rick managed to cast a cold glance over the room, then turned, at Quist's side, to face the bar.

Redwood Tolliver towering above them was looking sharply at Rick, as though wondering whether or not to doubt Quist's words. Quist said, "Don't bother to set out a drink, Tolliver. We're not indulging."

Slowly Tolliver's small eyes came back to Quist. "That's all right too," he said sowly. "What's on your mind?"

"I don't think I have to tell you," Quist said, and his voice was dangerously calm now. "I sent Bailey with word I wanted some information. I didn't get it. Somebody unleashed a slug in my direction this morning. I don't like that sort of thing. Who was it?"

"I ain't the least idea," Tolliver said coldly. "Sure, I got your message. I've questioned the boys. Nobody staying with me is responsible——"

"That I can well believe," Quist said sarcastically. "That's not the point. I asked you to get some information. You haven't done it. Why?"

Tolliver swore an oath. "I'm getting just a little tired of being at your beck and call, Greg. I've already told you none of my boys flung that lead at you. That settles it."

A harsh laugh left Quist's lips. "That's what you think. How'd you like it, Redwood, if I came out here with some riders, some night, and took this place apart—and you with it, as my own personal job?"

Tolliver's big frame swelled. "You wouldn't dare—even if you were man enough. I'm sick of bein' crowded, Greg. You may have somethin' on a heap of these hombres, but you've got nothing on me—see?" He repeated, "I'm sick of bein' crowded. From now on, you scrape up your own information. I've broken none of El Paso's laws. I've had nothing to do with your railroad. I don't owe you anything. I'm in the clear and I don't aim to be pushed no farther."

One of the men Quist had crowded from the bar gave a hoot of derision. "That's telling him, Redwood! It's about time Greg Quist got his comeuppance——" A low growl of approval ran through the room.

The man stopped short, mouth open as Quist turned toward him. There was a swift movement of Quist's right hand and his gun flashed into view, the barrel describing a short arc that landed, with considerable violence, on the side of the man's head. A pained groan left his open mouth, his eyes became glassy. He managed for a small moment to stay erect, and then as though he were making a deep bow to Greg Quist, his body bent at the waist and he nose-dived toward the floor.

Tolliver swallowed hard and craned his neck across the bar to look at the stricken man. "Well, now," he commenced slowly, "it might be Lippy had that comin'. He'd no right to interrupt our *habla*——"

Quist snapped, "Keep this room covered, Trigger."

Rick had already reached for his gun and it was out now, bearing on the men crowded about the big room. Their growled approval of Lippy's words had been abruptly silenced. At the same moment, Quist's left hand had darted out and, seizing Tolliver by the throat, he dragged the big man halfway across the bar. Tolliver struggled and threw himself about, his hands endeavouring to tear Quist's fingers from his throat, but Quist only squeezed the harder. Finally, when the big man had started to grow purple, Quist loosened his grip somewhat. Meanwhile, no other man in the room had made a move.

His eyes and gun still covering the crowd, Rick heard Quist's voice, something of the chill of frozen wastelands in the tones: "Don't ever again, Tolliver," Quist was saying, "tell me I'm not man enough to take you apart, or I'll crowd you even worse. And don't try to tell me I haven't anything on you." He laughed harshly. "Let me remind you of a certain bank robbery that took place nine years ago, in Sacramento, California. They are still looking for the robber, Tolliver." Rick caught Tolliver's startled gurgle, then Quist's cold tones again, "Yes, I know all about that too. I've got it all down, black on white, and cached away in a safe place where it will be made public, if anything should suddenly happen to me. Just as I've a pile of similar papers covering other men in this room——"

"Quist—you devil!" Tolliver gasped.

"Not quite," Quist stated coldly, "though I can make it hot as hell for anybody that crosses me." Rick heard the big man's heels thud on the floor, back of the bar, as Quist released him. "Now, do you get busy, or do I have to crowd you some more?"

"I'll do what I can," Tolliver said sullenly. He seemed to be having trouble with his voice.

Quist laughed softly, suddenly congenial. "Why, Redwood, that's right reasonable of you. It's all any man could ask. I'll be expecting to be hearing from you before too long. . . . Come on, Trigger, let's slope. . . . See you again, boys." Arrogantly, Quist turned and, followed by Rick Hamilton, started for the doorway. At the exit he paused, pushed one door open for Rick to pass, glanced quickly about the room, and then stepped outside.

Neither man spoke as they climbed into saddles, though Rick caught the long pent-up breath of relief from Quist as he settled to his horse's back. For five minutes they walked their ponies and Rick discovered suddenly that his forehead was dripping moisture. He reached for his bandanna and heard a chuckle from Quist, as he started to mop his face.

"Pretty warm back there, Rick?"

"Not half as warm as I was expecting it would be," Rick managed. Indignation crept into his tones and he added reproachfully, "Trigger Hamilton! The man who ran Billy the Kid out of Tutumcari! My God! Don't you give a damn what lies you spill?"

Quist laughed. "Not when they achieve proper results. I wanted to give that gang something to occupy their minds, and it worked. If they'd stopped to think, they'd realized you weren't old enough while the Kid was alive to do anything like that. Just like Tolliver, when I grabbed him by the throat. He had a gun in his holster. If he'd grabbed it, he might—just might, mind you—have had a chance to plug me. But, no, he busied both his hands trying to get his throat free. Another instance of not thinking. We ran a bluff and got away with it——"

He paused as the sound of drumming hoofs at their rear interrupted the words. Glancing back, Rick saw a large body of riders closing in fast. He started to reach for the gun in his waistband, when Quist said sharply, "Hold it! It's all right." They swung their ponies off the road as the riders thundered past, grim-faced, angry, sullen, but each man riding as though his life depended on it—as perhaps, in some instances, it did. As they passed, Rick recognized many of the faces he'd seen at Tolliver's Hotel, but not one of them paid him any attention as he flashed by.

Quist and Rick waited for the dust to settle before they again started on. Quist laughed softly, "It sure looks like Tolliver had put a brand-iron under the seats of their pants."

"But, what——? I don't understand."

Quist explained. "Tolliver's hounds on the scent. They'll fan out once they hit town and ask questions. Eventually, they'll get a line on our unknown gunman. You see if I'm not right. Come on, let's move along." They put the ponies into a lope and within a half hour had reached El Paso. . . .

It was after midnight, that night, and Rick and Quist were seated at a table in Weinkoff's saloon on El Paso Street. It was quiet; there was only a scattered handful of customers at the bar. Rick and Quist had wandered about the town and eventually had dropped in for some iced beer. Finally Rick spoke, "Do you reckon we're going to have to make another visit to Tolliver's?"

Quist smiled ruefully. "Don't rub it in. I've not given up hope yet. These things take time."

"Whether your plan works or not," Rick said earnestly. "I want you to know it's been a pleasure seeing you work——"

Quist raised a derogatory hand in protest, but Rick went on, "I mean it. I recognize nerve when I see it and——"

"Nerve? Bosh! I ran a bluff and made it stick—and *you* helped me. I only wish it would produce results before you leave——"

"It would be mighty fine if you could return with me."

Quist shook his head. "That job's not for me, Rick. I don't want to dictate, but in your place I'd forget the whole business, before somebody gets hurt—somebody you wouldn't want to see hurt——" He broke off as Tug Bailey entered the saloon, glanced about and then approached the table where Quist and Rick sat. Quist motioned to the bartender who brought three fresh bottles of beer. At Quist's invitation, Bailey drew up a chair. Quist said, "Well?" His manner was confidant.

"I think we've got something for you, Mr. Quist," Bailey said. "We don't know who the man is—he's not one of our crowd——"

"Tolliver told me that much. Get on with your story."

Bailey eyed the ceiling, marshaling his thoughts. "This man arrived two days ago on a morning train—westbound T.N. & A.S.—carryin' a .38-55 Winchester. It happened one of our fellers was at the depot when he got off, so that part's easy. It took some castin' around for the rest, though——"

"Get to it!" Quist snapped.

"He got a room at a Chinese boardinghouse over on Montana Street, then went and asked directions to the T.N. & A.S. office. He went there. He was heard to ask for you, but he left right after you came in—waited across the street until you went out, then followed you to the Pierson Hotel. Yesterday morning he was at the Pierson early and after you went to breakfast, he went in the hotel. We don't know what for, but he didn't stay long."

"See, Rick," Quist said wryly, "that's the kind of detective I am. I didn't even realize I was being shadowed. Get on, Bailey."

"After this feller left the Pierson, he hired a hawss at Cox's Livery, then picked up his rifle at the boardinghouse. He was seen leavin' there, riding east. Two hours later he was back and returned the hawss to the livery. A couple of our boys rode out and read sign on him, found where he'd waited behind a rise. They picked this up."

Bailey dropped an exploded .38-55 Winchester shell on the table. Quist studied it a moment and thrust it into a pocket. Bailey continued, "Next this feller was seen on Second Street, talkin' to a Mex kid. He give the boy some money and a paper. Might be he was arrangin' to have a message delivered. Then he hurried to the depot. The first train to come through was headed east—Texas & Galveston road. He got on that."

Quist asked, "Where was he headed for?"

"He was routed to change to a T.N. & A.S. train at San Sabita, and his ticket was to carry him to a town named Hyperion." Quist and Rick exchanged quick glances. Bailey continued, "The ticket-seller told this feller if he'd wait just a half hour, he could get on a T.N. & A.S. train when it come through, and then he'd have no need of changin'. But the hombre said he wouldn't wait. He took the Texas & Galveston, and acted plumb impatient until it arrived."

"Sounds like he was in a hurry," Quist said. "Didn't he stop to pick up his baggage? Got a description of him?"

Bailey said, "The only baggage was his rifle, which he kept with him, after returnin' the hawss. Didn't even give no name at the boardin'house, or maybe the owners forgot it. He'd paid his money. That's all they cared. He was 'bout six foot tall, brownish complected; around thirty-five to forty. Mustache. Somethin' wrong with his left leg. He limped. Looked like a cowman. His clothes——"

"Never mind his clothes. They could be changed without trouble," Quist cut in. "That all you got?"

"That's all," Bailey said. "I think we done purty good."

Quist nodded. "I agree on that. Tell Tolliver if he'd got on the job when I first asked, I might have caught this fellow before he skipped town. Impress it on Tolliver I don't like that part at all, and that next time I speak, I want him to jump, quick and sudden!" Bailey said he'd tell Tolliver. Quist nodded and spilled some money on the table. "Pay for the drinks, Bailey. Keep what's left for your trouble. Come on, Rick." Brushing aside Bailey's thanks, Quist left the saloon with Rick close at his side.

Rick frowned. "I wonder why that fellow went to Hyperion."

"Probably headed back home," Quist said shortly.

Rick's eyes widened. "You mean he's somebody I might know?"

"I don't think there's the least doubt of it."

"I'll be dad-blasted!" Rick exclaimed. "I don't know who it could be."

They strode along in silence for a time, passing the lighted front of saloons and a few stores. Rick opened his mouth to speak on various occasions, but a look at Quist's frowning face checked him. Arriving at the Pierson Hotel, Quist went directly to the lobby desk. "Any message arrive for me?" he demanded.

"Yes, Mr. Quist. It came in after supper. The Mexican kid who brought it had been told not to deliver it until tonight."

Quist spoke over one shoulder to Rick. "Giving himself plenty of time to get clear of town." He tore open the envelope. His eyes narrowed as he read the brief message enclosed, then passed it to Rick Hamilton.

Rather crudely printed in lead pencil on a smudged sheet of paper were the words: "If you want to keep healthy don't leave El Paso." There was no signature on the note.

Rick lifted his troubled eyes to meet Quist's. Quist said, softly, "Almost sounds like a threat, doesn't it? Rick, who knew you were coming to see me?"

Hamilton frowned. "Just my father and sister, I guess."

"You guess? That means somebody else knew, whether you intended it or not."

"It looks that way," Rick said tonelessly, "though I don't see——"

"Forget it." Quist took Rick's arm and walked him away from the desk. His manner was lazy, nonchalant, as he summed up the details: "We're fairly certain that the man who wrote this note is headed for Hyperion. He doesn't want me to come to Hyperion. He has already demonstrated his markmanship in the hope he can scare me into staying in El Paso." Quist laughed softly. "To paraphrase our mutual friend, Mr. Tolliver, 'I don't aim to be pushed.' " He consulted his watch. "There's a T.N. & A.S. train due to leave here for Hyperion, in exactly thirty-three minutes. Time's burning fast, Rick——"

"You mean"—Rick was grinning widely, excitedly—"that you're coming back with me, after all?"

Quist drawled blandly, "Whatever gave you the idea I wasn't? Get over to the Grand Central and get your satchel packed. I'll meet you at the depot. Jump to it!"

Chapter V : A COLD TRAIL

The Terrapin Ranch, Gregory Quist was deciding, as he sat on the long, flagstoned gallery, with Rick and his sister, Tracy Canfield, was a mighty nice layout. The house was far more pretentious, with its whitewashed, rock-and-adobe walls and slanting shake roof, than was customary with ranch houses of that day. From the gallery, Quist could see, beneath the low-hanging branches of numerous live oak trees, the road that ran

through rolling grasslands to Hyperion. To the rear of the big
house, Quist had noticed on his arrival with Rick, the bunkhouse with adjoining messhouse, barns, stables, and corrals.
A well-oiled windmill clanked steadily in the gentle breeze
blowing down from the Gunsight Mountains.

"You're sure you and Mr. Quist have had your dinner?"
Tracy was asking her brother. "I can go in and fix up something——"

"Tracy!" Rick laughed. "Where's your mind? It must be
somewhere else. That's the third time you've asked that question. Did you forget? Like I told you, we got off the train in
Hyperion a couple of hours past midnight, and slept at the
hotel. We combined breakfast and dinner, then went to the
livery stable——" He broke off. "I told Greg that once we
got out here I'd see that he got a decent horse. The livery
didn't have much to offer."

"Of course," Tracy said politely. "We should have some
saddlers that need exercise. I'll ask Tom Jenkins. If Mr. Quist
decides to stay here"—she hesitated meaningly—"we can have
one of the boys return the livery animal."

"I think I'd best stay at the hotel in Hyperion," Quist said,
"though I'll be glad of the loan of a horse." He had already
sensed in the girl a certain resentment of his coming here, a
resentment that was in conflict with her natural custom of
hospitality. She was a tall girl, and slim, with blond hair like
pale gold parted in the center and drawn severely back in a
heavy knot at her nape. Her eyebrows, strangely enough, were
dark, and her very fair hair was in strange contrast to her
deeply tanned smooth skin; her lips looked as though they'd
been stained with crushed raspberries. Tracy Canfield's features resembled greatly those of her good-looking brother's,
though they were finer, the nose arched and sharply chiseled
with sensitive nostrils; her chin showed a great deal of deter-
mination. The girl wore a white blouse with short sleeves that
displayed well-rounded arms, and a long, full-flowing skirt that
might have been designed in Mexico. On her bare feet were
low Mexican sandals of braided leather. It wasn't at all the
sort of costume in which one generally received guests in that
day and age. Quist judged she had donned the clothing for an
afternoon's comfort. The unexpected arrival of Gregory Quist
appeared to bother Tracy Canfield not at all—so far as concerned her appearance.

Quist's gaze came back to the pale-gold hair and he thought
of a yellow rose. And in the next instant he remembered
thorns, as well. There was something fine, patrician, about
Tracy Canfield, but the lips of her generous mouth were a

trifle too tight and in her off-guard moments he had certainly detected a definite haunting fear in the velvety brown eyes. A fear of what? Despite Rick's assurances, Quist felt quite sure, now, that Mrs. Canfield hadn't wanted any investigation of the year-old murder. The girl rose after a few minutes and went into the house, dropping over one shoulder a remark that had to do with giving her guest something to drink.

"I had thought," Rick said somewhat uncomfortably, "that you'd stay here—sleep down at the bunkhouse, that is."

"If I make my headquarters in Hyperion," Quist said, "I'll feel freer to move around." He smiled. "To tell the truth, I'm not sure I'd be too welcome here."

Rick flushed. "I doubt it would make any difference to Tracy. You can see how she is, I imagine—doesn't seem to give a damn about anything."

"I wouldn't say that," Quist replied. "As a sort of defense she's built up a hard outer shell, but she's not as hard as she'd like to make out——"

"Defense against what——?" Rick commenced; then, "I see what you mean. She's put on a don't-care attitude for anybody who might choose to think she killed Nash Canfield."

"Something like that," Quist nodded.

The girl returned within a few minutes with tall cool glasses containing an amber liquid. The drink, when he had tasted it, was very satisfactory. Bourbon and something tart—lime or lemon. He dropped a remark to the girl concerning the drink's excellence. She thanked him in a cool, impersonal voice and said nothing more. Quist started to manufacture a cigarette. Rick produced his own "makin's" and rolled a smoke.

Silence reigned until the men had finished their drinks. Finally, Tracy seemed to come to some decision. She brushed a wisp of the pale-gold hair from her tanned forehead and said, "Rick, Mr. Quist came here to make an investigation. I suppose there's no use losing time. He'll probably want to look at the house. Do you want to show him through? I suppose you've told him all there's to be told. I'll answer any necessary questions, but I know no more than you do."

"We'll let the questioning go for another time," Quist said. "I would like to see the house, though."

The girl remained seated on the porch, while Rick and Quist entered the wide front room, Rick closing the door behind him. Quist glanced about the big room with its wide fireplace, comfortable leather chairs and Navajo rugs. Paintings of the western country on the walls caught his eye and he commented on them. Rick nodded, "Nash Canfield bought those from an artist in San Antonio at the time this house was being built. They set him back a pretty penny——"

"I can see he had the pretty penny to spend, just by looking at this house."

Rick nodded. "He had it all right."

Quist asked quietly, "Who stood to benefit most from his death?"

Color flowed into Rick's face. "Why—why, Tracy, of course, as his wife—you understand. She inherited everything. Nash had no living relatives—but look here, Greg, don't rush to conclusions—"

Quist looked surprised. "Just what conclusions am I rushing to?"

Rick said shortly, "Forget it," then went on, "There's where Nash was sitting when I first arrived that evening,"—indicating a chair near a big table. "When I returned a second time he was throwing himself about, at just this spot, I'd say," a pointing finger indicating the location where Nash Canfield had died. "And Tracy was just a couple of yards—maybe more —from the open front door."

Quist asked various questions, checking on details Rick had already related, then went on, "You mentioned that an overturned lamp had spilled oil on one of the rugs. Which rug?"

Rick glanced dubiously about. "I'm not sure, now. It should be that rug under the table, there. Still, I don't know—wait! I'll go ask Tracy."

"It doesn't matter," Quist protested.

"I aim to see you get answers to any questions asked." Rick hurried to the front door, stepped outside a minute, then returned. "The rug," he explained, "is around some place. Tracy had the rug washed out, but the colors ran and she decided not to use it any longer. I imagine she didn't want to be reminded of what had happened, each time she saw that rug."

"I imagine," Quist nodded carelessly. "But doesn't this house, and Canfield's money, remind her of things?"

Rick flushed angrily. "You may not believe it, but she earned every cent she ever received due to Canfield's death. Good God, Greg! Where would you have her go? This is her home."

"She didn't care to return and live with you and your father?"

"No, she didn't," Rick said flatly. "Mother's been dead for years, and we'd liked to have had her. On the other hand, Tracy doesn't seem to care for the Circle-H any more. She goes to see Dad regularly, but never stays long."

Quist nodded. "You said once only your father and your sister knew that you were coming to El Paso to see me. We know by now that somebody else knew. I may be mistaken, but your sister impresses me as not being too keen on having me here."

"We-ell," Rick spoke hesitatingly, "she did say before I left that she didn't see what good it would do, and that you'd have only a cold trail to read, but I didn't think she actually objected." The younger man looked troubled.

"How did your father feel about me coming here?"

"To tell the truth," Rick admitted frankly, "he was dead set against the idea——"

"Why?" Quist snapped.

Rick frowned. "I'm not sure. He just said he didn't think it would do any good at this late date. He, too, brought up that matter of a cold trail. To be honest, Greg, I think he was afraid you might uncover some evidence damaging to Tracy."

"You mean he believes your sister killed Canfield?"

Rick shook his head. "Not knowingly, that is. But Dad might think she'd done something when she was only half-conscious, as she was when she arrived here that night. That's the only thing I could think of, Greg, though I may be all wrong."

"That's to be seen," Quist nodded.

They continued the inspection of the house. At the far end of the room, opposite the front door, a second door led into a wide hall which ran parallel to the front of the house. At either end of this hall a door led into two wings of the building, between which was an open space, also paved with flagstones, and from the center of which grew an ancient live oak tree. There were several benches placed against the walls in this patio, and Quist could believe it would be a very pleasant place to sit at certain seasons of the year.

One wing of the building was occupied by a large dining room, and beyond it a kitchen containing an iron range, table, cupboards, and so on. Quist said, "You mentioned the Terrapin cook——"

"Trunkfoot Wagner."

"That's the name. You said the night Canfield was shot, Wagner entered the house from the rear. Would he have come through this kitchen?"

"That's it. Well, I suppose this is the way he came in. It would be the natural thing to do. There's a back door opening from the other wing, but I doubt any of the Terrapin hands have ever entered there."

Quist nodded, as he glanced through the window in the back door down a gentle slope to the bunkhouse and other buildings. "Yes, I suppose he would, naturally, come in this way. What about the other wing, Rick?"

They came back through the dining room, walked along the hall and entered the door to the other wing. Here, too, was a hall, but narrower than the first, with a door at the far end giving access to the outside. Spaced evenly along this hall were four other doors, which Rick explained led to bedrooms. "The first is Tracy's, then comes the one that Canfield used. The other two were for guests. Tracy and Canfield didn't have guests after the first six months they were married."

Quist glanced into the bedrooms and then with Rick returned to the gallery. Tracy was seated as they had left her. She glanced up as Quist resumed his seat. "Through so soon, Mr. Investigator?" she asked, something brittle in her tones. "I suppose you can already tell us who the guilty person is."

Quist shook his head. "I'm not that smart, Mrs. Canfield." He added dryly, "I might even require another day of investigating." The girl stared at him. Quist laughed and she saw he was joking. Something that had been hard left her lips, her eyes softened a trifle. Quist went on, "Mrs. Canfield, who else beside you and your father knew that Rick was coming to El Paso to engage me? Who have you told?"

"I've mentioned it to no one. I did hear Dad, the day after Rick first proposed the idea, say something about it to Gabe Bedell."

Rick groaned. "Gabe Bedell—of all men! Gabe never did know how to keep his mouth shut." Quist asked a question and Rick explained, "Bedell runs the Rocking-B outfit. He's an old crony of Dad's. Straight as they come, Gabe is, but his tongue hangs in the middle and waggles in all directions."

"Oh, it's no secret you were coming here, Mr. Quist," Tracy laughed. She spoke to Rick, "Yesterday when I was in town, that nosey Mrs. Flaglin said she heard you'd gone to get a detective to solve—well, you can guess how she went on."

"What did you tell her?" Rick asked.

"Told her your business was your own and that I'd have you report to her when you got back."

Rick grinned. "Gentle with her, weren't you? Can't blame you, though. She's the worst gossip in seven counties." He turned to Quist. "I guess it's no use trying to keep secret what business brought you here?"

Quist shook his head. "I've known that ever since that shot was fired through my hotel window."

"You were fired on?" Tracy Canfield looked startled.

Rick told the story, going into minute details regarding the visit to Tolliver's. A certain respect for Gregory Quist ap-

peared in Tracy Canfield's eyes. "You mean to say that you
went to that dive this Tolliver man ran?" she asked Rick.

"Certain," Rick laughed. "Greg couldn't have got along
without his gunman, Trigger Hamilton."

"Pshaw! It's a good thing Mr. Quist didn't have to depend
on your markmanship, Rick. He surely doesn't know how bad
you really are. Or didn't it matter? I'm commencing to think
you're fooling me, that you've concocted this whole story out
of your imagination. I believe you're both frauds."

"Let's say you're fifty per cent right, Mrs. Canfield," Quist
chuckled. For a few moments something of the real girl had
shown in Tracy's manner, and Quist was admiring what he
saw. "You'll have to decide, though, whether Rick or I am
the fraud. You're probably partial to your brother——"

"Therefore," Tracy interrupted, "I'll have to consider him
the fraud."

"Aw, Tracy," Rick protested. The other two laughed. Some
of the tension left the air. In a short while, however, Rick came
back to more serious business. "While you're here, Greg, do
you want to question Trunkfoot Wagner regarding what happened that night?"

Quist considered. Finally, "I'll pass that up for the time
being. You've already told me what Wagner did that night. I
gather from what you've told me that your cook didn't tell the
same story on the stand. I'd just as soon not bring that matter
to light, and I'm sure you agree with me, until it becomes
absolutely necessary."

Tracy's brown eyes narrowed slightly. Rick appeared somewhat relieved. "Is there anybody else you want to talk to?" he
asked.

I think you said the Terrapin foreman went into the bank
with Mr. Canfield that day. I'd like to ask him a few questions——"

"I don't think Tom Jenkins can tell you anything," Tracy
said. "Tom wasn't even here when it happened."

"You're sure of that, of course," Quist said dryly.

"Of course I am." Tracy bridled. "Tom and the rest of the
hands had already started to Hyperion before Nash arrived
here."

"He might have had time to return, too," Quist pointed out.
"As I get it, Mrs. Canfield, at the time of the shooting you were
in no condition to know who was here." Tracy fell silent. Quist
went on, "So if you don't mind too much, I'll talk to your foreman."

"You can talk from now until doomsday for all I care,"

Tracy said in hard, even tones. "But you'll learn that Tom Jenkins had nothing to do with the business."

"Then he has nothing to fear," Quist said quietly. "You apparently think pretty well of your foreman——"

"Oh, everybody likes Tom," Rick broke in.

"Known him long?" Quist asked.

"All my life. Tom was born not far from Hyperion. He's a straight-shooter—I mean he's honest. For that matter, he *is* a straight-shooter. I don't think there's a man in the Gunsight country can touch him, using a rifle."

"That's open to argument, Rick," Tracy put in. "You'll remember two years ago, at the Fourth of July celebration, Homer Pritchett got first place in the rifle contest."

"Shucks!" Rick protested. "Tom Jenkins just had some bad luck that day. Nine times out of ten, Tom will beat him."

"Who is Homer Pritchett?" Quist asked idly.

"Foreman on Cody Thatcher's Wagon-Wheel Ranch."

Quist sighed. "And I don't even know who Cody Thatcher is. It seems there are a lot of people I have to get acquainted with. Friend of yours?"

Rick said he was. Tracy added she'd known him for years, though again hard lights had entered the girl's eyes when she spoke. Quist went on, "How long has Jenkins been rodding the Terrapin?"

Tracy said, "Something over two years, going on to three, I guess. He's a good foreman. I don't know what I'd done the past year without him to handle the running of this place."

"He sounds capable," Quist said, then turned to Rick, "You said, when we arrived, Jenkins wasn't here. Any idea when he'll be back?"

Rick looked to Tracy for an answer. The girl sat looking out across the open country and didn't turn her head as she replied, "Tom is at the Diamond-Box, over in Sanchez County. The Diamond-Box wanted to buy some feeder stock from us and Tom went to arrange a deal. He should be back today ——" She broke off as a step sounded at the corner of the house and a long-jointed man with black hair and rather swarthy features rounded the corner of the house. He was in cowman togs and appeared in the vicinity of thirty years.

"Speaking of the devil," Rick laughed. "Here's Tom now."

Tracy said, "We were just wondering why you weren't back. Have a good trip, Tom?"

"Pushed my horse some," Jenkins replied. "The trip was successful, if that's what you mean." For a moment he spoke more directly to the girl. "The Diamond-Box will take those feeders whenever we push them over to their range. I got a right good price, too, Tracy." He broke off, looking at Quist.

Rick introduced the two men and they shook hands, meanwhile sizing each other up. Jenkins' handclasp was hard and firm; he looked capable, and possessed a lean, muscular jaw. Tracy said, "The rumor seems to have spread, Tom, that Rick was bringing a detective here, so there's no use trying to keep the secret from you. Mr. Quist is the man." Quist noticed Jenkins stiffen a trifle at the words, but he said nothing beyond:

"I wish you luck, Mr. Quist. If there is anything I can do——"

"You can," Quist said. "Mrs. Canfield has been good enough to loan me a horse. It's up to you to say what I can have in the way of horseflesh."

"That's easy enough," Jenkins replied, smiling, and Quist saw that his teeth were very white and even. He looked thoughtful. "The pick of our extra saddlers settles down to three—there's a little *grulla* that's a goer, but a trifle light, maybe; then there's a black gelding that *I* like, though you'd have to show him who's boss. There's a chestnut I can recommend——"

"I'll leave it to you," Quist nodded.

"Suppose we leave it to *you,* when you see the horses. You'll be staying the night, I reckon." Quist explained that he planned to get back to his hotel in Hyperion that night. He wondered if it was actually a look of relief that crossed Jenkins' face when he spoke. Jenkins went on, "Well, that's up to you, too. We've extra bunks. Howsomever, if you do plan to ride in tonight, I can ride with you and see how you like the horse." Quist said that wasn't necessary. "I've got some business in town, to 'tend to, anyway," Jenkins said.

"What business makes it necessary you should go in tonight?" Tracy asked in some surprise.

"Oh, just some odds and ends I want to get cleared up, early in the morning," Jenkins said evasively. The girl didn't say any more.

Rick got to his feet. "Well, I'd best slope along to the Circle-H and let dad know I'm back. Greg, I'll drop into town tomorrow and see how you're getting along."

A few minutes later, the three men strode down to the corral, and Rick got into his saddle, while Quist and Jenkins busied themselves at another corral. In the end, it was the black gelding that Quist chose. By this time the cowhands were coming in off the range, and after eating supper, cooked by Trunkfoot Wagner who eyed Quist with a suspicious gaze, Jenkins and Quist saddled up and headed toward the road to Hyperion.

Chapter VI : SHOTS IN THE NIGHT

The sun had long since dropped below the tops of the Gunsight Mountains by the time Jenkins and Quist departed from the Terrapin, and it was nearly dark. They ran the horses for the first couple of miles to give Quist an opportunity to try out his mount. Finally they pulled the animals to a walk to breathe them. "How do you like him?" Jenkins asked.

"Suits me fine," Quist said truthfully, "though I can see he needs a firm hand on the reins. A rider wouldn't dare get careless with him."

"You called it. That little black is a horse! You won't have any trouble, though, once you've showed him who's top man."

They rode in silence for a time, the road taking them between low hills, dotted with post oak, cedar and mesquite. Here and there clumps of cactus contrived with other brushy growth to make a dense thicket on either side of the hoof-chopped road. By this time there was only a faint light left in the western sky.

Jenkins said abruptly, "Well, start your questioning."

Quist laughed softly. "I didn't think you had any particular business to take you to Hyperion, so you took this way——"

"Certain, I did," Jenkins said harshly. "I knew it would be right difficult to talk around the bunkhouse, so I thought we'd get it over with quickest this way."

"No, the bunkhouse wouldn't have been any place to talk," Quist acknowledged. "I wasn't missing the fact that your hands weren't what is called friendly. Dammit, Jenkins, the air was almost hostile at supper."

"You've got to expect that attitude in other directions too. Mr. Quist, please get it through your head you won't be popular in these parts. Everybody knows what you've come here for. Why in hell couldn't you let well enough alone?"

"You forget, Jenkins, that I was asked to come here. And when somebody throws a Winchester slug in my direction, in an attempt to scare me into staying in El Paso, it makes me just that more determined to learn what is going on in these parts——"

"T'hell you say! When did this happen?"

"Is it necessary to tell you?" Quist asked.

Jenkins snapped, "I'm asking for information."

Quist related the story briefly. When he had concluded, Jenkins said furiously, "Goddammit! I was afraid of something like that. Though I didn't figure it would happen until you got here——"

Quist interrupted, "You're sure you've been at the Diamond-Box the past few days? I understand you're mighty handy with a rifle."

"I can prove it," Jenkins flared, after a moment's hesitation.

"Prove that you're handy with a rifle?"

"That, too, if necessary. But I can prove I was at the Diamond-Box."

Quist nodded. "You may have to, eventually. For the present I'll take your word for it—so long as your looks don't tally with the description of the man who did the rifle work. But a description can be changed——"

"Meaning I'm under suspicion?"

"Practically everybody who ever had anything much to do with Nash Canfield, in the Gunsight country, is under suspicion," Quist replied, "until he's proved innocent——"

"He?"

"Or she, if you must have it."

"Now, look here, Quist, Tracy isn't——"

"Let's drop that angle," Quist said sharply. "I've made no accusations, yet, so don't go off half-cocked." Jenkins fell silent and Quist continued, "The way your crew behaved at supper didn't inspire any confidence in me. I figure you wanted me away from the Terrapin. You were afraid of trouble."

"I didn't want you shot at while you were at the Terrapin," Jenkins said frankly. "One or two of my boys are right quick-tempered on occasion. I can handle my men, but sometimes trouble starts too fast to be handled. What you can't seem to realize is that Tracy—Mrs. Canfield—and Rick are right popular around here. Nash Canfield deserved killing if ever a man did, but that's over now—we've hoped—and friends of Rick and Tracy have been satisfied to let things lay as is. Rick never should have brought you here, though that fact alone should prove him innocent——"

"Not necessarily," Quist put in.

"Have it your way," Jenkins said sullenly. "Anyway, if you got any sense at all, you can realize why I wanted you away from the Terrapin. There isn't a man on the outfit who wouldn't fight to protect Tracy and Rick Hamilton. And you not even wearing a gun."

Quist didn't mention the gun in his shoulder holster, covered by his coat. He said, "I gave up slinging a gun at my hip several years ago."

"I don't think you're smart."

"That's open to argument," Quist said dryly. "I haven't been killed yet."

Jenkins said darkly, "You forget there's always a first time."

"Is that a threat, Jenkins?"

Jenkins swore. "It wouldn't do any good for me to deny it. I will tell you this, Quist—if any man, in any way, hurt a friend of mine, I'd sure as hell even the score."

"Revenge is an Indian trait," Quist pointed out.

"I'm one-sixteenth Cherokee, if it interests you."

"I'd guessed at something like that. You should be mighty proud of your Indian blood, Jenkins. The Cherokees were, are, a great people, with a culture far above what most people think."

"I *am* proud of it," Jenkins said, somewhat mollified.

"I think you were overly pessimistic about fearing trouble at the Terrapin, Jenkins, but, anyway, you did get me away—with my consent, of course—and now you're even accompanying me to town as a bodyguard."

The foreman was silent for a moment. "You're pretty damn' sharp, Mr. Quist. But I'm repeating, I just don't want anything happening to you while you're at the Terrapin, or on the way there, or coming back."

"Meaning my presence isn't welcome at the Terrapin?"

"I didn't say that," Jenkins growled.

"You meant it."

"That's whatever," Jenkins said angrily. "Once we're in Hyperion, my responsibility is over."

"Just when did my safety become your responsibility?" Quist laughed.

"The instant you crossed Terrapin holdings. I don't want any more charges leveled at Tracy or Rick. That old trouble is ended and I don't take it kindly that it's being dug up again."

"Exactly what are you afraid of, Jenkins?" Quist asked directly.

Jenkins didn't reply at once. Finally he said in a weary tone, "Oh, hell, ask your goddam questions and get it over with. If you think you can pin anything on me, you're welcome to try."

It was completely dark by this time and too early for the moon to be up. The only light came from scattered stars overhead. The two horses scuffed through the loose sandy soil at an even-gaited walk while their riders talked. Crickets chirped in the thickets at the side of the roadway; now and then the momentary flashing on and off of the pale greenish lights of fireflies cast some small illumination in the path of the advancing riders.

Quist marshaled his thoughts. "Jenkins," he asked first, "I'd like to know exactly what your actions were the day Canfield was killed."

"We-ell," Jenkins commenced slowly, "it was this way. Canfield had been drunk for days and hadn't bothered to see to paying the men——"

"I know about that," Quist cut in. "Mrs. Canfield got him out of bed and sent him to Hyperion, to the bank. Later, she sent you after him, as Rick told it. Why?"

"That's simple enough. Tracy got to figuring he might not even go to the bank, or if he did that he'd spend the money before he returned to the ranch. She sent me in to see that the money was brought back."

"That's clear. What happened when you got to Hyperion?"

"I found that Canfield had been making the saloons on both sides of the street. I caught up with him in Calydon's Saloon and after some argument persuaded him to go to the bank with me. We drew out the money and started back——"

"Just a minute," Quist interrupted. "There was an argument in front of the bank, wasn't there?" Jenkins didn't reply at once. With some apparent difficulty he remembered, finally, that an argument had taken place, though he claimed it didn't amount to anything. Quist said, "Let me be the judge on that score. What was the argument about?"

"As we left the bank," Jenkins said reluctantly, "Canfield saw Rick passing. He called him a couple of names." Quist interjected a question. Jenkins swore and continued, "All right, if you got to have it. Rick and Canfield weren't on friendly terms at all. Rick, on Tracy's account, had been riding Canfield, more or less, trying to get the man to straighten up. Canfield said something that made Rick lose his temper and Rick started to take a punch at him. I stopped him——"

"What was it Canfield said?"

"Damned if I remember," Jenkins snapped.

"Don't lie, Jenkins," Quist said softly.

Jenkins drew a long breath. His voice sounded miserable: "Well, it was something about me being too friendly with Tracy—and more stuff that I won't repeat. Now, look here, Quist——"

"You've told me what I wanted to know. We'll skip details. I'm surprised, though, that you didn't take after Canfield yourself."

"If you've got to know the truth," Jenkins flamed, "that was what I aimed to do—after I got Canfield out of town where there'd be no interruptions."

"You'd have killed him?"

"I might have," Jenkins stated bluntly. "Once I had him out of town, I cooled down. He was too drunk to remember what he'd said."

"I can understand that. When Canfield and Rick had their fuss, did Canfield pull his gun, or anything?"

"Canfield didn't wear a gun."

"I understood from Rick that Canfield had been shot with his own gun."

"That's right. But he never wore it. He was just too plumb careless about throwing lead promiscuous when he felt like celebrating. Finally, Sheriff Nixon ordered him to leave his gun off when he came to town. I don't think he ever wore it again."

"Who could get hold of that gun?"

"Practically anybody who knew where it was. It always hung in that hall, back of the ranch-house main room, where hats and coats and things were put. There's a row of hooks right near the door to the big room——"

"I remember seeing them now. In that case, anybody coming in the back way could get that gun."

"If he wanted to. If you ask me, I think Canfield got the gun himself and committed suicide."

Quist laughed softly. "Now you know better than that, Jenkins." Jenkins didn't reply. Quist continued, "All right, you've just stopped Rick from taking a punch at Canfield. What happened next?"

"I told Rick to clear out. There was a crowd of men around, so I told them to take care of Canfield—the bustard could scarcely stand alone—while I hunted up his horse. That took some time. I finally found the pony at the far end of town, at the hitchrack of the first saloon where Canfield had entered Hyperion. I brought the pony back and got Canfield into the saddle."

"Anything unusual happen while you were gone?"

"I reckon not. Canfield was sitting on the bank steps, in a sort of half-stupor. Somebody had stuck a bottle of whisky in his arms, and the crowd was still standing around laughing at him. I tried to take the bottle away, but he woke up and started to act ugly so I figured what the hell!—let the louse keep it and drink himself into an early grave. The doctor in Hyperion had warned him more than once about his drinking——"

"I know about Canfield getting the d.t.s. and so on. So you got him on his horse and headed out of town. What next?"

"Well, like I say, I'd cooled down by then. I was carrying the crew's wages, and I just couldn't get him to hurry. He couldn't have stayed on his horse, had it gone faster than a walk. So I left him to come on alone, while I rode on ahead to pay off the crew. Then we all got into saddles, excepting the cook, and headed back to town. We passed Canfield on the way in, and he hadn't progressed much farther than when I'd left him. I suppose the horse stopped to crop grass and such."

"Did you feel it was wise leaving your employer alone, considering his condition?"

"You're damned right I did," Jenkins said savagely. "I was hoping he'd fall out of the saddle and break his neck."

"You're frank."

"Why not?" Jenkins snapped. "I thought of a lot of things that could happen to him, if he was left to himself. The horse might get startled and run. Maybe he'd fall off and cut his throat on the bottle he carried, if it smashed——" He broke off. "Cripes! You're likely getting the wrong idea of me, but that's the way it was, where Canfield was concerned. Any decent man felt the same way. You didn't know Canfield the way we did——"

"All right, we can pass up that too. It's pretty firmly established in my mind that Canfield was a skunk and generally hated. During this altercation he had with Rick, was any other woman—besides Mrs. Canfield—mentioned?"

"What makes you ask that?"

"Just idle curiosity, I reckon," Quist said carelessly.

"Where Canfield was concerned, there were any number of women who might have been mentioned," Jenkins said evasively.

"You haven't answered my question."

Jenkins said testily, "All right, something was said about Camilla Peters that didn't set right with Rick."

"Who's Camilla Peters?"

"She owns the Bon-Ton."

"Dance hall?"

Jenkins swore. "Dammit, no! It's a hat store—women's hats."

Quist said mildly, "I'm sorry, but I couldn't be expected to know, remember. There's a Bon-Ton dance hall in two or three towns I've passed through in my time."

"I forgot you were a stranger here."

Quist asked for information regarding Camilla Peters. Jen-

kins said, "Now don't get any wrong ideas about Camilla, and
if you do, don't mention 'em to Rick. Rick's right interested in
that direction. So was Canfield before he died. Does that answer your question."

"Not completely, but it's enough for the present. Go on."

"There's not much left to tell. I was in Calydon's Saloon
that night when Rick hit town for the doctor. He told me
Canfield had been shot, so I headed for the Terrapin right off.
The doctor and sheriff both came out; neither could help Canfield by that time——"

"You mean the sheriff probably didn't care to, and the doctor came too late."

"All right, have it your way. You probably know that Rick
was arrested, brought to trial, and declared not guilty. The
upshot seems to be that Canfield met his death at the hands of
someone unknown."

"And since then," Quist said ironically, "the sheriff has
been running himself ragged trying to apprehend the unknown."

"There's no law against you thinking that, if you like."

"Only you figure me as a damn' fool if I do," Quist laughed.

"Draw your own conclusions," Jenkins growled, and fell
silent. He spoke again after a time, changing the subject,
"We're making the eight miles to town in right good time,
considering the slow gait we been traveling at." Quist agreed
that they were. Jenkins went on, "I don't know if you remember or not, but this road narrows, just ahead, and dips across
an arroyo. You'd best let me ride in front and show the way."

Without waiting for a reply, he pushed ahead of Quist's
pony. Quist felt the hoofs of the black gelding descending
sloping ground and heard them clatter on loose rock. The way
leveled off after a minute and commenced to rise. Just ahead,
the road cut between two thickets of dense brush rising on
either side. Jenkins was already climbing out of the arroyo,
the darker mass of his shoulders and sombrero silhouetted
against the night sky. He called back over his shoulder, "You
coming all right, Quist?"

"Coming all right," Quist replied, eyes peering ahead
through the gloom.

The words had scarcely left his lips, when the shot came.

To Quist's right, and slightly ahead, there was a brilliant
burst of orange fire, screened by the tangled branches of mesquite and chaparral, and a leaden slug passed dangerously
close to Quist's face.

Two bullets had already left Quist's underarm gun, before

Tom Jenkins got his six-shooter into action. For a brief few moments the night was made hideous by the detonations of exploding gunpowder and lead.

Chapter VII : SUSPICIONS

The guns fell silent. There'd been only the single shot from the brush, and Quist had replied to that so quickly the noise of his shot had blended with the echoes of that from the hidden assailant's weapon. Quist had dismounted from his pony and standing behind it, shielded from view of the brush and Tom Jenkins, was busily engaged in shoving fresh loads into the chambers of his .44. Up ahead a short way, he could hear Jenkins cursing in the darkness.

Jenkins called, "You hit, Quist?"

"It was close, but no bull's-eyes scored," Quist said shortly.

He was still peering toward the brush. Something that had been making thrashing sounds in the thicket was now silent, though after a moment there was a long-drawn groan.

"By God!" Jenkins said, as he stumbled over loose rock in Quist's direction. "You did have a gun on you." Quist could hear him reloading, as he approached.

"Underarm six-shooter," Quist said.

"You took me by surprise," Jenkins said lamely, "when I heard that shooting at my rear, I thought we'd been surrounded. For a second I couldn't get my own hawg-laig to working."

"So I noticed."

Jenkins swore again. "I been afraid of something like this." He came close, peering into Quist's face. "Look here, you got any suspicions I had anything to do with this?"

"I didn't say that," Quist replied quietly.

"But you're thinking it."

"Think about it yourself, Jenkins," Quist responded coldly. "This is ideal for an ambush. You pull away from me—oh, hell, we're wasting time talking. Let's investigate. If you're not in the clear, I'll learn it soon enough."

Jenkins started to speak, then remained silent. The two men separated and made their way into the brush at different points. It was Jenkins who located the hidden gunman, now sprawled, unconscious, at the side of a huge clump of prickly pear. Meanwhile, Quist had stumbled on the man's horse, tethered a few yards away. Jenkins called to Quist and scratched a match.

The man was on his stomach, one outflung hand still clutching a six-shooter. His hat had fallen off and lay nearby. His clothing was the usual kind worn in the western country—high-heeled boots, overalls, somewhat shabby; denim shirt and a skimpy vest. Quist turned him on his back and saw two bullet holes, bubbling with crimson, widely spaced on the man's middle.

"I suppose you don't know him, never saw him before," Quist commented.

"Certain I know him," Jenkins said testily. "Know who he is, leastwise. He's no pal of mine, if that's what you're hinting."

"Who is he?"

"Webb Bascom." Jenkins scratched another match.

"That doesn't tell me much."

"There's little I can tell you. Bascom is just a hanger-on in Hyperion. He's worked for most of the outfits hereabouts but never holds a job long. Lazy, I reckon. I don't understand ——" Jenkins paused.

"What don't you understand?"

"Why Bascom should be throwing lead your way. From what I know of the man, he wouldn't care whether you came here or not. He had nothing to do with Canfield, so far as I know."

Quist drew a deep breath. "He's still breathing. We'd better get him to town. Maybe when he comes to, he can tell us something."

"About what?"

"That's what I'm aiming to learn."

The match burned down in Jenkins' fingers. "Look here, Quist." He spoke through the darkness, voice trembling with the effort to repress anger. "Maybe I was a mite slower, but my .45 was throwing out lead along with your weapon. It might not have been you that hit him."

"If we can get a doctor to probe out the slugs, that can be settled quick. I use a .44."

"Then you can see," Jenkins said earnestly, "that if the bullets, or even one bullet, is a .45, I'm not a party to this bushwhacking."

"Not necessarily," Quist pointed out. "I've known of hombres to kill off evidence after a killing had been arranged."

"By God!" Jenkins flared. "You're going to be a hard man to get along with."

"I'm glad you realize that, mister," Quist said coldly. "I wouldn't want folks to get any wrong ideas about me. Let's get this hombre packed out of here. I'm anxious to learn if it was a .44 or a .45 that stopped him—or maybe both."

He went to get Bascom's horse. There was a rope on the saddle and within a short time they had the unconscious man lashed across the saddle and, themselves mounted, started once more toward Hyperion.

There were still plenty of lights burning along Hyperion's main thoroughfare—Huisache Street, as it had been named—when the two riders, their unconscious burden loaded between them, reached town, but Jenkins cut over to a side street, with the comment there were always a lot of curious people abroad at night and he didn't feel like answering questions.

"I don't mind attracting attention," Quist laughed shortly.

"I've noticed that," Jenkins growled.

At the corner of Austin and Crockett Streets he drew rein before a large house, painted white, with a picket fence surrounding it. "You wait here," Jenkins said, "while I see if Doc Sturven is in. There's lights in the windows, but it might be only his wife is there." He climbed down from the saddle, passed through a gateway in the picket fence and knocked at the house door. A woman opened and Jenkins passed inside; the door was again closed. A man came sauntering on the pathway that ran before the buildings ranged along the street. He started to pass, then stopped and came out to the edge of the road.

"What you got there, mister?" he asked. "Somebody been hurt?"

"I've heard rumors to that effect," Quist replied. "Fellow named Bascom. Know him?"

"Webb Bascom?" The man came closer and squinted at the wounded man on the saddle. "Damned if it ain't Bascom. What happened to him? There's blood drippin' down that saddle."

"I'm not surprised. You a friend of Bascom's?"

"Me? Not much. I don't reckon he's got any friends—not real pals, that is. What happened? Did he get shot?"

Quist didn't reply. The house door had again opened and Jenkins emerged, followed by the doctor. The two came out to the street. Jenkins introduced Dr. Sturven to Quist. The doctor nodded, but made no offer to shake hands. Instead he glanced at the passerby. "This is none of your business, friend, but if you want to be helpful, look up Sheriff Nixon and say I'd like to see him." The man hastened away. Sturven went on, "Let's get this fellow into the house where I can see what's what."

Quist and Jenkins carried the wounded Bascom into a bedroom indicated by the doctor and helped him strip off Bascom's clothing and get him into bed. The doctor commenced his examination by the light of an oil lamp. Now and then he delved into the black bag on a table near the bed. Quist and Jenkins waited in silence. There were movements at the rear of the house, but the doctor's wife didn't put in an appearance. After a time the doctor straightened up, frowning, and turned to Quist and Jenkins. "Bascom's pretty badly hurt," he announced. "I don't know as he's got much chance. I'll do what I can, of course."

"That's to be expected," Quist nodded. He studied the doctor a moment and saw a tall, spare, middle-aged man with a lined face and thin graying hair. "For certain reasons," Quist said, "Jenkins and I are anxious to see the bullets you probe out of Bascom——"

"I'll get to that when I can," Sturven said testily. "This man is bad hit, he's lost a lot of blood. I don't know as it's going to be worth while probing out those bullets. I've got to see how he picks up after the shock of being hit."

"Is he likely to regain consciousness soon?" Quist asked.

Sturven shook his head. "I've given him a hypodermic. It will likely be days before he'll be in a condition to do any talking—providing he lives. Just as soon as I know anything about the bullets I'll let Tom Jenkins know and he can tell you."

There was a definite dismissal in the doctor's tones and Quist took the hint. To his surprise, Jenkins departed with him. As the door closed behind them, Quist said in an amused voice, "Certainly friendly people in this town. I'll have to reverse my opinion of Texas."

"Look," Jenkins said, as they walked toward the gateway, "Doc Sturven is a mighty close friend of Tracy's and Rick's. I've warned you how folks will feel about anybody that comes meddling around here. If Sturven doesn't take to you, that's too bad. But he's a good doctor. He'll do all possible for Bascom. Just as soon as I learn anything, I'll pass it on to you——"

He stopped. As they passed through the gateway, Quist saw a tall man approaching along the walk. The light from the doctor's windows glinted on a metal star pinned to the approaching man's vest.

Jenkins said, "Looks like the sheriff." He raised his voice, "That you, Bard?"

"It's me," Sheriff Bard Nixon replied, in a deep voice, as he came within the arc of light thrown from the house. He was a big, rawboned man with a stern face beneath his tilted-back gray sombrero. Spreading mustaches adorned a tight-lipped mouth and his gray eyes were penetrating. He looked to be in the vicinity of forty-five, but may have been younger. A holstered Colt gun hung at his right thigh.

Jenkins performed introductions and, as in the doctor's case, the sheriff made no move to shake hands. "Howdy," he nodded shortly, and the tone was definitely hostile. "I heard some detective or other had arrived in town. Well"—turning to Jenkins—"what's this I hear about Bascom having some trouble?"

"You want my story or Jenkins'?" Quist put in.

The sheriff directed a brief glance at Quist. "I'll listen to Tom's version. I know him."

Quist suppressed the anger that rose within him and listened while Jenkins gave the sheriff an account of what had taken place. When Jenkins had finished, Quist admitted to himself that Jenkins had told the tale exactly as he, Quist, would have done. The Terrapin foreman hadn't skipped any details.

When the story was concluded, the sheriff asked, "How much chance does Doc Sturven give Bascom?"

"Not a great deal," Jenkins replied.

"Hmmm. . . ." Nixon considered that for a moment, then turned to Quist. "If Bascom should die, Quist, I'd have to hold you for the murder, you understand."

"No, I don't understand," Quist said tersely. He waited a moment, then said softly, "I guess you're a close friend of Mrs. Canfield and the Hamiltons too."

Color rose in the sheriff's face. "Certain, I am, but that has nothing to do with it. You'll be held for murder if Bascom dies."

"I fired in self-defense," Quist said in a steady voice. "For that matter, Jenkins fired too. It may have been his bullet—you see, that can easily be determined, once the bullets are probed out. I use a .44—Jenkins a .45."

"I've a hunch," Nixon said meaningly, "both slugs may prove to be .44s. Besides, there's so little difference between them calibers, and a slug generally gets battered when it hits, that it's going to be difficult to decide what the slugs are. A mite of lead knocked off a .45 could easy bring the weight down to .44 caliber. Yep, Quist, this looks serious."

Tom Jenkins laughed harshly. "Quist, did you say you were anxious to learn the caliber of the slugs taken out of Bascom?"

Quist ignored the remark and said in a steady voice, "Sheriff, I repeat, I fired in self-defense——"

"You've no proof of that," Nixon broke in heavily. "Maybe Bascom fired at Jenkins. How about it, Tom?"

Jenkins hesitated. "Well, I don't know why Bascom should

shoot at me. I was already past the point Bascom fired from, so I couldn't say where his aim was directed."

Nixon turned back to Quist. "You see how it is. Maybe you were just hasty in triggering your lead. Maybe you've made a damn' bad mistake, Quist."

Quist said in a disgusted tone, "Oh, hell! I've never yet found any way to out-argue stupidity. If I'm under arrest, let's go through with it—but I warn you——"

"Take it easy, Quist," Nixon said sharply. "I don't like folks warning me. No, you're not going to be arrested—yet. Bascom ain't dead—yet. I'm not preferrin' charges of any sort until I see what happens. You're a free man, so far as I'm concerned. There's not a thing I could do should you suddenly take it into your mind to leave town on the train that stops here within the next half hour."

"So that's your game?" Quist suddenly sounded amused. "I don't bluff easy, Sheriff—and I'm not interested in that train. Matter of fact, I expect to be staying around for quite some time. And I'll hand you another warning. Don't try to stop me."

Nixon's face flamed. He started to speak, stopped, then finally managed to say in a stiff voice, "On your own head be it, Quist." Turning, he walked quickly to the doctor's door, knocked, and after a moment stepped within the house.

An uncomfortable silence followed before Jenkins said, "Don't get Nixon wrong, Quist. He's a good man——"

"The stand he's taking, I couldn't get him any other way but wrong," Quist said bitterly. "That goes for practically everybody I've encountered since I hit this neck of the range. You'd better take that black gelding back with you, Jenkins. I made a mistake. I should have ridden that livery nag back to town——"

"Take the black back with me? What do you mean?"

"I don't like to be under obligation to people who don't like me," Quist said crisply.

"Now, look here"—Jenkins fumbled for words—"Tracy isn't going to like what happened any better than you do. She'll be hurt if you refuse that horse. I'm asking that you keep him, Quist, and if you think Nixon's idea of trying to scare you out of town was any of my doing, you're bad mistaken. I know better than that—now. I've seen you in action." He added morosely, "It might have been better if Bard Nixon had, too. He went off at a tangent that surprised me, though maybe it shouldn't have." Jenkins changed the subject: "But that's neither here nor there. I'm asking again that you keep that black gelding while you're here. Tracy won't take it kindly if I let you return the pony, now."

Quist nodded carelessly. "So long as you put it that way, I can't refuse. I wouldn't want to offend Mrs. Canfield."

They climbed into saddles and, leaving Bascom's horse for the sheriff to dispose of, walked their horses to the main street. After leaving the black gelding at the livery stable, across from the hotel, Quist announced that he guessed he'd saunter around town for a spell and get acquainted with the place. When he refused Jenkins' offer to buy a drink, the Terrapin foreman turned his mount somewhat huffily and said he'd be getting back to the ranch. Quist said good night and watched Jenkins spur rapidly out into the dusty street.

Later, when Quist entered the hotel, the desk clerk asked, a trifle coldly. "How long do you expect to be staying with us, Mr. Quist?"

"That," Quist replied somewhat cryptically, "hasn't yet been decided for me." Getting his key, he mounted the lobby stairway to the second floor.

Chapter VIII : QUIST TALKS TURKEY

Quist was in the hotel dining room the following morning, eating breakfast, when, glancing up, he saw Rick Hamilton's blond head in the doorway. Quist motioned him to a table, saying, "How about a cup of Java, with me?" Rick nodded and sat down. Coffee was brought.

Rick said, "Danged if you aren't an early riser. I'd hoped to get here in time to eat a second breakfast with you, but I see I'm too late." The smile left his face. "I hear you and Tom had some trouble on the way to town, last night."

"No particular trouble for me," Quist said quietly. "You been talking to the sheriff?"

Rick nodded. "I ran into him just before I came here." He frowned. "Darned if I know where Webb Bascom enters into this business. He couldn't be concerned, one way or the other."

"His gun could be hired, perhaps, if he's the sort of man I hear he is—or is it was?"

"Bard Nixon said he was still alive, but unconscious. Bard wouldn't talk much. He acted like he was mad about something."

"He was—and is, I imagine. You've got to get it through your head, Rick, that your friends don't like you bringing me here. They think you've done something awfully foolish; maybe you have."

"I don't figure it that way," Rick answered. "Say, what did happen last night?"

Quist told the story. When he had finished, Rick shook his head in perplexity. "I still don't understand it, any more than I can understand why that fellow shot at you in El Paso, Greg. I've been thinking about that. Why wouldn't it be a good idea to go down to the depot and inquire who got off the train that arrived before we pulled in?"

"I tried that, last night," Quist smiled. "The stationmaster can't seem to remember who got off, if anybody. He seems to have a very poor memory. In short, I gathered he didn't care to talk to me any more than was necessary. He must be a friend of your family."

"Who? Hodge Wood? Sure he is. I'll bet I could get him to talk. I used to call him uncle—though he's no relation."

"I doubt that you could, Rick. You forget that you're tarred with the same brush that smears me. Even showing him my T.N. & A.S. credentials didn't help. He thinks more of you Hamilton folks than he does of his job, I figure, but I've a hunch his memory wouldn't be any better for you than for me. Right now, Rick, even your friends seems to feel you've done a mighty foolish thing in bringing me to Hyperion. You'll find they'll continue to humor you in your ideas—but not to the extent of co-operating with you in same."

Rick looked curiously at Quist. "You seem to have learned quite a bit about me."

"That's part of the job. I sashayed around town and talked to a lot of folks, here and there, last night. And I didn't find anybody who acted friendly, so I had to judge by what folks left unsaid, rather than what was said." Quist smiled ruefully. "Yep, I'm right unpopular here, and you are, too, so long as you insist on digging up old bones."

"Dad sort of hinted at something of the kind, this morning," Rick said.

"How did he take the news that I had arrived?"

"Said he couldn't see what good you coming here would do. He was right grumpy, but he'll get over it after he knows you. I was thinking we might ride out to the Circle-H today, so you could meet him—unless you have something else——"

"Nothing more important." Quist nodded. "We'll start any time you say."

"Fine." Rick hesitated. "There's some business I'd like to 'tend to first, then——"

"This business," Quist smiled. "Could her name be Camilla Peters?"

Rick flushed. "We-ell—say, who told you about Camilla?"

"Tom Jenkins told me a few things last night, Rick. You forgot to mention that her name was brought into that quarrel you had with Canfield in front of the bank, that day he was killed."

Rick's flush deepened. "Aw-w, I couldn't see any reason for bringing her name into it. She had nothing to do with Canfield's death."

"It might be a good idea to let me be judge on that score."

"I tell you she didn't," Rick persisted. "I think a heap of Camilla. I—I'm going to ask her to marry me when—when ——" He swallowed hard. "I suppose now you're going to suspect me of——"

"You're no more under suspicion than you ever were, son," Quist stated. "If you want to marry the girl, why not ask her?"

Rick shook his head. "I couldn't do it, not so long as a lot of folks think I killed Canfield. I wouldn't like people to think that Camilla had married a murderer."

"Bosh! You're too idealistic. Rick, I'd like to meet Camilla Peters."

"There's nothing I'd like better, Greg. Once you know her you'd realize she didn't have anything to do with that killing. It's too early for her Bon-Ton shop to be open yet, but we can sashay around town until we see the shades raised in her windows. C'mon, let's go."

They left the hotel dining room and stepped into the street which was washed in morning sunlight. Hyperion, seat of Castaneda County, with a population crowding two thousand residents, looked prosperous, as befitted a booming cattle center. Along Huisache Street, the main thoroughfare, stretched an almost unbroken line of hitchracks at which stood waiting ponies and wagons. Saloons were numerous; there were four general stores, two drugstores, a Stockman's National Bank, three hotels (though two of them were more nearly akin to boardinghouses), and various other enterprises. Buildings were constructed of rock-and-adobe, or rock only; many were of frame construction, and there were several brick structures. High false fronts were common as were the wooden awnings stretching out over plank sidewalks. A brick county house stood on Huisache Street, just a few doors off Fannin Street. Other cross streets, running north and south, were Crockett, San Jacinto and Brazos. To the north, running parallel with Huisache, were residential thoroughfares: Austin, Franklin, and Gunsight Streets. At the end of Gunsight, going east, was the cemetery, known as Boot Hill. Beyond Huisache, to the south, ran the T.N. & A.S. rails, with a spur and clutter of whitewashed cattle pens at the eastern end of town, rarely in use except during the shipping season following beef roundup. On the far side of the tracks was open country, dotted here and there with scattered adobes occupied by Mexicans and railroad section hands.

Rick and Quist strolled west on Huisache Street and, returning, stopped at John Calydon's saloon, a low-ceilinged place with a bar running along the right hand wall, and a few chairs and tables occupying the remainder of the room. There was a scattering of men at the bar. Rick introduced Quist to Calydon, a bulky-middled man with slicked-down gray hair and pale blue eyes, who was behind the bar. Calydon nodded briefly and asked them what they'd have. Quist got a cigar and Rick took a bottle of beer. After Calydon had moved away down the long counter, Rick said, "I'm commencing to see what you mean, Greg. John Calydon is usually a right genial man, but he acted like he didn't like to see you here. I'm sorry. This is generally considered the best bar in town."

Quist shrugged. "I'm pretty thick-skinned, Rick."

Two men pushed their way through the swinging doors. The first, something under thirty-five years, was broad-shouldered and lean-hipped, with reddish hair and good features. The second was about five years older, with a lean, angular frame in the vicinity of six feet; his brownish hair was streaked with gray and he wore a thick mustache. Both men wore cow country togs—overalls cuffed at the ankles of high-heeled riding boots, woolen shirts, sombreros, and holstered six-shooters at their right thighs.

Rick hailed the first man: "H'are you, Cody! What you doing in town so early? Hello, Homer."

The older man just nodded after casting a sharp glance at Quist. The younger replied, "How's it going, Rick? I rode in to see about buying some grain. I reckon Homer just come along to keep me company."

Rick introduced Quist to the two men: Cody Thatcher, owner of the Wagon-Wheel brand, and his foreman, Homer Pritchett. Quist was busying himself replacing a bit of loose wrapper on his cigar, so didn't offer to shake hands. It was just as well; neither Pritchett nor Thatcher offered a handclasp. Both nodded carelessly and continued on their way to the far end of the bar. Quist gazed after the two with narrowed eyes, remembering a description he carried in mind: close to six feet, brownish complexioned, between thirty-five and forty, mustache. . . . He turned to Rick. "Isn't that the Homer Pritchett who's supposed to be so handy with a rifle?"

"Yes, why? Sa-ay, you don't think he's the one who fired that Winchester in El Paso——?"

"The description fits, Rick—except I didn't notice any limp in Pritchett's left leg. He don't walk like he was lame."

"I reckon not." Rick frowned. "I think you're on the wrong track, Greg. Pritchett wouldn't be concerned in your doings——"

"Dammit," Quist said irritably, "I've got to proceed on the premise that everybody's concerned in what I do, until facts prove otherwise." Somewhat dubiously, Rick agreed. Quist looked thoughtful. Finally he said, "Rick, before we leave, try and think up an excuse to speak to Thatcher again. I'll follow along and get in a few words with Mr. Homer Pritchett."

Rick lingered over his beer while Quist smoked the cigar down to half its length. Then Rick sauntered down the long counter until he came to where Thatcher and Pritchett were drinking. "Cody," Rick asked, "can I buy you a drink?"

Thatcher was about to accept, then he glanced at Quist and shook his head. "Thanks, no, I reckon not, Rick. We'd just dropped in to slosh down our tonsils, after we left the feed store. It's hot walking this morning."

Quist joined them. "It is that," he said, "and cowman's boots were never made for walking." Pritchett and Thatcher nodded short agreement. Blandly, Quist asked Pritchett, "How is your blister? Bother you any?"

Pritchett shook his head. "Not any. I bathed it with turpentine, then smeared on some vaseline and wrapped a rag over it and——" He stopped suddenly, eyes widening, "Sa-ay, how did you know I had a blister?"

"Left foot, wasn't it?" Quist said. Frowning, Pritchett said it was the left foot, right side of the heel. Quist went on, carelessly, "I don't know who it was mentioned it—somebody down to the depot said you were limping when you got off the train just before the one that brought Rick and me to Hyperion. Well, glad to hear it's better."

Pritchett's frown deepened. "Ye-es," he said uncertainly, "it was still hurting some when I got off'n the train. I'd—I'd been over to Tonkawa Springs to visit with my brother."

"That so?" Quist said with disarming carelessness. "I can't seem to remember that Tonkawa Springs is on the T.N. & A.S. line."

"T'ain't," Pritchett said. "It's some distance off the line." He was thinking faster now. "I expected my brother would meet me with a horse, but he was late. I'd started to walk and made about five miles afoot before he showed up."

"That was tough," Quist said sympathetically. "Walking was bad enough, but to be loaded down with a .38-55 rifle made it worse."

Pritchett just stared for a moment. "Somebody down to the depot," he blurted at last, "sure must have told you a lot about me."

"Somebody," Quist agreed, "sure must have. You want to be real careful about picking up blisters the way you did—or you might die sudden. Such a blister can cause a man a heap of trouble, sometimes." Pritchett didn't reply. There was a puzzled expression on Cody Thatcher's face, but he didn't say anything. Quist nodded, "Yep, Pritchett, you'd best walk mighty careful from now on. I'd hate to have anything happen to you." He turned to Rick, "Come on, son, let's get moving. We've got business ahead." Together they pushed through the swinging doors and made their way to the street.

They had crossed Fannin Street before Rick again opened his mouth. Then his words came in a rush: "Greg! Do you think he's the one? How did you know about that blister? What will Pritchett do now? Will you——?"

"Whoa up!" Quist's topaz eyes twinkled. "Not so fast, youngster. In the first place, Homer Pritchett answered the description we had, right down to being a crack man with a rifle. All except the limp. That bothered me for a minute. Then I got to thinking that cowman's boots aren't built for walking, and whoever shot that slug my way had done a lot of walking around El Paso the two days he was there. I figured a blister could be the result and a blister makes a man limp, sometimes. All the rest, of course, was pure bluff. I'll bet it won't be long before Pritchett heads for the depot to learn who's been talking about him."

"Darned if you aren't the smart one," Rick said admiringly.

"That's not smart," Quist disagreed. "That was just plain common sense."

"Anyway, Greg, you sure talked turkey to Pritchett. He knew what you meant, and I'm betting he'll not try any more tricks."

"If he was the one who did the shooting, he knew," Quist pointed out. "Otherwise, anything I said was just idle conversation. How do we know he wasn't visiting his brother in Tonkawa Springs?"

Rick's face fell. "Then you're not sure about Pritchett——?"

"Not absolutely. Certain things point in his direction, but I can't feel positive."

"Maybe you're right, at that," Rick said disappointedly. "Come to think of it, neither Cody nor Pritchett would care if you came here, as I see it."

"You don't always see it right, Rick. If Thatcher and Pritchett happened to be interested in protecting the Hamilton family, I'll have to judge 'em by the way other folks hereabouts are acting."

Rick didn't have any reply for that. A few steps farther on he said, "Here we are. She's open!"

Quist chuckled. "Do you have to act so damn' tickled about it?" He glanced at the small, neat shop before which they'd halted. On either side of the entrance door was a window displaying women's bonnets. Quist followed Rick through the doorway and saw within a carpeted floor and a long shelf, holding more hats, along one wall. At the opposite side were a couple of mirrors with chairs before them. A small table held a couple of potted geraniums and ferns. Camilla Peters was nowhere in sight, however.

Rick raised his voice, "Hey, Camilla! You got company."

A door at the rear of the shop opened, beyond which Quist had a brief view of living quarters, and a trim figure in checked gingham came into the shop. "Rick!" she exclaimed. "I'd heard you were back with——" She broke off upon seeing Quist. Rick performed introductions and the girl offered her hand. Quist liked the handclasp the girl gave him. "That's most unusual," he chuckled. The girl looked at him, puzzled. Quist explained: "I haven't found folks here quite so cordial in their greetings."

"Oh!" The girl tossed her head with some irritation. "Don't pay any attention to Hyperion. Folks will like you well enough when they get to know you, Mr. Quist."

"I hope so."

Camilla Peters was small with a rounded form and an unusually clear complexion. Petite was the word that sprang into Quist's mind when he first saw the girl. And pretty. Her eyes were a very deep violet; her thick dark hair was parted in the center, braided, and then the heavy plaits were brought up to encircle her small head, leaving her nape bare. Camilla pointed out chairs, and the two men and the girl talked idle commonplaces for a few minutes. Nothing was said about the Canfield murder, nor did Camilla refer to the business that had brought Quist to Hyperion.

Finally, Quist rose. Rick started reluctantly to accompany him, but Quist said, "You wait here for me, Rick. I've got something I want to see to. I'll pick you up here before we start for the Circle-H."

Rick sank back. "You're sure you won't need me?"

Quist smiled. "I've an idea you'll enjoy Miss Peters' company for a while, rather than mine. I'll be back within the hour."

He bowed to the girl, mentioned it had been a pleasure to meet her, and strode out to the street once more.

Chapter IX : BAD MEDICINE

Quist left the Bon-Ton Shop and, turning east, walked a block and then crossed diagonally toward the corner of Huisache and Fannin streets, where the sheriff's office and county jail were located. The bright sun made black shadows along the street. One or two pedestrians glanced sharply at Quist, but no one offered even a casual nod. The sheriff's building was a one-story rock-and-adobe structure with a sign reading: "Sheriff's Office—Casaneda County" jutting from one of the uprights supporting the wooden awning above the sidewalk. Quist crossed the narrow porch that fronted the open doorway and glanced inside. Within, placed near a right-hand window, stood the sheriff's desk. A few straight-backed chairs were scattered about. On the walls were calendars from packing companies, a topographical map of the county, and a rack of guns and handcuffs. A closed door at the rear showed the way to the jail cells. The sheriff was seated at his desk and next to him was a younger man wearing a deputy sheriff's badge. The two were engrossed in some papers on the sheriff's desk.

Quist stood nonchalantly against the doorjamb, surveying the scene. Neither the sheriff nor his deputy had glanced up. Finally, Quist said, "Is this a plan to ignore me, or didn't you really hear my step?"

The heads of the two men jerked up, the sheriff's long, sunbleached mustaches fairly bristling at sight of Quist. A certain color flooded into his stern features. "You, eh?" he growled. The deputy sheriff didn't say anything.

Quist said, "You called it. Aren't you going to ask me in, or do I have to have a special invitation to come here?"

"Generally, when I ask folks to come here I got a good reason for it," Bard Nixon said ominously.

"I can understand that," Quist said quietly, "but that's speaking generally. How about a particular case?"

Sheriff Nixon snapped, "Come on in!"

Quist said "Thanks" in a dry tone and entered the office.

The sheriff didn't offer him a chair. "What in hell do you want, Quist?"

"A mite of civility, if you don't mind," Quist said quietly. "Also a little talk. That you can suit yourself about, but you aren't going to get any place trying to rough-ride me around Hyperion." His voice took on a brittle tone. "I'd like to be friends, but if you can't see it that way, that's all right too. Personally, I don't give a damn how you act, but common sense, if you have any—and I'll admit it's a mighty scarce article these days—should tell you that more flies are caught with honey than with vinegar."

"Have I said I wanted to catch any flies?" Nixon snapped.

"Perhaps I should have said hornets," Quist remarked.

Nixon growled an oath. "Draw up a chair and get it off'n your chest. This is my deputy, Joe Menzell."

Menzell started to offer his hand, glanced quickly at Nixon and withdrew it, then by way of apology rose and offered Quist the chair on which he'd been sitting. Quist smiled thinly and said, "Thanks, Joe." The deputy's face reddened and he mumbled, "Don't mention it."

Nixon said testily as Quist sat down, "All right, get talking, Quist. I ain't too much time to waste on you."

Quist said, "You've apparently decided not to arrest me."

"I will when the right time comes," Nixon said angrily. "What do you want, anyway?"

"Has Doctor Sturven probed the slugs out of Webb Bascom yet?"

The sheriff hesitated. "Yeah. Doc got 'em out a couple hours ago."

"What were they?"

"Slugs from a six-shooter." Nixon's voice was sarcastic.

An edge crept into Quist's tones, though he held them even. "Sheriff, you can save that brand of humor for somebody who appreciates it. I'm not in the mood for humor, at present. I'm asking for the caliber of those slugs, as you damn' well know."

Somewhat reluctantly Nixon said, "One was a .44. The other was heavier but some damaged where it had struck bone. It might be a .44, too——"

"You know mighty well it wasn't," Quist cut in. "If it was heavier than a .44, it had to be a .45—shot from Tom Jenkins' gun. All right! Sturven took out a .45 and a .44. Now, Sheriff, if you arrest me, you've got to take in Jenkins as well, if Bascom dies."

"I ain't so sure of that," Nixon said cautiously. "I got to think things over for a spell before I act. I still think you'd be wise if you got out of Hyperion, Quist."

Quist shook his head. "I like it here. There's so much going on to arouse a man's interest. Is Bascom able to talk yet?"

"Doc says he won't be able to talk for quite some spell, as he sees it. He's still unconscious. Now, Quist, I warn you that——"

"Don't say anything you'll be sorry for, Sheriff," Quist interrupted sternly. "I'm commencing to wonder if you're not unconscious too."

"What do you mean?" Nixon bridled.

"If you're not unconscious, Sheriff, you certainly are not using your mind. I want certain information. I'd hoped to get it from you, but all you can do is warn me to leave town. You're just not showing good sense."

"That's my business," Nixon said sulkily.

"You're a damn' poor businessman then."

Nixon's jaw dropped, then his lips tightened as he strove to hold his temper. He said finally, in a strained voice, "What information do you want?"

"Everything you know that's connected in any way with Nash Canfield's death."

"Why bother me with things like that?" Nixon flared, then he forced a short laugh. "Go to the county house and look into the records. Hell! I'll send my deputy along to help you dig 'em out." He turned to Menzell. "Joe, you go along with Mr. Quist and help him find what he needs——"

"Never mind, Joe," Quist cut in, then swung back to the sheriff. "What I want isn't in the records, Nixon."

"I don't know what you mean by a statement of that sort," Nixon blustered. "You talk like evidence had been covered up, or something. I won't stand for talk like that in my office."

"T'hell you won't," Quist snapped. "Nixon, how long have you been sheriff of this county?"

"Huh! What?" Somewhat taken aback the sheriff gazed puzzledly at Quist. Quist repeated the question. Nixon said belligerently, "What's that got to do with it?"

"I'm asking."

"Long enough to know my business better than you do, anyway. If you got to know, this is my fifth term in office."

"Fifth term, eh? . . . Nixon, that looks as though the county had faith in you——"

"Certainly, folks got faith in me." The sheriff's chest swelled.

"—but," Quist continued, as though he hadn't noticed the interruption, "like a good many politicians who stay in office a long time, you've grown too big for your job—in your own mind. You think your word is law in everything and you ride rough-shod over anything and anybody you don't like. You've

become arrogant, opinionated, narrow-minded—and impracticable——"

"By God, Quist!" Nixon leaped upright. "You can't talk
that way to me! I'll throw you in a cell so fast——"

"See? That's what I mean." Quist smiled thinly up at the
sheriff towering over him. "There's a touch of your arrogance
now. You just can't stand anyone crossing your ideas. That's
damn' impracticable. The wise man will listen to what an
opponent has to say, at least." His hand shot out suddenly
against the sheriff's middle and he shoved hard. Nixon sat
abruptly down in his chair. Quist's voice had suddenly gone
cold. "Now you're going to listen to me whether you like it or
not. And I'd like to see you throw me in a cell. Go ahead, try
it, if you want to get your sit spot burned."

"You can't buff me," Nixon gasped.

"Get it through your thick head I'm not bluffing," Quist
snapped. The sheriff mumbled something about taking this
matter to a higher authority. Quist laughed harshly. "All right,
let's take it up with the Capitol. We'll see who has the most
pull there, you or an employee of the T.N. & A.S. Railroad.
I've a hunch my word will carry a mite more weight than that
of any two-bit, tin-pot sheriff. I've come here looking for co-
operation and you've treated me like a suspected criminal.
Suppose we take that matter up with the governor? I can
promise you a hearing. He happens to be a friend of mine. It's
your play, Sheriff, only remember, I'm getting damn' sick of
your evasions."

Silence fell on the room while the glare in the sheriff's eyes
slowly died away. Deputy Joe Menzell was open-mouthed,
speechless, as he watched the two men. The words came hard
when the sheriff finally found his voice: "All right, Quist. What
exactly do you want?"

"Co-operation, in the first place. There's some damned bad
medicine been brewed around here. I've been shot at in El Paso
to keep me from coming to Hyperion"—the sheriff's eyes
widened at the words—"and I've had lead slung in my direction since I arrived. I've been threatened by you. And I'm getting almighty sick of your stupidity. For all I know to the
contrary, you were back of those shootings——"

"S'help me God, I wa'n't! I didn't even know there'd been
any trouble in El Paso——"

"You could have known if you'd been willing to listen, instead of shooting off your big mouth all the time," Quist
half-snarled. "But no, you didn't want to listen to anything I
wanted to say, nor would you come through with information
I wanted, until I'd dragged it out of you. You know, Nixon,

you're not the only person who holds an opinion on the Canfield killing. I hoped to get the correct information from you, but if you don't talk, I'll just have to get it any place I can. But I'll get it, by God, and if you happen to get hurt, that's your tough luck. This town is full of gossipy people who'll tell what they know and think. Some of the information I'll get will likely be wrong, but don't blame me if you get your tail burned. You've had your chance. I've tried to talk reason to you. Now, you can go to hell! I'm through trying." Quist shoved back his chair, hard lights gleaming in the topaz eyes, and got to his feet.

A thin grudging smile had appeared on the sheriff's face. "You needn't to get mad, Mr. Quist. That's mighty rough talk you handed me. I don't know as I——"

"The time had come when you needed rough talk," Quist snapped.

Nixon eyed him curiously a moment. "I won't go so far as to say you're wrong, Mr. Quist, but I ain't so sure you're right, either. Sit down. Maybe we'd better thresh this out a little." Quist reseated himself. Nixon glanced up at his deputy. "Joe, why don't you drift across the street to Calydon's and get yourself a beer, while Mr. Quist and I *habla* a mite? There's one or two things I'd like to get him straightened out on."

"Sure, Bard," Joe replied, suppressing a grin. He nodded to Quist. "Hope I'll be seein' you again."

Quist said he hoped so, too, and the deputy disappeared.

Nixon didn't speak for a moment, while he picked up a sack of Durham and papers and twisted a cigarette. Then he passed the "makin's" to Quist with a grunted, "Peace pipe?"

Quist smiled and accepted, manufactured a cigarette of his own. The sheriff scratched a match and held the flame while smokes were lighted. Quist said, "Maybe I'd best take back what I said about you being a two-bit, tin-pot sheriff. I'm commencing to think you're human, after all."

"Sometimes I ain't so sure but what that two-bit, tin-pot name hits the nail on the head," Nixon said moodily. He exhaled a cloud of gray smoke. "What's this about being shot at in El Paso?"

Quist told the story briefly, leaving out mention of his suspicions where Homer Pritchett was concerned. When he had finished, Nixon said, "But you got the description of the feller. Damn' smart the way you done it. I'll keep an eye peeled for anybody that tallies with that description." Something like a chuckle welled up from his chest. "Trigger Hamilton! That makes me laugh, as it would make anybody else laugh that knows Rick. The youngster is right mild-tempered, unless he's pushed. Then I figure him as a wildcat."

"Rick's a good kid, got a good head on his shoulders," Quist commented.

"Generally, I agree with you," Nixon said heavily. "But I don't know as he was smart to bring you here——"

"Hold it, Sheriff," Quist said quickly. "You're starting to crawl back in your shell again, just when we're getting acquainted. The way folks act hereabouts I don't know whether they're afraid of being accused of Canfield's murder, or whether they know who did it and are covering up to save the Hamilton name—or somebody else."

"Who else, for instance?"

"That's what I don't know. All I have is what Rick told me about the case. Then, last night, Tom Jenkins mentioned Camilla Peters."

"In what way?" Nixon demanded, scowling. "Camilla's a mighty nice girl."

"I thought that myself when I met her this morning. Don't get Jenkins wrong, Sheriff. He merely said that her name had been mentioned during that quarrel Rick had with Canfield, the day of the murder. Look here, I'll run over the information I had from Rick, then I'll expect you to fill in anything that's missing."

"There ain't too much I can tell you," Nixon said warily.

"We'll see." Quist talked rapidly for several minutes. When he had concluded, Nixon said, "You've got the story, Quist. What else do you want that you think I can tell you?"

"First, I want to know everything you know about Canfield. When he came here, what he did, who he associated with. I know he did a lot of drinking and there were women too. Who were they?"

"That's a large order," Nixon growled. "Women! My Gawd! I couldn't begin to name 'em all. There weren't many that amounted to anything though. Canfield wasn't choosy, after he'd been here a while. And he had money. Anything with a skirt on was likely to get him started. Then when he got to messing around with decent girls, folks commenced to warn him. Don't ask me what folks. My memory ain't big enough to hold all the names. Just say that nobody in Hyperion had any use for him the last year he was alive. And a long time before that. There was a few, of course, that refused to hear what was being said about him, and there was them that heard it too late."

"Meaning the Hamiltons?"

"Among others. Canfield hadn't really commenced to slop over at the time he married Tracy, so Rick and Chris Hamilton, her father, hadn't really had a chance to know what Tracy had got." The sheriff swore an oath. "They found out soon enough, afterward."

"Who did Canfield pard around with when he first arrived in Hyperion?"

"He kind of took up with Tom Jenkins right at first——"

"You mean the Terrapin foreman?"

"The same. Hard to understand, ain't it? Tom's a nice feller. But he was sort of wild those days. And then there was Cody Thatcher; he was right friendly with Cody for a spell, until——" The sheriff paused.

"I'm listening."

Nixon drew a deep breath. His voice sounded miserable, "I reckon I'd better tell the story in correct order, but I don't want you to jump to no conclusions."

"This doesn't happen to be my day for jumping."

"Canfield arrived in Hyperion about four years back. Stayed at the hotel and it was given out he was here for his health. I reckon he was just out here to recuperate from a bad spell of drinking. Anyway, he didn't do no drinkin' at all, at first. Then he gradually began gettin' back in his old habits. About that time, Tom Jenkins had sort of slipped off his rocker and was paintin' the town at every opportunity, so him and Canfield took up together in their drinkin'——"

"Had Jenkins always been a wild one for drink?"

"Hell, no. Tom was a right steady boy at one time, as he is now. I've knowed him since he was a little shaver, knowed his pa, old Morg Jenkins, the wolfer."

"Wolfer?"

"You know, makes a livin' trappin' and killin' wolves around this range when they get to devastatin' the stock. Morg Jenkins has still got a little place over on the Circle-H holdin's. Like I say, Tom used to help his father kill wolves and coyotes. Evenutally he went to ridin' for different outfits and made a top hand. Everybody liked him."

"What made him go wild?"

Something like a groan escaped Nixon's lips. "If you ain't the damnedest man to weasel information out of a fellow," Nixon said resentfully. He drew a long breath, "Well, if you got to know, it was Tracy Canfield—Tracy Hamilton, them days. Her and Cody Thatcher." Quist asked a question. Nixon explained, "Jenkins had been going right steady with Tracy for sometime. I don't say they was engaged or anything, but folks had commenced to gossip a mite about a coming marriage. Then, somehow, Cody Thatcher got the inside track with Tracy and eventual their engagement was announced. That's what threw Jenkins and he commenced hitting the redeye. And it was about that time Canfield arrived in Hyperion. Them two," Nixon said reminiscently, "sure painted this town on occasion."

"Where does Camilla Peters come into this picture?"

Nixon glared at Quist. "Damned if you ain't a mind reader. I was hopin' you wouldn't ask about her. Camilla used to work as a waitress at the hotel. She's an orphan and had to support herself; but she had ambition. Camilla and Canfield got acquainted, and the next thing we knew, Canfield had loaned her money to open her Bon-Ton female's gear store. Camilla gave Canfield her note, though, all legal, and I happen to know the money was paid back, with interest, inside a year."

"Just how friendly were Miss Peters and Canfield?"

"Don't get any wrong ideas, Quist. Camilla is square as a die. She and Canfield went to dances and rides and such. I reckon it was serious for a spell, because for a time they were engaged to be married. I suppose Canfield appealed to the girl. He had money and he was a handsome jasper to boot. One night at a dance, Canfield was introduced to Tracy by Cody Thatcher. Shortly after, Tracy broke her engagement to Cody and there was a breakup between Camilla and Canfield. Followin' that, it wa'n't long before Tracy and Canfield got engaged."

"Right busy girl, Tracy," Quist said dryly.

"I told you not to jump to any conclusions," Nixon snapped. "Remember, she was only eighteen. You can't expect good sense from no girl at that age, where men are concerned."

"You could be right. So Tracy and Canfield were married. How did Thatcher take that?"

"I figure he didn't like it, naturally, but he never took to drink like Tom Jenkins did. Figure yourself how you'd feel in his boots, if somebody swiped your girl. But it wa'n't long, I guess, before Tracy realized she'd got the wrong man and made a bad mistake. Canfield soon started his hell-raisin', but Tracy's purebred and never complained. Canfield was no stockman, of course, and Tracy has largely had the running of the Terrapin. Canfield never could keep a foreman, though. He quarreled with every one of 'em——"

"Any of those foreman around here now?"

"Not that I know of. They've all left the country, and I don't figure any of 'em ever got mad enough at Canfield to kill him. Like I say, no foreman ever lasted more than three months—there was four of 'em the first year. Then one night, when Canfield and Jenkins were both pretty well plastered, Canfield offers Tom the job of roddin' the Terrapin. To everybody's

surprise, Tom took the job, and what surprised 'em more was
the way Tom straightened up from that day and did a real job
of handling Terrapin interests. Tom Jenkins is a solid citizen."

"He looked that way to me." There was silence for a few
moments as Quist mulled over the information Nixon had
given him. He shot his next question with disarming carelessness: "Sheriff, was it Tracy or Rick who killed Canfield?"

"To tell the truth I'm damned if I know——" Nixon commenced, then stopped. "Hold up! I don't say neither one done
it, Quist. You can't——"

"You've said enough, Sheriff," Quist interrupted. "In your
own mind you're certain one of them is guilty, and you can't
tell me different." The sheriff's eyes were on the floor and he
didn't reply. Quist went on, "Now why didn't you do your
sworn duty and try to find out who was guilty?"

Nixon said sullenly. "Canfield got what he deserved. I
arrested Rick——"

"But you didn't try to dig up any evidence against him,
did you?"

"Damn it, Quist," the sheriff flared. "I've knowed Tracy and
Rick ever since they were born, and their father before them.
Chris Hamilton's the best friend a man ever had. He helped me
out one time when I needed money right bad. I was in a tight
fix——"

"So you were just repaying that obligation? It never occurred
to you you might be obstructing justice?"

Nixon's face reddened. "Look at it any way you please," he
growled. "I acted according to what I thought fit. Chris Hamilton is a big man in this country. Anythin' he gets is owin' to
him. In the early days he fought the Comanches and helped
drive 'em out, so folks could live in peace. Nobody who was
needy ever had to ask Chris twice for what was needed. Without Chris Hamilton, this country might not be as law-abidin'
and prosperous as it is now——"

"Law-abiding except for an occasional murder," Quist said
dryly. "Not to mention a little bushwhacking——"

"A murder that was damn' well needed," Nixon snarled.

Quist said mildly, "I'll take your word for it." He got to his
feet. "Nixon, don't ever get an idea I'd hold it against any man
for backing a friend. . . . Thanks for the talk. I'll be seeing
you again."

Before the sheriff could reply, Quist had vanished through
the open doorway.

Chapter X : SHARP PRACTICE

It was only a little after ten o'clock that morning when Quist, after getting his black gelding and picking up Rick at the Bon-Ton, was headed in the direction of the Circle-H Ranch. The two men loped their ponies over the hoof-chopped and wheel-rutted road that pointed almost due west out of Hyperion. Five miles out of town they reined their ponies to a walk to cross the shallow Gunsight River, the horses' hoofs making hollow thumping sounds across the plank bridge stretching over the slowly flowing stream. Both banks of the water were lined with a heavy growth of ancient cottonwoods. Once across the bridge, neither man urged his pony to a faster gait. Rick jerked one thumb over his shoulder. "It was among those cottonwood trees, t'other side of the river, that Tracy got her knock on the head that day, so near as we can figure it, and from what she tells."

Quist glanced back. "It would be mighty easy to get knocked off a horse if he took it into his head to bolt through those cottonwoods. You say your sister walked from there, clear to the Terrapin?"

"I don't know how else she could have got to the ranch." Quist asked how far it was from the river at that point to the Terrapin. Rick replied, "Around seven miles I'd say, off-hand."

Quist looked quizzically at his companion. "That's a mighty long distance for an injured person to walk, one that's only half-conscious."

Rick agreed. "It's possible, though," he persisted. "Remember, it was morning when the accident took place and after dark when Tracy reached the Terrapin."

"It's possible," Quist conceded. "Did the horse ever turn up?"

"The following morning. It came to the Terrapin corral of its own accord. Probably got tired of running loose, once it had its freedom for a spell."

"I suppose," Quist nodded. The horses moved side by side in an easy walk that kicked up dust along the trail, the way leading through rolling hill country, the hills growing higher as they advanced toward the distant Gunsight Mountains. Post oak, mesquite and prickly pear grew in profusion over the slopes on either side of the road; now and then a tall pecan tree lifted its lush yellow-green foliage toward the blue sky against which fleecy white clouds made a slowly moving pattern.

Quist said abruptly, "Rick, you've been holding out on me?" Rick looked startled and asked what Quist meant. "I mean," Quist explained, "that you neglected to tell me that Canfield had once been engaged to marry Camilla Peters."

Rick crimsoned. "I reckon I forgot——" he commenced, then abruptly his eyes met Quist's. "No, I won't say that. Damn it! How could I forget anything like that? To tell the truth, Greg, I hoped it wasn't necessary——"

"I know,"—sarcastically, "you expected me to be a miracle man and work out the problem without information that might hurt somebody. Jeepers, boy! I'm no mind reader. I count on you to tell me things."

"I'm sorry, Greg. I should have told you. There's something else you should know, maybe. Camilla once borrowed some money from Canfield——"

"And repaid it with interest," Quist said cherrfully. "I got all that from the sheriff, if you're interested."

"Bard Nixon?" Rick looked surprised. "I didn't think Bard would ever show you any co-operation."

"Neither did he, at one time," Quist smiled. "Howsomever, I persuaded him to see things my way. He told me the answer to everything I asked."

Rick laughed. "I'm commencing to think you are a miracle man." Quist merely grunted a protest and for a few minutes the horses moved on in silence. Finally, Rick lifted one arm to point toward the distant Gunsight Mountains, indicating a point somewhat to the northwest. "See those two twin peaks with the flattened tops and sort of a notch between 'em, with a shoulder of rock protruding into the notch? . . . Those are Gunsight Peaks; they give the name to that range of mountains."

"Sure enough." Quist eyed the distant twin peaks thoughtfully. Something had clicked in his mind. "The Gunsight country. Rick, there's a fairly wide, level pass through that notch, isn't there?"

"How did you know?"

"I'll tell you in a minute."

"Sure, it's the only pass through that range where a wagon can travel. The rest of the range, while not so high as some mountains, is right steep, making a stiff climb even for a horse. There's darn' little growth on those limestone bluffs. It's rugged country."

Quist gave the matter some consideration. "Rick, if a line

was drawn due east from that notch between those two peaks, it would cross Terrapin holdings, wouldn't it?"

"Correct—and after it had crossed the Terrapin, it would then cross Cody Thatcher's Wagon-Wheel spread."

"Rick, who did Canfield buy that Terrapin land from?"

"Cody Thatcher," Rick said promptly.

"So? Tell me what you know about the deal."

"We-ell"—Rick's forehead furrowed in thought—"as I remember it, the original Wagon-Wheel holdings stretched clear to the mountains. When Cody's father died, Cody inherited, of course. Some years back, the cattle market fell off pretty bad, and Cody had a hard time catching up—financially, I mean. He was deep in debt. About the time Canfield was preparing to marry Tracy he got his idea of owning a cattle outfit. He looked the country over and liked the Wagon-Wheel range where it swelled up to the mountains. So he asked Thatcher to sell him the land. At first, Thatcher wouldn't hear of it."

"Why? You say Thatcher was pressed for money."

Rick explained. "In the first place, Thatcher hated to cut up the land his father left him. Also, he had heard that some railroad planned to build in that direction and go through Gunsight Peaks—sa-a-ay, come to think of it, it was your road, the T.N. & A.S."

"That's right." Quist nodded.

Rick continued, "Thatcher had it in mind that the railroad would pay him a good price for the right-of-way. Canfield said he could understand that, and dropped the matter temporarily. A week later, he came to Thatcher again, and told him the T.N. & A.S. had decided not to build toward Gunsight Peaks, because a better route had been located farther north. Thatcher believed him, particularly when Canfield flashed some correspondence he'd had with the railroad and displayed some T.N. & A.S. stock—though Thatcher said afterward that he never did get a good look at the correspondence. Well, with Thatcher needing money, and certain now the railroad wouldn't buy his land, he finally consented to divide the Wagon-Wheel and sell Canfield the western half of the property. Canfield got the land at a fraction of its value, and started construction on the Terrapin ranch house even before he and Tracy were married."

"Canfield wasn't above double-crossing a friend, was he?"

"He sure wasn't. After the deed was signed and the money paid over, he had a big laugh at Thatcher's expense. He admitted then that the T.N. & A.S. still intended to build through Gunsight Peaks, and he rubbed it into Thatcher by telling all over town the big price he was going to soak the railroad for a right-of-way. For a spell, there were pretty hard feelings between the two men. Thatcher called Canfield a crook. Canfield called Thatcher a sucker. Thatcher swore he'd square the account some day. However, the railroad never did build, and in time Canfield and Thatcher patched up their differences to some extent, though they never acted real friendly again."

"I can't say I blame Thatcher," Quist commented. "Considering the two had been friends, I'd term that pretty sharp practice on Canfield's part. I remember, now, why the T.N. & A.S. didn't go through with its plans for a road through Gunsight Pass. I'd forgotten the name of the party, but I remember that the owner of the land demanded such an exorbitant price for a right-of-way that the road practically told him to go to hell. The plan was dropped for the time being, but, if I'm not mistaken, the road would like to build another line in that direction eventually. Hell! That's the only available pass for a good many miles to the north. If the price was right, your sister— or whoever held the property at the time—might make some money some day."

Rick reined his horse around a low out-cropping of granite at the side of the road, cut past a mesquite bush and rejoined Quist. "Look here, Greg, do you think Thatcher could have held a grudge long enough to have killed Canfield?"

"Not knowing the workings of Thatcher's mind, I couldn't say. Some men will kill at the least effort, while others can be pushed to their limit without raising a finger."

Neither man spoke for a time, after that. The horses were again spurred to a lope and a panorama of rolling country dotted with cactus, post oak, mesquite and cedar flashed swiftly past. They slowed once to rest the ponies, then pushed on again.

The sun had passed meridian when they first sighted the Circle-H buildings, located on sloping ground with a scattering of live oaks casting shadows around them. There were the usual buildings—blacksmith shop, barns, corrals, a main house built of cedar logs, bolstered here and there with adobe and slabs of limestone. The vanes of a wood-framed windmill turned rapidly in the steady breeze blowing down from the Gunsight Mountains.

Rick and Quist drew their ponies to a slower gait. Rick said, "There's Dad and Brasadero on the gallery now."

"Who's Brasadero?"

"Brasadero Banning, the Circle-H foreman, though he spends more time nowadays acting as a nurse and companion for Dad—that's been his job ever since Dad had his accident."

Rick hesitated. "If Dad acts sort of grumpy, don't pay him any mind. He's always been a pretty big man in the Gunsight country and very active. But ever since he received his injury a couple of years back, all he can do is sit in a chair or lie in bed, and it goes against the grain. He gets mighty bitter at times. He was so angry at me when I first said I intended to bring you here that I moved over to the Terrapin for a spell, so I could keep out of his sight."

"If Banning acts as your father's nurse, I don't see how he can rightly 'tend to rodding the outfit."

"Gus Diehl—he's one of our oldest hands—can pretty much run things. Gus can take care of Dad, too, when something happens that Brasadero isn't here."

"I suppose the rest of the Circle-H crew is fully as capable."

Rick nodded. "Every man on the payroll has been with Dad for years, and everyone is completely loyal, so you'll have to be prepared for a rather chilly atmosphere at first. But they'll like you fine, once they get to know you."

Quist said dryly, "I just hope, under the circumstances, I get to know them too."

Chapter XI : CORNERED

By this time Rick and Quist had drawn to a halt before the gallery and were getting down from saddles. The two men seated on the porch said not a word beyond nodding shortly when Rick greeted them. Both were eyeing Quist sharply and there was a definite feeling of hostility in the air. Chris Hamilton appeared to be about sixty years old. He had thick shoulders, bushy eyebrows and a thatch of bristling gray hair. A heavy gray beard covered the lower part of his face; the rest of his features were seamed and hard, and he possessed a pair of flinty, penetrating eyes. From the waist down, his legs and feet were encased in a wrapping of woolen blankets. A Winchester rifle rested against the arm of his chair.

Brasadero Banning, seated on Hamilton's left, appeared in the vicinity of forty, with brownish hair streaked with silver. Quist judged that, erect, Banning would be close to six feet tall. His features were tanned and leathery, except for his upper lip which, having been recently shaved, was much lighter than the rest of his face. A six-shooter was stuck in the waistband of his overalls.

Rick started to perform introductions, but old Chris Hamilton cut him short with a growled, "Never mind them formalities, Rick. You likely already told your friend who we are, and we know from your description he's Gregory Quist, the railroad dick."

Quist smiled, "Well, I'm glad to meet you, anyway."

"Too bad I can't say the same," Hamilton said bluntly. "But I reckon Rick's told you how I feel about you comin' here."

"He hinted at it," Quist nodded.

"Jeepers!" Rick exclaimed. "You shaved off your mustache, Brasadero. What happened, did the razor slip?"

Banning smiled sourly. "I reckon I just got tired of shavin' around that hawsstail, so I clean clipped her off this mornin'."

"We can talk later," Chris Hamilton cut in. "Rick, you'd better take Mr. Quist down to the cookhouse if you want any dinner. We had ours half hour since, but I guess the chow will still be warm and some of the boys will be eating yet. Soggy will growl, of course, but you tell him the Circle-H even feeds enemies when they arrive at meal time."

Quist said "Thanks" in a dry tone of voice and accompanied Rick around the house, heading in the direction of the cook shanty. The crew was still at the table when Rick and Quist entered. Rick introduced Quist to five men: Brose Fox, Jake Currie, Tim Baird, Nick Logan, and Gus Diehl. Soggy Hannan, the cook, growled something sarcastic about folks that arrived late for dinner, but as this is the manner of all cow-country cooks, Quist thought nothing of it. The other men merely nodded acknowledgments of Rick's introduction and made room at one of the long benches that were ranged on either side of the table.

While they ate, Quist had time to size up the Circle-H crew. It was a shade older than most ranch crews and, taken all in all, looked like a pretty capable bunch, sinewy-jawed, hard-bitten, with skins and frames very reminiscent of a length of rawhide. A very rough crew to tangle with, Quist commented mentally, especially the two youngest members, men in the vicinity of thirty years, Brose Fox and Jake Currie, who, from the rather hard looks they directed at Quist, gave the appearance of welcoming trouble. None of the men spoke to Quist, and any of Ricks' attempts to make conversation was answered with a plain "yes" or "no." Soggy Hannan, a long-nosed, bald-headed man who presided over the kitchen, had nothing to say when he entered now and then to replace platters or slam a fresh pot of coffee on the table. The crew seemed in a hurry to finish, and shortly after they had, one by one they left the messhouse, and Quist heard them saddling up and riding away. When he and Rick had concluded their meal, Quist called a "much obliged" to Hannan, who was banging pots and pans in the kitchen, but received only a short grunt in reply.

A minute later, walking back to the house, Quist said, "Nice friendly crew, Rick."

Rick said uncomfortably, "I apologize for the Circle-H. I reckon I never should have brought you here."

"Forget it, son, it doesn't bother me any."

"I'm damned if I know what's got into 'em," Rick frowned. "They're generally a right congenial bunch. It's just that they're loyal as the devil to Dad, and they'd hate to have anybody make trouble for him in any way. If it's any satisfaction to you, they've been as unfriendly with me as they have you, since I got back from El Paso."

"Don't let it get you down, Rick. Maybe, later, they'll change their tune."

He and Rick rejoined Hamilton and Banning on the gallery. More chairs had been set out and Banning had produced a bottle of bourbon and a box of cigars. Apparently, Chris Hamilton's natural feeling for hospitality had, to some extent, overcome his hostility toward Quist. The atmosphere, if not more friendly, was at least less strained than that of the mess-house had been.

"Draw up a chair, Mr. Quist," Chris Hamilton invited, "and test out some of my bourbon. Hope you had a good dinner." Quist said he had and thanked the owner of the Circle-H. Hamilton gave a grunt in reply. Banning poured glasses of whisky and passed the cigars.

Rick said, after a time, commenting on the six-shooter in Banning's belt and on the rifle at his father's side, "Why all the armament?"

Old Chris Hamilton explained, leveling one gnarled fore-finger to a point some distance out from the ranch house, "There's a damn' gopher throwing up a hill yonderly. I been trying to nail him, but didn't have any luck. Brasadero wa'n't no more successful with his hawg-laig——"

"We might of hit him, at that," Brasadero speculated. "I ain't seen him throw up no dirt for 'most two hours now. Boldest damn' bustard I ever see. He'd stick his head up, ever' so often, like he was just laughin' at Chris and me. Then at the slightest move, he was gone back into his tunnel. I don't cater to them little beasts none; a hawss sticks his leg in one of their holes, and you got a hawss to shoot 'cause of a broken leg."

"I don't reckon Mr. Quist come here to listen to you spiel about gopher pests, Brasadero," Chris Hamilton cut in. Quist, seated on Hamilton's right, had been sizing up the Winchester resting against the arm of the old man's chair, and saw that it was a .44-40.

"That's a good gun," Quist commented, motioning toward the rifle. "Don't know why more men don't use that and the .44 six-shooter. Then there's only one ca'tridge to carry."

Chris Hamilton's eyes ran rapidly over Quist. "Rick tells us you carry a .44 underarm gun, under your coat——" He broke off. "And neither did you come here to talk about guns, Mr. Quist. You want to question me about Nash Canfield's killing. Well, I'll tell you, there's not one damned bit of information I can give you—nothing that Rick ain't already told you. You'll hear a heap of rumors of one sort and another around town, probably, but don't you pay 'em any mind. Hell's-bells! There was even a rumor at one time that I'd gone to the Terrapin and shot Canfield—me that can't even walk, let alone fork a horse."

"Just how did your accident happen, Mr. Hamilton?" Quist asked.

"Couple of years back it was," Hamilton said. "I'd rounded up a bunch of strays over in a draw in the Gunsights and was herdin' back to open grazing. One ornery steer didn't take to bein' herded and he spooked off through the brush with me after him. Give me quite a run, he did. It commenced to grow dark and my horse didn't see where he was headed, when we both went can-over-appetite down a cut-bank. I'd loosened my feet from the oxbows the instant I felt the pony going. Pony didn't get hurt none, but when I tried to pick myself up, I found my back had sort of come unhinged. So I just had to lay there. Eventually, the boys set up a search and located me. But I ain't never walked since."

"Can't the doctors do anything?" Quist asked.

"Doctors!" Chris Hamilton snorted. "I've had Doc Sturven and another sawbones from Hyperion. Sturven brought in specialists from Denver and San Antone'. One man come from the East—Kansas City. None of 'em could do any more than Sturven done in the first place. Somethin' happened to my spine and it affected my legs—paralyzed 'em—I ain't got no feelin' in 'em from the thighs down. No, them doctors couldn't do anything. There was some talk of an operation, but they finally decided it was too ticklish a job and might kill me. Hell! I'd be better off dead than half-alive, like I am now. Best the docs could offer me was that the injury might wear off in time and things right themselves through Nature—but I realize now they was just lettin' me down easy." He added fervently, "God damn it!"

As though to punctuate the remark, Brasadero Banning's six-shooter roared suddenly. Dust kicked up in the vicinity of the gopher hole. Chris Hamilton hooted derisively. "You never even come close."

"I spied that head of his'n peekin' up above ground,"— Banning was shoving a fresh load into his six-shooter—"but he was gone before I even had a chance to draw a good bead on the cuss."

The black powder smoke drifted away. Flies buzzed about the empty whisky glasses. The men drew on their cigars in silence for a time. Chris Hamilton finally said, "Mr. Quist, I don't see why you had to come here pokin' your nose along a cold trail. You can't do no good."

"You forget," Quist said mildly, "that I was asked to come here." He didn't turn toward Hamilton as he spoke; his eyes were fixed on the gopher mound where he thought for a moment he'd seen a slight movement.

"Yes, I know," Hamilton said testily. "Rick asked you to come here. He had some fool idea——"

"But, look here, Dad——" Rick commenced a protest.

"I'll do the talking, Rick," Hamilton interrupted in a heavy tone. "Maybe I've lived long enough to know what's what. You haven't." He turned back to Quist. "I ain't sayin' you don't know your business, Mr. Quist. Rick has told us what happened in El Paso. I admire the way you handled that——"

"That man in El Paso who did the shooting," Rick broke in eagerly, "might be Homer Pritchett."

"Whatever gave you that fool idea?" Hamilton demanded.

"I'm not sure, of course." Quist took up the explanation. He mentioned Pritchett's description and the cause of the man's limp, while in El Paso.

Chris Hamilton shook his head. "I think you're wrong, Quist. Why should Pritchett care whether you came to Hyperion or not? He wa'n't concerned in Canfield's killing, one way or t'other. I've known Homer for quite some years too. Fact is, he worked for me for a time, until he got a chance to rod for Cody Thatcher——" He broke off; then, "So far as your description goes, take a look at Brasadero here. He fits that description. Not only that, but he's got an old bullet in his leg that makes him limp, now and then, when the weather gets damp." Hamilton chuckled sourly, "He even cut off that chunk of brush on his upper lip, this morning. Maybe he was gettin' rid of some evidence." Hamilton gazed up at Banning. "How about it, Brasadero? You been to El Paso to throw lead at Mr. Quist?"

"Now you know better than that, Chris." Banning smiled in rather sickly fashion as his eyes went to Quist to see how he was taking Hamilton's remarks.

"You're damn' well right I do," Hamilton snorted. "You never could hit anything with a rifle."

"Here's something else, Dad," Rick said. "You say that Pritchett wouldn't be interested in Greg coming here. What interest would Webb Bascom have in trying to drive him out, or kill him?"

"Webb Bascom!" Hamilton snapped. "What's that lousy, two-bit bum got to do with Quist?"

"That's what I'm trying to find out," Quist said quietly. "Bascom took a shot at me last night——"

"T'hell you say!" Hamilton exploded. "Tell me about it." Quist told what had happened on his way from the Terrapin to Hyperion the previous night. When he had finished, Hamilton slowly shook his head. "I can't understand Bascom doing that, Quist. He wouldn't be interested in your coming here—wait! maybe you've got a clue there. Perhaps it was Bascom that killed Nash Canfield."

"I somehow doubt that," Quist said. "What would a lousy, two-bit bum"—quoting Hamilton's words—"have to do with Nash Canfield?"

"That I can't answer," Hamilton growled. "But Canfield mixed with all sorts. Look, Mr. Quist, whoever killed Nash Canfield done a good job and nobody regrets Canfield's death. He made life a hell for my daughter and, if the truth was known, for a lot of other folks as well. Why can't you just forget this whole mess and go back to your railroadin'? It's not your business and——"

"Any time I'm shot at it becomes my business," Quist said quietly. His gaze was again on the gopher mound.

"All right," Hamilton growled, "if you get into trouble snoopin' around, don't blame me. You're not wanted here. And if that sounds like a threat, make the most of it. I don't give a damn——"

"Dad!" Rick commenced to protest. "I don't think——"

"You keep your mouth shut, Rick," Hamilton snarled. "I aim to——"

He paused as he saw Quist's hand steal out to the rifle leaning against the arm of the chair. The men fell silent, their eyes on Quist as he looked over the rifle, then carefully, slowly, raised it to his shoulder. His right forefinger curved about the trigger, tightened, as the muzzle came gradually to bear on the loose dirt of the gopher mound. Quite suddenly, the rifle cracked; fire and smoke spurted from the muzzle. Out near the gopher mound a small brownish furry form leaped convulsively into the air, fell back to earth, squirmed a moment and lay still. The haze of black powder smoke dissolved in the breeze.

"You got him, by Gawd!" Banning exclaimed, and leaped from the gallery, running in the direction of the dead gopher.

Quist levered another cartridge into the Winchester's chamber and started to set it back against the chair arm. Abruptly, the rifle slipped from his grasp and nearly fell to the gallery floor, but Quist's left hand, darting out, retrieved the falling weapon and caught it in time, though as he swung it up, the solid walnut stock struck with some violence against Chris Hamilton's right leg. There was a sudden half-savage exclamation from Hamilton.

Quist took a firmer hold on the weapon and set it carefully against Hamilton's chair. "I seem to be getting clumsier every day," he smiled ruefully, then stopped.

Hamilton's face had gone sheet-white, the old man's eyes blazed, and there was a twitching of his facial muscles. Quist said, "I sure hope I didn't hurt you, Mr. Hamilton. I didn't intend to bang that gun against you in such fashion. It just sort of slipped out of my hands for a second——"

"Hurt me?" A harsh, sarcastic laugh left Hamilton's bearded face. "How can you hurt a man with no sense of feeling in his legs? That ain't what riled me, Quist. Being you're strange here, I'll overlook it, but I'll make it plain, right now, I don't like strangers using my guns without permission——"

"I'm sorry as the deuce——" Quist commenced.

"Well, just remember what I told you," Hamilton grumbled. "Don't you ever touch no gun of mine again. Not unless I give you permission. We'll forget it, now——"

"Cripes, Dad!" Rick said. "Greg didn't hurt your rifle."

"I didn't say he did," Hamilton crabbed. "I just don't like other folks usin' my guns. You ought to know that. I've told you more than once——" He broke off, growling under his breath, as Brasadero Banning came striding back to the gallery.

"You nailed him all right, Mr. Quist," Banning said. "Blew the head clean off'n the little bustard. That's damn' smart shootin'."

"It's smart shooting, all right," Hamilton conceded jealously. "But I could have done the same, long ago, could I have wanted to. I just been pleasuring myself shooting around that little pest, past couple of days. It helped pass the time. Now I got to find something else——" Rick cut him off with a protest.

"I'm sorry about the whole business, Mr. Hamilton," Quist said. He smiled. "I regret spoiling your pleasure. If you like I'll round up some gophers and send them out for you to shoot at."

"Let's drop the matter," Hamilton said irritably. "And I can't think of any other subjects that might interest you—leastwise anything I'd give you information on."

Quist nodded. "That being the case, I reckon I'd best get along back to town. I'll water my horse before I leave, if you don't mind———"

"Let me take him down to the trough for you, Mr. Quist," Banning offered, stepping down from the gallery and picking up the black gelding's reins. He spoke to Rick, "You ridin' back to Hyperion too."

"Not unless Greg wants my company back."

Quist shook his head. "No sense you going back with me, Rick. I reckon I can find my way all right."

Banning, with the reins of both horses in his hand, rounded the corner of the ranch house. There was silence for a few minutes. Finally Chris Hamilton said, "I don't want you to get any wrong idea of our hospitality, Mr. Quist, but I don't think you're going to do any good here. You might as well head back to El Paso."

"Supposing I don't agree with you?" Quist asked.

Hamilton shrugged. "That's your business, of course. But just remember, Mr. Quist, should anybody belonging to me get hurt, in any way, I'm holding you responsible———"

"And then what?" Quist asked.

"If they get hurt through you," the old man said in a hard, level voice, "I'll be squaring matters. I may be a cripple, but what I can't do myself I can get done, one way or another. I'm sorry we can't be friends. I appreciate your kindness to Rick. But I think everybody would be better off if you got out of Hyperion on the next train."

Rick protested, "That almost sounds like a threat, Dad———"

"It's not meant to—not unless Mr. Quist stirs up something I don't like." He looked directly at Quist. "I can still put up a fight, Mr. Quist, if I have to."

"I can appreciate that, Mr. Hamilton," Quist said quietly. "I'm sorry we can't see eye to eye in this business, but until I've actually stepped on your toes, can't we be friends? I'd like to shake your hand."

Hamilton glanced sharply at Quist, then a slow, grudging smile showed through his gray beard. "I reckon it wouldn't actually hurt me none, if you did step on my toes. No sense of feeling in 'em. But I know what you mean." He thrust out his gnarled hand and Quist took it, as Hamilton continued, "This is good just so long as you don't step on them aforesaid toes, y'understand?"

"I understand," Quist nodded.

"Good. Drop out again when you find time—but remember, I can't give you any information about Canfield."

A few minutes later, Brasadero Banning returned with the black gelding, and after saying good-by all around, Quist climbed into the saddle and turned his mount toward the road to Hyperion. . . .

He had progressed some seven miles toward town, with the setting sun warm on his back, when, rounding a curve in the road between two gigantic Spanish oak trees, he caught a movement in the high brush on either side of the trail. Abruptly, three riders pushed their ponies out to the center of the road, effectively barring further progress. One rider had already drawn his gun. His voice was definitely hostile as he exclaimed: "Hold up a minute, Quist! We're aiming to settle something with you, right now!"

Quist eyed the hard, determined faces of the trio and pulled the black gelding to a halt. "Just as you say," he replied in level tones.

There was nothing else to do. Quist realized he was cornered.

Chapter XII : FLAMING GUNS!

The three men crowded closer as the black gelding stopped. Two of the men Quist recognized as Circle-H hands, Brose Fox and Jake Currie. The third man was Homer Pritchett, Cody Thatcher's foreman.

"It looks," Quist observed quietly, "as if the Circle-H and the Wagon-Wheel had ganged up on me." He spoke directly to the two Circle-H men. "I can't believe this is any of Chris Hamilton's doings. What you men got in mind?"

"Chris doesn't know anything about this," Brose Fox said. "This is our own idea. You just keep your hand away from your gun, Quist, and nobody's going to get hurt."

"Aw, he ain't wearin' any gun," Homer Pritchett said, casting a quick glance toward Quist's right thigh.

Jake Currie spat and said, "I understand he totes a hide-out gun under his coat, but he's goin' to have too much sense to pull it against three of us. Just keep your hand away from that shoulder holster, Mr. Quist, and we'll have a nice friendly talk." He was a dark-complexioned man with a hard, lined face. Brose Fox was chunkily built, with a wide mustache.

Quist said, "Get on with your talk. I want to get to town."

"You ain't goin' to Hyperion, Quist," Pritchett stated. "We figure to have you turn your hawss south from here. You can catch a train for El Paso, at Wolf Gap station. If you want us to, we can get your satchel and stuff and send it to the hotel in El Paso."

"What hotel in El Paso?" Quist asked idly.

"Pierson Hotel, of course———" Pritchett commenced promptly, then caught himself and stopped.

Quist smiled. "You seem to know considerable about my El Paso doings."

"That's whatever," Pritchett said sullenly.

"You know, Pritchett," Quist said, "the next blister you get may not be on your foot. What was your idea in coming to El Paso, and———?"

"Cripes! I ain't been in El Paso in ten years," Pritchett said.

"You're a liar, of course," Quist said quietly, "but let it pass. Who sent you to El Paso to find me?"

"I don't know what you're talking about," Pritchett said. One hand curved a trifle more tightly about the six-shooter he held in his hand. "I reckon we'd better drop the subject."

Brose Fox and Jake Currie were looking curiously at Pritchett. Currie said abruptly, "Take it easy, Homer. We don't want any shooting—unless necessary." Neither he nor Fox had drawn their guns.

Fox said, "Look here, Quist, we don't know what your trouble is with Pritchett and we're not interested. We're just interested in one thing———"

"The same being?" Quist asked calmly.

"That you get out of the Gunsight country *pronto!*"

"Why should I?"

"You're not wanted around here. You're messing into something that is none of your business. We Gunsight folks aim to settle our troubles in our own way—and we don't need any nelp from outside."

"Not even when help is brought in by one of your own people?"

"Not even then," Currie said flatly. "Rick Hamilton is a good kid—but he doesn't always think straight."

"You act like you're afraid of something," Quist accused.

"Maybe we are," Fox conceded. "That's why we're asking you to get out———"

"Asking hell!" Pritchett snapped. "We're telling you, Quist."

"And suppose I don't see it your way, Pritchett?"

"That," Pritchett said, in a hard voice, "will be just too bad. You'll either leave now—or you won't ever leave."

"Take it easy, Homer," Currie said sharply. "I don't think we are going to have to threaten Mr. Quist. He'll listen to reason——"

"What sort of reason, Currie?" Quist broke in.

"The only sort that appeals to a reasonable man, and I figure you're going to be plumb reasonable."

"My idea of reason may not line up with yours, Currie." An edge had crept into Quist's tones. "I don't like to be pushed around."

"Look here, Mr. Quist"—Brose Fox's voice sounded almost pleading—"we don't want any trouble with you. All we ask is that you go away and not mess into things that aren't your concern."

"Supposing I refuse to see it your way?" Quist demanded.

"In that case," Fox said testily, "we're going to have to use force. Dammit! Can't you understand we're giving you a chance——?"

Pritchett swore an oath. "We've wasted too much time already. We want a flat answer, Quist. Are you going, or do we have to——?"

"Cut it, Homer!" Currie rasped. "This can be handled——"

"Handled hell!" Pritchett snarled. "I'm sick of all this palaverin'. I want some action. All Quist has to do is say yes or no, and this whole business can be settled pronto."

Fox sighed. "I guess that's how it will have to be, Quist. Pritchett is plumb impatient and I don't know as how I can blame him, maybe. You comin' here has sort of upset things. So what's your answer?"

Quist considered the situation. Directly in front of him, horse turned sidewise in the road, barring a quick getaway, was Jake Currie. To Quist's left, his pony's head close to Quist's mount, was Brose Fox, whose hand was now resting on his gun butt. And to Quist's right, perched tensely in his saddle, sat Homer Pritchett, one finger already curled around the trigger of his six-shooter, though Quist noticed that the man's curved thumb hadn't yet drawn back the hammer.

"It looks like I'm cornered," Quist said calmly, at last. "If I consent to leave the Gunsight country, I satisfy you—but I don't satisfy myself. If I tell you I'm staying——"

"That won't satisfy you, neither," Pritchett rasped. "It all settles down to whether you leave here with a whole skin, or whether you stay and get said skin perforated. Make up your mind—fast!"

Quist looked questioningly at Fox and Currie. Both nodded. Currie added heavily, "That's the way it is, Mr. Quist."

Quist studied the features of the three men. This was something, he realized, he couldn't talk his way out of. There had to be some other method. A slow smile curled his lips. "It looks as if you hombres held all the cards," he conceded quietly. "Give me a couple of minutes to think it over. It might be we can reach some sort of compromise."

He dropped one hand to his coat pocket and produced a sack of Durham and cigarette papers. "I've got to smoke on a proposition like you men hand out. Join me?" He extended the "makin's" to the three men, but each shook his head in refusal. Carefully, deliberately, Quist sprinkled yellow grains of tobacco into a paper and curled it into a cylinder which he thrust between his lips, after twisting one end of the cigarette. He dropped the sack, which had been dangling by its string from his little finger, into a pocket, and searched for a match. His hand came out of his pocket empty, and he tried the other side of his coat. Again, his hand came forth empty. Quist asked the man on his left, "Have you got a match you're not using, Fox?" His voice sounded casual, almost careless.

Lulled into a feeling of security by Quist's easy manner, Fox said, "I reckon I have," and thrust his right hand into his pocket. Currie said, "Here, I got one."

Fox's hand emerged first and extended a match to Quist, while Currie was still fumbling in his pocket.

Quist said "Much obliged" in the same careless voice and put out his left hand to take Fox's proffered match. Instead of accepting the match, however, Quist did three things simultaneously: the fingers of his left hand closed like steel around Fox's right wrist, jerking the man suddenly forward, a movement that was intensified by the abrupt plunge of Quist's black gelding, as the startled horse, knee-guided by its rider, felt spur rowels thrust savagely into its flanks. At the same instant, Quist's right hand darted beneath his coat to shoulder holster and emerged again in a burst of smoke and white flame.

Even as he fired, Quist felt the breeze of Pritchett's bullet fan his cheek, then Pritchett swayed in the saddle. The black gelding, at touch of the spurs, had reared, then thrust ahead, its front hoofs slashing violently over Jake Currie who frantically shifted his weight to one side. At that moment, the gelding came down, the impact of its solid weight crashing against Currie's pony and overthrowing it. By this time, Quist had already released his grip on Fox's wrist, allowing the man to pitch headlong to earth.

Flying hoofs scrabbled in dust and gravel, as Quist again

got a firm hold on his reins, checking the excited black gelding and whirling it on hind hoofs to face his enemies once more. Through the rising haze of dust, Quist saw that Fox had scrambled to his feet and was raising his gun. Quist thumbed one quick shot at Fox, shifted aim and fired again at Pritchett who was bringing his six-shooter into action with his right hand, while his left, gripping the saddle horn, was holding him upright on his horse's back.

Booming echoes of gun explosions rolled through the hills. Quite suddenly, Pritchett slumped sidewise in the saddle, his nerveless fingers relinquishing his six-shooter and sliding futilely down the reins as he crashed in the roadway.

Currie was struggling to extricate himself from beneath his struggling horse whose hoofs, thrashing wildly about, were kicking up dust and gravel. Fox was on his knees now, one hand bracing his weight from the earth, the other dangling helplessly from the shoulder. His gun lay in the road a couple of feet away, and he was doing his best to get to it. Still pinned under the fallen pony, Currie was swearing and trying to pull his weapon from the holster pinned beneath his leg.

"Hold it!" Quist called sharply, reining his pony toward the men. "It's your finish if you try to go on with this. Use your heads!" He was holding his .44 ready, his eyes narrowed and alert.

Brose Fox said "Oh, hell," and staggered uncertainly to his feet. Currie swore some more and managed to get out from under his horse. He made no further move toward his gun as he scrambled upright. An instant later, his horse was again erect, shaking itself.

Quist said, "Currie, take your gun out real carefully and toss it in the brush."

Currie managed some further cursing but obeyed orders. Fox had dropped back to earth, but was maintaining a sitting position. His left arm hung helplessly at his side; his shoulder was stained with dark crimson. He glanced up at Quist, grudging admiration mingling with the pain in his eyes. "You—you wily devil," he grated.

Quist shrugged, smiling thinly. "You forced me into it, fellows. I didn't want trouble, but you forced my hand——"

"Talk won't get us no place," Currie growled. "Can I take a look at Brose, Quist, and see how bad he's hit?"

"I was about to suggest that very thing."

Quist moved his pony a few steps farther, got down from the saddle and kicked Brose Fox's gun well out of reach. Then he went to Homer Pritchett who was huddled on his side in the roadway. First casting a quick glance toward Currie who

was occupied with Fox, Quist swiftly reloaded his .44 and replaced it in his holster. Then, after picking up Pritchett's gun
and sticking it in the waistband of his trousers, Quist knelt by
the silent form and turned it over to learn where the bullets
had struck.

Quist's first slug had entered Pritchett's body low, beneath
the left ribs; the second had gone in just over the heart.
Pritchett's eyes were already glazing. Quist drew a deep breath,
then lifted the limp form from the road and placed it across
the saddle of Pritchett's horse which stood quietly nearby.
There was a lariat on the saddle and Quist proceeded to lash
the body firmly in place. Then he strode over to Currie and
Fox. Fox was on his feet, his head, resting on one arm, bowed
against the saddle of his pony. Currie glared at Quist.

Quist said, "How bad was the damage?"

"You smashed his shoulder, damn you," Currie snarled. "I
plugged the hole up with chewin' tobacco and bound it as well
as possible with a couple of bandannas, but that don't help
much. What you aim to do with us?"

"I'll let Sheriff Nixon decide that," Quist said, cold-voiced.
"First, though, we'd best get Fox to a doctor."

Currie looked relieved and some of the hard lines vanished
from his face. "I reckon we made a mistake, Quist. Mebbe we
got out of line some, stopping you like we did."

"It's too damn' bad you didn't think of that earlier, Currie."

"I reckon you're right," Currie agreed in a toneless voice.
The fight was gone from him now. "Looks like Pritchett was
hit bad."

"No doctor can help him, any," Quist said meaningly.

"T'hell you say. Well, dammit, he had his chance——"

Quist interrupted, "Come on, let's get started for Hyperion."

Fox was boosted into his saddle, his lips tight, his face
streaming with perspiration. Beyond a suppressed exclamation
that had to do with the agony caused by his smashed shoulder,
he didn't say anything. Quist and Currie mounted on either
side of him, leading behind them Pritchett's horse with its
grisly burden. Nothing more was said as the horses got started,
and this silence held, except for an occasional groan from
Fox, for a mile or more. Because of Fox's wounded shoulder,
it was impossible to make speed.

Currie said finally, "I've been thinking, Quist, when I was
pinned under this fool bronc of mine, you could have plugged
me, easy as not."

Quist nodded. "I reckon I could've."

Currie cast a quick glance at Quist, then growled, "Much
obliged."

"Don't mention it," Quist replied with a sort of dry politeness.

The sun was below the Gunsight Mountains now and a dim half-light covered the land. Currie went on, after a time, "Yeah, it was a right fool stunt, I reckon."

"How'd you come to try it?" Quist asked.

Currie scowled. "We knew it didn't set right with Chris Hamilton, you bein' here, so we thought mebbe we could scare you into leaving. We never had any intention of drawin' on you—then when you started in—well, I reckon things got out of hand and we lost our heads."

"Why didn't Chris Hamilton want me to come here?" Currie looked at Quist a moment, then quickly looked away, without replying. Quist repeated his question.

Currie said, "Why don't you ask old Chris?"

"I'm asking you. You know, Currie, I can send you to prison for what you tried today."

Currie laughed harshly. "Hell! That much I'm expecting. I'm just countin' myself lucky it wa'n't worse. But don't expect me to tell you what's in Chris Hamilton's mind."

"All right, Currie," Quist smiled. "I like a man that's loyal to the man that hires him. Tell me this: how come you and Fox joined forces with Homer Pritchett?"

"We-ell, that just sort of happened," Currie frowned. "Me'n Brose got the idea we could scare you out—damn' fools that we were—so we rode out there where we stopped you, before you left the Circle-H. While we were waiting for you to show up, Pritchett came along. We asked where he was going. He said no place in particular, that he was just riding around——"

"For his health, I presume."

"If it was," Currie growled, "he took the wrong road. He asked if you had been to the Circle-H. We said you was there at the time. One thing led to another when your name was mentioned. Pritchett seemed to hold some grudge against you, but he wouldn't tell us why——"

"I'm quite sure he took a shot at me in El Paso."

"Why?"

"Trying to scare me away from Hyperion."

"Why?"

Quist employed Currie's remarks of a moment before: "Why don't you ask old Chris?" And added. "Or somebody else. I don't know who sent Pritchett to El Paso."

"I'm bettin' it wa'n't none of Chris Hamilton's doin's."

"How come you're so certain?"

"Why should Chris," Currie demanded, "send a Wagon-Wheel man to do what his own hands could have done?"

"Maybe his own hands didn't take to the idea," Quist suggested.

"You're talking fool talk, Mr. Quist. The Circle-H hands will back Chris Hamilton to the last ditch, as will a hell of a lot of other people in the Gunsight country."

"Even to breaking the law?"

"*Anything* Chris Hamilton wants," Currie said earnestly, "he can have for the asking, in these parts."

"That much is settled, anyway," Quist said carelessly. "Now I'd like to know how you and Fox happened to join up with Pritchett."

"Like I said, your name was mentioned. One thing led to another. Pritchett remarked that he'd like to see you run out of the country. Brose and I agreed, and—well—you know what happened. Though I swear we never—Brose and me—figured it would end in gunplay. That wa'n't our intentions a-tall."

"You just figured all you had to do was say 'Booh!' and I'd run?"

Currie swore. "You know better than that. All right, so you've stopped Brose and me, but that just means other people will be trying——"

"What other people?"

"That's for you to find out," Currie said sullenly. "My advice still holds good. You'd better get out of the Gunsight country."

"I don't agree."

"That," Currie snapped, "is just your tough luck, then."

Fox moaned that he'd like a drink. Currie told him the river was only a mite farther on. Darkness had settled over the range by this time. The horses pushed steadily toward Hyperion.

Chapter XIII : WAR TALK

Lights burned along Huisache Street when they entered Hyperion. Before Quist and the others had proceeded a block they had a following of curious men, demanding to know what had happened. Quist didn't reply. Currie threatened in an ominous tone to "burn their backsides with hot lead" if the crowd didn't shut up and keep away from them. No one noticed that Currie's holster was empty and the threat had some effect. Most of the crowd fell farther to the rear, while three or four ran ahead to tell the sheriff.

By the time the horses had stopped before the sheriff's office, another crowd had collected. Lights burned from the window and from the open door of the building where Bard Nixon stood silhouetted against the illumination. "Now what's happened, for cripes' sake?" he snapped irritably, striding out to the hitchrack where the horses had stopped. He paused to yell at the crowd to clear out, then repeated his question. The crowd moved across the street, but refused to leave the vicinity.

Quist said, "I've got one dead man for you and one wounded man, Sheriff——"

"My God! What happened?"

Currie said in a humorless voice. "Brose Fox and Pritchett and me tried to scare Mr. Quist into leaving the country. We made the wrong play."

"You fools! You utter damned fools!" Nixon said wrathfully. "I could have warned you not to try anything of that kind."

"You weren't there to warn us," Currie said, adding, "I wish to Gawd you had been."

Quist said, "You do as you see fit, sheriff. Fox ought to be taken to the doctor, soon as possible. But it's out of my hands. I'm heading for the nearest restaurant. I'll talk to you later."

He turned the black gelding and rode a block to the corner of Crockett Street where he turned the horse into the Hyperion Livery. "Give that pony a good rub-down and a feed of grain," Quist told the stableman in charge. "I owe a lot to that pony for his work today."

"He don't look like you'd been pushing him hard," the stableman said.

"He was on the job when I needed him, though," Quist said.

"Well, that's all you can ask from any horse," the man said. "Say, I noticed a crowd heading toward the sheriff's office a short spell back. You heard anything about any trouble?"

"No trouble that I know of," Quist replied, and made his escape before the stableman could pursue the matter further.

Leaving the livery, Quist went first to his hotel room where he cleaned up. By the time he'd descended to the lower floor the supper hour had passed and the hotel dining room was closed. Quist stepped into the street and strolled along Huisache until he saw a restaurant with the words "T-Bone Cafe" painted on its windows. Within was a long counter with stools at one wall, while the rest of the room was devoted to space for tables and chairs. A door at the back gave into the kitchen. Quist seated himself at a table near the front, and a girl who had been standing behind the counter came and took his order.

For the next half hour Quist occupied himself with a thick steak, stewed corn, fried potatoes, and hot biscuits. Later, the waitress brought coffee and dried apricot pie. There was no one else in the restaurant besides Quist and the waitress, so he was left alone with his thoughts of the day's events.

Quist was about to leave when he saw Sheriff Nixon entering the T-Bone. The sheriff came in, slammed the door behind him and scowled at Quist. "There's something almighty funny has got to be cleared up," Nixon said explosively.

"Sit down and we'll see what we can do about it," Quist suggested. He beckoned the girl to bring more coffee and a cup for the sheriff. "What's on your mind?"

Nixon jerked out a chair and slammed himself on the seat, his long mustaches bristling with indignation. "That blasted liar!" he swore.

"Who's a blasted liar?" Quist asked. "And you don't want to get too excited, Sheriff. It's bad for your blood pressure."

"Jake Currie!" The sheriff paused and lowered his voice. "Do you know what Jake Currie told me?"

"What did he tell you?"

"Jake told me—and he must think I'm an awful fool if I believed him—that he and Brose Fox and Homer Pritchett had you cornered, and that you turned the tables on them."

"What's wrong with that?"

"Ain't no man living can do that! All three are damn' smart with a hawg-laig—two, that is, with Pritchett gone. But what I want to know is, who was helping you?"

"Nobody. Maybe I was just lucky."

"Pshaw! Quist, I'm too old a man to swallow fish stories."

"What did Currie tell you?"

"Well——" Nixon drew a long breath. "He said that him and Fox and Pritchett cooked up a plan to corner you and tell you to clear out of the country, and that you listened calm to what they had to say, while you rolled a cigarette. Then you borrowed a match from Fox and the next thing Currie knowed, Fox was out of his saddle and hitting the dust, you'd climbed your pony halfway over Currie and shot Pritchett all at the same time. I told Currie plain he was lyin', and he allowed as how he didn't quite understand himself how it happened."

Quist smiled thinly. "That's about the story. I'll repeat, I was lucky."

Nixon snorted. "But Currie claims that Pritchett already had his gun out. Damned if I can see how——"

"Don't let your coffee get cold, Sheriff. Currie told the truth so far as he knew. Things were happening right fast, and he was down, pinned under his horse, part of the time. Those fellows just cooked up something that backfired on 'em, that's all. I'm fairly sure Pritchett was the hombre who fired on me in El Paso." Quist gave his reasons. "Whether Pritchett followed me out the Circle-H road to finish the job, or just scare me into leaving, we'll never know what his intentions were now." Quist drew Pritchett's six-shooter from the waistband of his trousers and shoved it across the table. "I forgot to give you his gun before. You figure you'll have to arrest me for the killing?"

Nixon examined the gun, muttered something about "three empty shells," then raised his head. "In view of this and what Currie told me, I'd be a fool if I tried." He paused. "Do you think old Chris Hamilton had anything to do with the business?"

Quist shook his head. "First, I think the old man is too smart to have anything like that happen so soon after leaving his place. Second, I can't bring myself to believe he'd think he could throw a scare into me. I think Rick convinced him I don't scare easy."

Nixon shook his head unbelievingly. "I still don't see how you got your gun out and shot so fast." Quist said dryly that it had been necessary. Nixon went on, "Chris ain't going to like it, I'll bet."

"In one way I'm glad that little ruckus happened."

"How you figurin'?"

"Maybe now folks will think twice before they try to crowd me. Maybe they'll realize I'm here to stay until I get damn' well ready to pull up stakes. I'll appreciate you spreading word how I feel."

"I'll not only spread that gospel; I'll add a warnin' to it," Nixon growled, angrily jerking up his coffee and spilling part of the brown fluid down the front of his shirt. He banged the cup back in the saucer, wiping his mustache with the back of one hand, and reached for tobacco and cigarette papers. Quist called to the waitress and asked her to bring a couple of cigars. The men smoked in silence for a few moments. Quist said finally, "How bad is Fox injured?"

"You broke his shoulder but Doc Sturven got the bullet out while I was there. Nice clean wound." Nixon hesitated. "Doc's going to take care of Fox tonight, but tomorrow we're goin' to let him return to the Circle-H, if you don't mind. I know Fox; he won't run off. He give me his word. Doc's got Bascom to nurse and will have his hands full. And I don't figure I could take care of Fox in jail. I can lay hands on him when I'm ready. Too damn' bad you didn't plug Currie the same way."

Quist shrugged his wide shoulders. "He and Fox were only

doing what they thought Chris Hamilton would want. You can't blame a man for loyalty to his boss."

"Damn me if you don't take things easy," Nixon snapped. "Loyalty is all right, but I don't intend to have no man breakin' the law, regardless if it's in favor of Chris Hamilton, or anybody else."

Quist laughed softly. "You seem to have changed your tune a mite since we had our little talk, Sheriff."

The sheriff reddened and said, "That's whatever," in a sheepish tone. He went on, "Pritchett's body's at the undertaker's. Cody Thatcher came in while I was there." A frown crossed Nixon's face. "I don't know but what you might have some trouble with Cody. He thought a lot of Pritchett and he's right well worked up about the whole business. I warned him not to start any trouble, though, while I was around——"

"Meaning he can go the limit when you're not in sight?"

"Now, dammit, Quist, you know better than to say a thing like that," Nixon protested aggrievedly. "Sometimes you act like you're just lookin' for trouble."

"Maybe I am," Quist conceded. "The more people get mad at me, the sooner they'll give me an opening, perhaps. . . . What did you do with Currie?"

"I've got him locked in a cell. That's something else, Quist. What charges do you want preferred against him and Fox? I figured first, 'assault with deadly weapons,' but damned if I can see where you got assaulted any—not when you killed one, wounded another and captured a third. I'd look sort of silly bringin' up a charge like that in court." He paused, shaking his head, "Just who assaulted who is what I want to know."

Quist shrugged. "Suit yourself. I didn't start the fracas."

"All right; then you're the injured party—and that sounds crazy too. You tell me what charge you want brought."

"Have I asked you to charge 'em?"

Nixon's eyes widened. "What the hell! You want 'em put where they won't make you no more trouble, don't you? I'll throw Fox into a cell, too, just as soon as he gets healed some. T'tell the truth, I wouldn't be surprised to see Chris Hamilton kick him out, if Hamilton really didn't have anythin' to do with stoppin' you——"

"I've yet to see a paralyzed man do any kicking."

"You know what I mean."

Quist nodded and considered the matter. "Look here, Sheriff, I don't want to infringe on your authority. If you want to bring charges against Fox and Currie and take 'em into court, suit yourself, but don't expect any help from me."

"You mean they can go free as far as you're concerned?" Nixon exclaimed.

"Exactly that."

"Moses on the mountaintop! What's got into you?"

"The Circle-H is hostile enough without me giving 'em something else to make 'em mad. I figure Fox and Currie have learned a lesson. Particularly Fox. They won't be wanting to start anything against me for quite a spell. And they might prove to be helpful, in the long run."

Nixon looked thoughtful. "I guess I know what you're drivin' at," he said dubiously. "Maybe you got the right idea. When I get back I'll let Currie go free. If you don't want him and Fox brought to trial, there's no use of me antagonizin' the Circle-H either."

Quist nodded. "You might tell Currie, in case he's forgotten, that his and Fox's six-shooters are laying out near the trail where they stopped me. Tell 'em I'm willing to forget the whole business, if they are."

Nixon looked curiously at Quist. "If you ain't the damnedest hombre. Most men would be all for gunning the life out of anybody that done what them hombres did."

Quist smiled. "You forget, Sheriff, that I'm trying to get along with folks hereabouts. So far, nobody's given me much chance to be friendly."

"I'm commencing to agree with you," Nixon said slowly. "What did you learn at the Circle-H today? Anything you want to tell me?"

"I guess there's nothing I can pass on. Hamilton went on record as not knowing anything Rick hadn't already told me. He made it clear I wasn't welcome in the Gunsight country. He got sort of riled at me for a spell——"

"Chris is right testy-tempered at times. What did you say that upset him?"

"It was something I did. I picked up his rifle and potted a gopher that he and Banning had been shooting at all morning."

Nixon chuckled. "That sounds like Chris. He fancies himself with shootin' irons and hates to be outdone on anythin'. He'll get over it."

They conversed a few more minutes, then Quist paid the score and they left the restaurant. The two men strolled east on Huisache Street which was almost deserted by this time. Most of the buildings along the thoroughfare were dark, though here and there a saloon or pool hall cast a rectangle of yellow light out to the dusty unpaved roadway. There were only a few pedestrians abroad. A number of ponies were scattered along the hitchracks. At the corner of Crockett Street,

Quist paused and gestured toward the Hyperion House where a single light burned in the hotel lobby window. "I reckon I'll go over to the hotel and hit the hay," he said. "It's been a long day."

"I'll be turning in myself, just as soon as I've released Jake Currie," Nixon replied. "Well, take care of yourself. I'll see you come *mañana*."

Quist said *Adios,* and headed for the hotel on the opposite corner. The Hyperion House was of two-story brick construction, with a short flight of steps running to the first-story porch that fronted two walls of the building on Huisache and Crockett Streets. The hotel bar entrance, now dark, gave off the porch on the Crockett Street side. Quist stepped to the sidewalk, his high-heeled boots making hollow clumping sounds on the rough boards and started to ascend to the porch. Just as he reached the top, a shadowy figure straightened from its leaning position against one of the porch uprights, saying in a tense voice: "Just a minute, Quist. I want to talk to you."

Quist faced the man and saw in the faint light from the lobby window that it was Cody Thatcher who barred his progress. "Thatcher, eh?" Quist said. "What's on your mind?"

Thatcher said, his voice trembling with anger, "You killed Homer Pritchett today. I'm aiming to square that account, Quist."

"You might as well jerk your iron and go to work then," Quist invited coldly. He made no attempt to draw, as Cody Thatcher was standing with his arms well out from his sides.

"Not yet." Thatcher shook his head. "I want to make sure first."

"Sure of what?"

Thatcher paused. "I've been told a damn' queer story by the sheriff, Quist. He claims that Currie, Fox, and Homer cornered you, and you shot your way out of the trap."

"That's how it was," Quist said quietly.

"You're a liar!"

"Now you're making war talk, Thatcher. You'd best be ready to back up that kind of *habla*."

"I'll back it up when the time comes," Thatcher rasped. "But first I want to get this story straight——"

"You've got it straight, Thatcher."

"No. There's something funny about the whole business. Who did you have helping you?"

"I was alone."

"I can't swallow anything like that. Nixon tells me Homer already had his gun out. I knew Homer. He was damn' fast.

No man on earth could beat him to the shot under those circumstances."

Quist said sarcastically, "I guss I must have been awfully lucky, then, Thatcher, but that's the way it was——"

"You lie!"

"That's the second time, Thatcher. I don't take that word very often. You'd better get ready to back up your words. I'm losing patience. Go on. Yank your gun—or shut your damn' mouth!"

Thatcher tensed, then a long pent-up breath left his lips. "All right," he conceded slowly, "I could be wrong. But just as soon as I get a chance to talk to Jake Currie I'm aiming to learn the right of this. If Currie tells it your way, we'll drop the matter, but if he doesn't, I'm warning you you'd better leave this country fast, or I'm coming after you with a blazing gun——"

"I don't scare easy," Quist laughed. "Pritchett tried it in El Paso. He tried it again today. I'm still in circulation, Thatcher. So you're not going to frighten me into leaving either——"

"What do you mean—El Paso?"

"Are you trying to tell me you don't know?"

"I'll swear I don't."

"And now I think you're a liar."

"Take it easy, Quist! I'm warning you——"

"Warn and be damned! I suppose you'll deny that Pritchett was away a few days before I arrived here, and got back on the train just ahead of me."

"No, I won't deny that. Homer was visiting his brother in Tonkawa Springs, and——"

"Are you ready to produce proof of that, Thatcher? It can be easily checked up, you know."

Thatcher was silent for a moment. "We-ell, no, I haven't any exact proof, but Homer said——"

"I don't care what Homer said. I'm interested in learning who sent him to El Paso, and just the minute I find out——"

"I don't know a thing about it. If you think Homer had anything to do with Canfield's death, you're on the wrong track. And certainly I didn't."

"Have I mentioned in any way that I thought you were connected with Canfield's murder?" Quist demanded.

"No, but everybody knows that's what brought you here."

"What are you trying to hide, Thatcher?"

"Nothing. What makes you think——?"

"You've tried to scare me into leaving Hyperion. There must be something you don't want uncovered."

Thatcher said angrily, "Hell! You're crazy!"

"While we're on the subject, just where were you the night Canfield was killed?"

"The trial records will give you that."

"I'm asking you!"

"All right." Thatcher's voice was suddenly cold and steady as though he felt himself on more even ground now. "I was called as a witness when the trial came up. I had seen Nash Canfield in town, I had seen him leave town long before I did. I didn't leave until late afternoon. At the time he died I must have been somewhere between Hyperion and my Wagon-Wheel ranch house. That satisfy you?"

"Nothing satisfies me that doesn't give me what I'm looking for, Thatcher. And if you want to see Jake Currie and learn what happened today, I'd advise you to go down to the jail. Bard Nixon should be releasing him about now."

"Releasing him? But isn't he——"

"Nixon's letting him go. I'm not asking that he be charged with any law violation——"

"By God, Quist! This makes things look queerer than ever. You've framed Homer Pritchett into something——"

"Pritchett wasn't framed. Pritchett deserved everything that happened to him. Now if you want to make anything of that, Thatcher, get busy. Otherwise shut your mouth and get out of here. I'm going to bed."

For just a moment, Thatcher stood glaring at Quist, then with a muttered curse, he brushed past, ran down the steps from the hotel porch and hurried off in the diection of the jail. Quist gazed after him a moment, laughed shortly, then entered the hotel. He awakened the clerk who was sleeping behind the desk, secured his key and ascended the lobby stairway to his bedroom on the second floor.

Chapter XIV : WOLF TRAP

Cody Thatcher was waiting in the lobby when Quist appeared the following morning. Thatcher said, without preliminaries, "I'd like to speak to you a minute, Quist."

Quist looked sharply at the man, taking in his lean form, the even white teeth and reddish hair, and decided that Thatcher seemed rather nervous. "That's the way you started in last night," Quist stated coldly. "What was that? A rehearsal?"

"Now don't get me wrong." Thatcher forced a feeble smile. "I want to apologize."

"For what?"

"I sort of went off half-cocked, last night, Quist. I reckon it must be my red hair that makes me so quick-tempered——"

"If that's the case, a bottle of black dye might save you getting your head blown off, sometime. Thatcher, what's on your mind?"

"I talked to Jake Currie, after I left you, last night," Thatcher said uncomfortably. "He confirmed what you and Nixon said about yesterday's doings, so I guess I was wrong. Currie even went so far as to state that he and Fox and Homer were in the wrong, too, now that he's had a chance to think things over. I guess that business sort of got out of hand, once it had started." Thatcher paused, frowning. "I just can't understand what got into Homer. Why should he want to drive you out of this country?"

"Or kill me?"

"Shucks! I can't believe Homer Pritchett ever intended anything of that sort."

"His first slug fanned awful close, Thatcher."

"I'll have to take your word for it, but it's a puzzle to me."

"You know of any reason why Pritchett would've killed Canfield?"

Thatcher's frown deepened. "There were a lot of folks had reasons for killing Canfield."

"You're not answering my question."

"We-ell, Homer did have some trouble with Canfield one time."

"What about?"

"Crooked dice. Canfield took better than seven hundred dollars off of Homer, one time. Homer took his loss like a gent, until one time Canfield got drunk and got to boasting about the dice he'd worked into the game. After he was sober, he denied the whole business, of course, and the dice weren't available by that time for Homer to prove anything. There were some pretty hot words passed between the two men, but it didn't come to anything—unless——" Thatcher paused as though reluctant to go on.

"Unless what?" Quist demanded.

"Damned if I like to accuse a dead man, especially anyone as close as Homer was——" Again the pause. Thatcher cast a quick glance about the lobby. The clerk on duty behind the desk was busy with his own affairs. Excepting the clerk, Quist and Thatcher, no one else was present, though through an open door in one lobby wall came the clatter of breakfast dishes from the dining room. "I tell you, Quist," Thatcher went on, "the more I've thought things over, the more I figure maybe Homer did kill Canfield."

"How?"

"Hell! I couldn't say as to that. At the same time, I'm not thoroughly convinced that Homer would kill Canfield over a sum as small as seven hundred dollars."

"Your mind is certainly trying to be neutral," Quist smiled. "Suppose that amount had been larger? Do you think in that case Pritchett would have had cause for murder?"

"It's entirely possible."

"In that case, Thatcher, how do I know you didn't kill Canfield? He certainly cheated you out a much larger sum when he bought his Terrapin holdings from you. On top of that, he married the girl you'd been engaged to——"

"Who told you all that?" Thatcher's face clouded up like a thunderstorm.

"I've more than one way of learning things," Quist evaded. "It's all true, isn't it?"

"Well——er——yes, I reckon it is." Thatcher appeared flustered. "Look here, Quist, you're not suspecting that I——"

"I'm suspecting everybody until I've got the facts. Now if you have any other facts that might help to clear you, you'd best let me have 'em——*pronto!*"

Thatcher drew out a blue bandanna and mopped his forehead. "I'll swear I had nothing to do with Canfield's death."

"Most murderers take a similar stand."

"But I tell you, Quist, you're off on the wrong track. I'll admit there wasn't any friendship between Canfield and me at the time he was killed. I'll go so far as to say I was almost glad to hear of his death. He was a skunk of the first water. But folks around here will tell you I'm not the man to commit murder——"

"I'm still asking for facts that might clear you. You're getting in deeper all the time, Thatcher, so you'd best start thinking fast."

"But I tell you I don't know anything."

"Not one single fact?"

"Not one——"

"It's your own skin you'd best be thinking of, Thatcher."

"But I don't——" He broke off suddenly, then lamely, "Well, I hate to say it, but there was something that puzzled me one time, shortly before Canfield was killed."

"Get to it," Quist snapped.

"God, I hate to say this, but it was something Rick Hamilton was doing." Again the pause. Quist spoke sharply, urging the man on. Thatcher continued with evident reluctance. "Well, I rode over to the Circle-H one time to visit Chris Hamilton. From time to time I'd hear some shooting down near the corrals. I asked Chris what was doing, and he said Rick was experimenting with some sort of contraption—he didn't know what it was. I went out to see later on. I found Rick out back of one of the corrals. He had a cocked six-shooter wedged between some chunks of rock, with a long strip of rawhide running from the trigger back of the gun, around another rock, and then forward again to where he had it tied to a whisky bottle—only the bottle was filled with water, at the time. Rick would take a sapling pole and touch the bottle, knocking it over, and the gun would go off. He had a fair-sized target cut out of a plank, and his shots were hitting it right regular."

Quist's forehead furrowed. "What was the idea?"

"That's what I asked Rick. He acted sort of sheepish-like and said he was fixing up a trap to shoot a lobo wolf that had been killing some stock."

"I thought Tom Jenkins' father was supposed to do all the 'wolfing' in these parts."

"He most generally does."

"Did Rick ever get his lobo?"

Thatcher shrugged. "I can't say. I never heard anything more about it."

"You think this is connected some way with Canfield's killing?"

"I didn't say so."

"Maybe you're thinking it. Maybe you figure you've thrown me off the track."

"What track?"

"Whatever track you're trying to cover, Thatcher," Quist said bluntly. "If you have anything to hide, now is the time to spill it. Confession is good for the soul."

"Now, look here, Quist," Thatcher bridled, "I won't take any such talk from you——"

Quist exhaled a bored impatient sigh. "Now, we're going right back to last night again. If you're through talking, Thatcher, I'm going in and eat breakfast. I've wasted enough time with you."

Thatcher said, "Oh, to hell with it! If you think you can get anything on me, go to it." He flung himself around and barged through the hotel doorway to the street.

Quist looked after him a moment. That hombre is sure scared about something, he thought. Oh well, if enough folks get scared, somebody will start spilling things soon. He turned and went into the dining room.

A half hour later, after he had returned to his room, strapped on his shoulder harness and gun and again donned his coat, Quist stepped on the hotel porch to see Tom Jenkins just ascending the steps. The men greeted each other, Quist adding, "What brings you to town, Tom?"

"Rode in to see if Webb Bascom had died or recovered consciousness———"

"I'll go along to the doctor's with you," Quist suggested.

Jenkins shook his head. His dark face looked very sober. "We're too late. I was just talking to Sheriff Nixon. Bascom died during the night. Nixon was on his way to tell you, but he had some other business and asked me to let you know." The Terrapin foreman drew a deep breath. "I reckon we both had a hand in it, Mr. Quist. Sturven said either bullet might have been fatal."

"We'll have to share the guilt, then," Quist nodded. "I don't know what else we could have done. Anytime, somebody starts throwing lead at me from the brush, I return the fire, if possible. It looks like self-defense to me."

"I didn't have the same reason———" Jenkins commenced.

"You couldn't be sure who Bascom was firing at, Tom. Not only that, you had a job protecting a visitor to your outfit. You did your job."

"Just the same, I hate the thought of killing———"

"You wouldn't have killed Canfield if you had a chance?"

Jenkins scowled. "That's a different matter."

Quist nodded. "Maybe it is; I'll keep it in mind. . . . Did Bascom regain consciousness before he died?"

Jenkins nodded. "He talked a little, not much, but enough for Doc to learn that Homer Pritchett had offered Bascom one hundred dollars to rub you out."

Quist whistled softly. "Why?"

Jenkins shook his head. "Bascom died before he could tell that, if he knew. He said that Pritchett had been in town when you got off the train with Rick, and a few hours later Pritchett made his offer. Bascom apparently didn't care why, so long as he earned the hundred."

"One hundred dollars," Quist repeated softly. "The price of a life. I can't say I'm flattered. Now I'll bet a Hamilton would have offered more———"

"Cut it out, Quist," Jenkins snapped. "The Hamiltons don't hire their killing done for 'em———"

"They handle them themselves?" Quist asked quietly.

Jenkins's scowl deepened. "Let's drop that line of conversation," he said shortly.

"Just as you say. What about an inquest on Bascom's death?"

"Doc Sturven—he's coroner, y'know—will call one, but Bard Nixon tells me there won't be anything to it. So far as Nixon and Sturven are concerned, we're both exonerated of any guilt in the matter, and Bascom didn't have any friends to kick up a fuss about his death. . . . Nixon tells me you killed Homer Pritchett last night, and put the bee on a couple of Circle-H hands. Just what happened?"

Quist told the story. When he had concluded, Jenkins shook his head, frowning, "There's two things I don't understand. First, how you ever got out of a trap like that. Oh, sure, Nixon told me just about the same story, but it's still hard to believe. Second, why was Pritchett so anxious to have you out of the way?"

"I can't answer that, either. Of course, he was Cody Thatcher's foreman."

"You mean Pritchett has just been carrying out Thatcher's orders?"

"It could be."

"But why—why should Thatcher——?"

"That's something I don't know. I'm still digging, however, and maybe one of these days——" Quist broke off. "Here comes Rick."

Rick Hamilton was just dismounting from his pony at the hotel hitchrack. He came around the end of the rack and stepped to the sidewalk, as Quist and Jenkins descended the hotel steps to meet him.

"Mornin', Greg! How's it going, Tom?" Rick said. He turned back to Quist, saying, "Dad wants that you should come out and see him, as soon as you have a chance."

"What's up?"

"He wants to apologize for the Circle-H."

"Now what's the Circle-H done?" Quist asked.

"That business with Jake Currie and Brose Fox—and Pritchett, last evening. Jake came back to the ranch this morning, before daylight. When Dad heard what had happened he hit the ceiling—that is, so far as a man can hit the ceiling and still stay in his chair. He bawled Jake to a fare-thee-well, and he'll do the same to Brose when he shows up. Dad's mighty sore about the whole business, and he wants it made clear that he didn't have a thing to do with it."

"I was right sure of that myself. Jake and Brose just got

overly ambitious on your father's behalf and went haywire for a spell."

Rick nodded. "Dad realized that they were trying to do him a favor. That's all that saved them from being fired, and they've been with the Circle-H a good many years, too."

Quist said, "I'll pay your dad a visit the first chance I get. This morning, though, I've got something else ahead of me. Just tell Chris Hamilton that I'm not holding any grudges"—Quist smiled—"and that I'll even come out and help him shoot gophers, if he'll lend me a gun."

"He would, like a shot! After you left yesterday he was ashamed he'd acted that way. It's just that being crippled the way he is, and forced to stay inactive, his temper gets a mite sharp at times."

Quist nodded. "I can understand how he feels. Rick, there are a couple of questions I'd like to ask you."

"Is this private?" Tom Jenkins broke in.

"I don't reckon so," Quist said. "If Rick doesn't want to answer he doesn't have to." He turned back to Rick: "Can you remember exactly what you did the day Canfield was killed—after you'd had the quarrel with him in front of the bank?"

"There's not much to remember," Rick said promptly. "I left town shortly after Canfield headed for the Terrapin, with Tom, here. I rode to the Circle-H. Dad asked for news. I told him what had happened. He got pretty mad, I recollect, and stated that Canfield needed killing——" Rick broke off in some confusion.

"Keep going," Quist said dryly. "Your father's remark merely makes it more unanimous. Every one seems to have felt the same way about Canfield."

"There's not much left to tell. I hung around the house until late afternoon, then decided to ride to Hyperion to see—to see——"

"To see about buying a new bonnet at the Bon-Ton, I suppose." Quist smiled.

"That's about it." Rick colored. "On the way to town I kept thinking about various things Canfield had said. Finally, I headed for the Terrapin, instead of going to town, in the hope of having a straight talk with Canfield and making him see reason. And then, after I got there—well, I've told you all that, about hearing the shot and going in and—well—I told you all that——"

"So you said." Quist looked thoughtful. "All right, skip the rest. Rick, do you suppose there was any way in which a gun could have been arranged, some place in that room, with a string from the trigger to some other object, so that when the object was touched, the gun would explode?"

Rick looked only slightly dubious. "Sure, something like that could have been fixed up, I reckon, but I doubt that it was."

"You didn't know of any such contraption?"

"Certainly not. I'd have told you if I had."

Quist eyed Rick quizzically. "That's open to argument too. Nobody ever seems to want to tell me anything until I worm it out of 'em." Rick started a protest then checked the words. Quist continued, "Why do you say you doubt anything of the sort was used?"

"Well, cripes," Rick said, "it stands to reason. The gun that shot Canfield was right there—his own gun."

"You're absolutely certain the gun you—well, we'll say the gun you saw in that room at the time of Canfield's death—was the one that shot him?"

Rick hesitated. "Not absolutely, of course, but I'm fairly sure. The slug that was probed out of Canfield's body was a .45, and Canfield's gun showed evidence of having been fired about that time. Anyway, I feel pretty safe in stating that Canfield was killed by his own weapon."

Quist had been watching Rick narrowly while he talked. "All right," he nodded. "I guess you've covered it, Rick."

"What's all this about a gun contraption?" Jenkins asked curiously. "Have you discovered something new, Mr. Quist?"

"Nothing for publication," Quist replied. "Tom, I'd sort of planned on riding to visit Mrs. Canfield, this morning, if you think she could bear the sight of me."

"I'm sure she could," Jenkins said promptly. "Tracy's been plumb upset about that Webb Bascom business. She wanted me to try and make it clear that the Terrapin had no hand in that. I'll be glad to ride back with you when you start."

"Give Tracy my best," Rick put in. "I'd ride with you, except I've got something here in town to see to——"

"The Bon-Ton wasn't open when I passed," Jenkins grinned.

"It is now, though," Rick laughed. "I noticed on the way in, Camilla had her window shades up."

Ten minutes later, Quist, on the black gelding, and Jenkins were loping along the trail that led to the Terrapin Ranch. Morning sun was bright on the mesquite, cactus and other brush at either side of the hoof-pounded trail. A fresh breeze blew down from the Gunsight Mountains, now etched sharply against the vivid cerulean sky. After a few miles had been passed, the men pulled their horses to a slower gait, while they rolled and lighted brown paper cigarettes.

Jenkins said, "During my talk with Bard Nixon this morning I sort of got the idea he's not so hostile to you as he was two nights ago. He actually acted like you were a friend."

Quist smiled. "Yes, the sheriff and I had a little talk and we got our differences straightened out. I still don't think he likes the idea of me being here, but he's showed me some co-operation, anyway. And he still insists that whoever killed Canfield did a good job."

"Can you blame him? After that mining stock deal?"

Quist pricked up his ears. "I reckon not," he replied, and made a wild guess: "That was pretty raw on Canfield's part."

"Raw was no word for it. Taking Bard's life's savings and——" Jenkins broke off. "Sa-ay, just what did Nixon tell you about that deal? Come to think of it, Bard never liked to talk about the matter."

"And he didn't," Quist said frankly. "This is the first intimation I've had that Nixon held a personal grudge against Canfield."

"Some day, mebbe, I'll learn to keep my big mouth shut," Jenkins said testily. "Oh, hell, I might as well give you all the story. . . . It happened about three years back. Do you remember when folks were all excited about the Red Gila gold strike?"

Quist nodded. "The papers were full of it. It looked like the strike of the century—until it was learned that a group of crooked eastern promoters had staged a fake strike to sell stock to suckers."

"That's it. Through his eastern connections, Canfield learned that the stock was worthless, before that news reached out here. As a favor to the sheriff—he said—Canfield unloaded a lot of the stock to Nixon, for something between four and five thousand dollars. You can guess how the sheriff felt when he finally discovered the stock wasn't worth the paper it was printed on. But there was nothing he could do; the transaction had been legal, and the law doesn't seem to cover a man's ignorance. So Nixon took his loss and shut up, but it's always been a right tender subject with him."

"Damn it," Quist growled. "Nobody ever tells me anything about themselves. I always have to learn from others. There's more suspects in this deal than a man can shake a stick at."

Jenkins said, "Good Lord! You don't think Bard Nixon killed Canfield to square that account?"

"Why don't I?" Quist demanded savagely. "Most any man will kill, if he gets mad enough at the proper time. I've uncovered a few things, since I've been here. Maybe Pritchett killed

Canfield because of a crooked dice game. Maybe Camilla
Peters got jealous enough to do the job."

"Hell! Not Camilla——"

"Canfield rooked Thatcher on some property and took his
girl away. There's a motive. Rick is in love with Camilla Peters
and he wanted to protect his sister. There's another motive.
Maybe Tracy Hamilton just got sick of living with a dirty so-
and——"

"Don't say anything against Tracy, Quist——" Jenkins
commenced sharply.

"God damn it!" Quist cut in. "Don't you try to get tough
with me, Tom. I''ve made no positive accusations. I'm only
pointing out motives. Maybe Chris Hamilton was responsible——"

"You forget old Chris is paralyzed."

Quist said furiously, "I knew you'd say that. I've forgotten
nothing of the sort. But Chris might have hired the job done.
If two of his men will try to get rough with me—me that never
harmed the Hamiltons—do you think it would be difficult for
Chris to find some Circle-H hand willing to do the job? For
that matter, the whole Terrapin crew, including you, look
ready to protect Tracy Canfield at any cost. You think, maybe
she did kill her husband, and you're afraid I'll discover that
fact." He brushed aside Jenkins' protests, and went on, "Apparently murderers can be hired right cheap in the Gunsight
country. Bascom was to get a hundred dollars—remember?
And with the hate there was for Canfield—hell! There's motive enough for fifty murders if there'd been fifty Canfields—"

"Thank God there weren't," Jenkins said fervently. He was
silent for a time, then, "Do you actually think that Nixon killed
Canfield?"

"Not positively," Quist replied irritably, "any more than I'm
positive you did it." Jenkins started to speak, but Quist cut
him short. "It's this damnable stupid way that everybody acts
that riles me. Everybody's so scared of falling under suspicion,
if they've ever had a run-in with Canfield, that they start concealing something the minute they see me coming. I don't
wonder folks hated the man. Is there anybody, hereabouts,
he didn't cheat, one way or another?"

"There might be," Jenkins said dubiously. "So far as concerns telling you things, you can't claim I've ever held out
on you——"

"The hell I can't!" Quist snapped. "You never did tell me
you used to pal around with Canfield and get drunk with him
and paint the town. I'd like to know what broke up that
friendship. Nor did you tell me that at one time you were

practically engaged to Tracy Hamilton, before Cody Thatcher got the inside track."

Jenkins' eyes widened. "Who told you that?"

"One of my secret spies," Quist said mockingly. "It's true, isn't it?" Jenkins replied in a muffled voice it was more or less true. Quist persisted, "What broke up the friendship?"

"I can't say it was exactly broken up," Jenkins said. "Canfield offered me the job of rodding the Terrapin, and I took it. It was more of a joke than anything at first. But once on the job, I decided it was my chance to straighten up and—and—well, look out for Tracy's interests."

"How damned unselfish," Quist said sarcastically. "And of course as Tracy had once been fond of you, there was a chance if Canfield should die suddenly——"

"Damn you, Quist!" Jenkins' eyes were blazing as he whipped out his six-shooter and leveled it at his companion. "You take that back *pronto,* or by God! I'll drill you——"

"Go ahead and drill," Quist glanced contemptuously at the gun. "I don't seem to be getting any place on this job. Killing me might save me from failure. Of course, Tom, you want to remember it is known that I left town with you. Another murder hereabouts would be hard to cover up."

Slowly the furious fires died from Jenkins' dark eyes. He slipped the gun back in his holster. "Jeez!" he muttered, shaking his head. "You can be a nasty bustard at times."

"You're right," Quist nodded. "In my work you have to get nasty at times—but often if I get a man mad enough he'll spill something he hadn't intended to say."

Jenkins gazed warily at Quist. "What did I spill?"

"The fact that you're still in love with Tracy Canfield," Quist said softly. "I could tell from your manner. But that was all, Tom, if it's any satisfaction to you. It's true, isn't it?"

"Come on. We'd better push these broncs a little," Jenkins replied roughly, and forged his mount ahead on the trail. Quist gazed after him a moment, then kicked his spurred boots against the black gelding's sides.

Chapter XV : TRACY'S STORY

Tracy Canfield was seated on the gallery of the Terrapin ranch house when Quist and Jenkins loped in about ten o'clock that morning. An opened book lay face down on the gallery floor at the side of her chair. Surrounding oak trees cast a pleasant shade about the building. The girl was in a costume very similar to that in which Quist had last seen her. She looked up as the men drew to a halt, and the smile she cast in Quist's direction was cordial if not exactly welcoming. The two men dismounted and came up on the gallery. Tracy mentioned Webb Bascom. Quist assured her he had never for a moment suspected the Terrapin of having a hand in the shooting. Jenkins explained that Bascom had died, and told of Pritchett's part in the affair.

The girl frowned. "I can't see why Homer Pritchett would want you killed, Mr. Quist." That led to the fight Quist had had with Pritchett and the two Circle-H hands the previous day, Jenkins telling most of the story. Tracy's frown deepened. "You've certainly been busy since you first met Rick, haven't you, Mr. Quist? . . . I'll bet Dad was furious when he learned that Currie and Fox had played a part in those doings."

"I understand from Rick that he was, Mrs. Canfield," Quist said. "He asked that I come out and see him. I was wondering if you'd care to make the ride with me. It's a nice day and——"

"And it would give you an opportunity to ask me some questions," the girl said with a cold smile.

Quist laughed. "I had that in mind too," he said frankly. "It has to be done sometime."

"I'm not so sure of that," Tracy said in a tight voice. "You already understand you're not welcome here, Mr. Quist. I wish the circumstances were different——"

"Maybe they'll be changed before too long," Quist pointed out. "At least, on Rick's account, I think I deserve a mite of co-operation."

The girl considered a moment. "All right, I'll go with you, just as soon as I can change my clothes. Tom,"—to Jenkins —"will you saddle up the chestnut for me? And have Trunk-foot Wagner make up some sandwiches in a package. If we don't wait for dinner, we can get started sooner. . . . I'll be back in a jiffy, Mr. Quist." She turned and headed within the house, while Jenkins, leading his pony, started toward the corral.

Twenty minutes later, Quist and Tracy were riding in a southwesterly direction across rolling grass lands, spotted here and there with a mesquite or pecan tree. Now and then, huge clumps of opuntia raised their spiney pads. Already Tracy semed a different girl than the one he'd seen on the gallery, Quist decided. She seemed at home in the saddle of her chestnut pony and more alive. Nothing fussy about her riding togs, either. A battered flat-brimmed black sombrero, scuffed ridingboots, a mannish flannel shirt and neckerchief, and well-worn deerskin riding skirt made up her costume.

When Quist didn't at once commence questioning her regarding Canfield's death, the girl lost some of her wariness and unbent a trifle. Instead, Quist avoided the subject for the time being, complimented her on her riding, spoke of the conditions in the Gunsight country so far as he knew them, mentioned his liking for Rick; he told her of various cases on which he'd worked, pointing out certain humorous aspects of the jobs, where they had occurred. Before long the girl's laughter was coming easily and naturally, and Quist could see she had commenced to enjoy the ride.

It was shortly past noon when they arrived at the banks of the Gunsight River, flowing wide and shallow at this point. Cypress trees grew along the near bank and there was some scattered growth of post oak. Quist and the girl drew the ponies to a halt. Tracy said, "Let's open that package and see what Trunkfoot's done for us. He's always telling me I should fatten up, so those sandwiches will probably be six inches thick." They got down from saddles. Tracy pointed some distance down stream. "See those cottonwoods beyond that rise—you can just spot the tops. That's where I was knocked off my horse that day—the day that——" She paused.

Quist said, "Remember, it's you who brought up the subject. I didn't, Mrs. Canfield. So I can't be accused of asking questions."

The girl didn't reply but busied herself with the package of food. Quist took the horses down to the stream bank and watered them. When he returned, Tracy had the sandwiches spread on a clean blue bandanna on the ground. The two sat cross-legged, opposite each other, and ate in silence. The trees threw cool shadows. Below the banks, the Gunsight River made a kind of murmuring music.

They sat quietly for a time while the nearby horses cropped sun-cured grass. Finally, Tracy said, "All right, Mr. Quist, I've enjoyed the ride. You haven't tried to corkscrew information out of me. All in all, I've had a good time so far. My defenses are down. When does the questioning start?"

Quist shrugged careless shoulders. "I doubt there's much you can tell me. I've talked to so many people. Rick has explained things pretty thoroughly. I know how you met your husband and the kind of man he was. Before you met him you were engaged to both Tom Jenkins and Cody Thatcher——"

"That was during my kid days," the girl cut in swiftly. "Does a girl of seventeen or eighteen know her own mind? After all, I'd known both Tom and Cody since we were quite small. It was a natural thing to have fun with them. Then Nash Canfield came along. He was from the East and had money . . ."

"Glamour, they call it," Quist said dryly. "No, I don't think you're to be blamed any for what happened those days. Let's say you just made a mistake. But that's no sign you should go on forever paying for that mistake. Rick tells me you've grown hard and cold and have lost interest in life. To tell the truth, I don't think you're nearly so hard as you'd like people to believe. You've just erected some sort of barrier so you won't be hurt——"

"And can you blame me?" the girl flashed, and her tone was bitter. "Half the folks in the Gunsight country believe I killed my husband. I can hear people whispering behind my back when I go to town——"

"But you didn't kill him, did you?"

The girl didn't answer for a moment. Finally she said in a low voice, "I don't know, Mr. Quist. I don't think I did, but I'm not *certain* that I didn't shoot him when I was only half-conscious of my actions." She smiled ruefully. "That sounds crazy, doesn't it?"

"Perhaps," Quist said carelessly. "This world's full of crazy things and crazy people. Often I think everyone is a little crazy at times."

"That," Tracy said soberly, "is exactly what I'm afraid of."

"You've got to learn to drop that fear," Quist said. "If you actually did kill Canfield, wouldn't it be better to learn the truth, than live in uncertainty? You're not the sort that fears the punishment that might follow, were you guilty. But you are afraid of learning the truth. That, in itself, proves that the thought of murder is abhorrent to you. You're wasting your life away in worry, and you're too pretty a young woman to do that. Why not just forget things? You had good times once with Cody Thatcher and Tom Jenkins. Maybe you can again. And there are other men, if you'll only realize——"

"I doubt Tom has ever forgiven me for passing him up in favor of Cody. He's a different man from the one I used to know. He manages the Terrapin very efficiently, but ranch business is the sole contact we have nowadays." Quist asked a question. The girl smiled. "Oh yes, Cody forgave me long ago for choosing Nash. He calls at the ranch quite frequently. He's asked me, more than once, to marry him."

"Maybe that's a solution to certain problems."

Tracy shook her head. "I couldn't while this business is hanging over my head. There's something else too; I don't know as I could ever trust Cody again. You see, by the time I'd realized my marriage was a failure, I'd learned how Nash cheated Cody on the Terrapin land deal. I swore I'd make that up to Cody someday. The first few foremen we had were useless. Nash paid no attention to ranch operation, so I had to look after things myself. I did a great deal of riding about our holdings, checking on stock, where cows were grazing, and so on. Eventually, I discovered that Cody was 'sleepering' Terrapin stock. In earmarking, the Terrapin underslopes the animals' ears, right and left. Cody would drive off a bunch of our calves before they'd been branded and cut our correct earmarkings, but not brand our iron. Later, when our punchers saw these earmarked calves in a herd, they'd take it for granted the animal had also been branded, and would pass them up. Still later, Cody and his men would pick up those same calves, burn them with the Wagon-Wheel design and change the earmarkings to that of the Wagon-Wheel—a right underslope and a gotch on the left." Tracy broke off. "But you understand 'sleepering' procedure. I merely explained the brands and carmarkings, so you'd understand how Cody worked his thieving."

Quist frowned. "You saw much of that sort of thing?"

"A very great deal. I've spied on the Wagon-Wheel men with field glasses. Then, later, I'd check on what they'd been doing."

"Does the Terrapin use stamp irons for branding?"

"During regular roundup. Otherwise, when our hands pick up any stock for branding a running iron is generally used."

Quist looked thoughtful. "There's a certain similarity in the two brands. I shouldn't be surprised if some of your running-iron-branded cows had been burned over and made into Wagon-Wheels. It would require some smart drawing, but it could be done."

"I suppose it's possible," the girl nodded carelessly.

"If Cody is stealing your stock, he's likely stealing from other outfits as well. Maybe that's it." The girl asked a question. Quist explained, "I've had a hunch that Thatcher was covering up something. It could be he's afraid that in my snooping around, I may uncover evidence of his thieving." Tracy said that, too, was possible. Quist asked. "Why haven't you told Thatcher you knew what he was doing, and warn him to stop?"

Tracy shrugged her slim shoulders. "The Terrapin can

afford the loss. And I keep thinking how Nash cheated Cody on that land deal. Maybe Cody Thatcher has a right to square accounts."

Abruptly, Quist changed his tactics. "Mrs. Canfield, did you ever, while he was alive, consider killing your husband?" He made the words sound as brutal as possible.

Tracy just stared at him a moment, shocked, jaw slack, eyes wide. All the color had left her face. "Why—why, no— certainly not," she stammered. "I—I—you have no right to ask such a question!" She looked quickly away and back. "You are insulting!" She had commenced to shake and Quist could see she was on the verge of tears.

"No weeping now," he said harshly. "I'll just laugh if you start fumbling for a handkerchief. Women look silly as hell when they cry, and you'll be no exception for all your good looks. And don't stall! Your good looks don't impress me either. I want an answer!"

Tracy's lips came tightly together. Her eyes blazed. Spots of angry color appeared in her cheeks. She started to rise from the earth where she'd been sitting cross-legged. Quist reached across and jerked her roughly back to the ground. "I'm still waiting for an honest answer," he snapped, tightening his grip on her arm.

Tracy's chin came up. Her voice when she spoke was filled with a kind of pent-up fury. "All right, if you have to know, that thought did enter my mind, more than once! Now, make what you will of that. You can't scare me, Mr. Quist, not for a minute. You won't understand, and I probably can't make you understand, just how unbearable Nash Canfield made life for me. I was ill most of our married life. Not a physical illness. Doctor Sturven said I was on the edge of a nervous breakdown. He wanted me to leave Nash. I'd wake up in the middle of the night, certain that I had already shot my husband, and then I'd realize it was only a dream. There were many, many nights like that. Under those conditions, how could I avoid thinking such things? Now you can take——"

"Exactly," Quist said quietly, "under those conditions, how could you avoid thinking such things? And they've been piling up inside you for years." His voice was suddenly humble. "I'm truly sorry I had to act like this, Mrs. Canfield, but it had to be done——"

"Act? What do you mean?" Tracy Canfield demanded.

"That's all it was—an act," Quist confessed. He'd still been gripping her arm, now he released it, and sat back. "My apologies to you, but—but you see I had to make you mad, somehow, so you'd blow off steam, get a few things out of your system. You've never before told anyone this, have you?" The girl, wide-eyed, shook her head. Quist went on, "You were sick before Canfield was killed and after. Rick tells me you were only half-conscious that night he found you at the house, with a gun in your hand. Considering those dreams you had, and your condition, it's no wonder you're only half certain you're innocent of Canfield's death——"

"Mr. Quist——!"

Quist looked quickly at the girl. "Remember what I said about weeping women——" he commenced warningly, then, "Oh, damn!" And rising, he walked quickly over to the black gelding and started making useless movements with its bridle bit. After a time he returned. The girl was still seated on the earth, but now she smiled up at him. Quist's lips curved and there was a warm light in his topaz eyes. "I take it all back, Mrs. Canfield. A shower sometimes improves a garden immensely."

"It was—it was darn near a torrent," the girl said.

"And probably good for you, Mrs. Canfield."

"I wish you'd call me Tracy—all my friends do. That—the Canfield name . . ."

Quist nodded. "We seem to be making progress. Mostly, I'm called Greg. Oh, I've been called a lot of other names, too —but not by friends. Y'understand?"

The girl was laughing now. After a time she sobered. "Then you don't think I killed Nash?"

"I don't *think* so—*right now,*" Quist responded warily. "I've a hunch if you'd been going to put those dreams of yours into action, you'd probably not have waited until a year ago to act. You're the direct type; you'd want to get a thing like that settled right off—the instant you'd found you were— well, disillusioned. If you didn't blow your top then, your type would be more likely to detach itself from the disagreeable things of life, so far as possible, and make an existence of its own, only contacting the disagreeable when it couldn't be avoided."

"That's comforting to hear, anyway."

"Mind you, that's not definite," Quist said, "but if I've eased your mind, that's something."

Tracy frowned. "The fact remains, I did have that gun in my hand when Rick arrived. I wish I could account for that."

"I can't explain it—yet. I'd have to know more of what happened. . . . Maybe you were framed."

"Who'd frame me—and why?"

"I can't tell you that, either. We know Cody Thatcher is

stealing your stock. From theft to murder isn't too big a step for some men. If you were accused and arrested, Thatcher could step forward in the role of staunch friend to the pretty widow, thus winning your gratitude. Later, when you were acquitted—juries rarely convict a pretty woman, you know—Thatcher could pay court, marry said widow, and gain ownership of the Terrapin."

"That sounds pretty cynical."

"I'm a cynical man, Tracy. Little that I've seen of life tends to make me otherwise. But what I said about Thatcher, remember, is only conjecture. It could have happened that way; I don't claim it did. I've got to learn more. Tell me what you can remember of that day. I know most of it, of course, from Rick, about you starting Canfield to town to get the payroll money, and then sending Tom Jenkins after him. But what about your part? What did you do after Jenkins' left?"

Tracy frowned. "Only the first part is clear. As soon as Tom left, I rode to the Circle-H. Dad had asked me the day before to take a message to Gabe Bedell———"

"He owns the Rocking-B, doesn't he, about fifteen miles southeast of Hyperion?" Tracy nodded and said Bedell was an old crony of her father's. Quist asked, "What was the message, did you know?"

"Not at the time. I found it months afterward in the pocket of the shirt I wore that day. It wasn't important. Dad merely wrote a short note to Gabe, saying he was lonesome and asking Gabe to ride over and see him sometime. Gabe was a pretty regular visitor at the Circle-H, anyway, so I imagine Dad, knowing how things were with me, was just giving me that errand to occupy my time."

"Probably," Quist agreed.

"I had started for the Rocking-B and had crossed the bridge over the Gunsight River, when something frightened the horse I was riding, and he suddenly bolted with me. He was a spooky sort of beast I'd been trying to gentle. When he ran he took me straight through that clump of cottonwoods. I remember a low branch suddenly looming up in front of me, while I was trying to manage the pony. From that point on I'm not sure what happened. Days later some of the boys went out and found my hat at that spot." Tracy screwed her forehead into a frown. "From the time I was knocked from my horse, I have only a spotty memory of what happened. I remember regaining consciousness under the cottonwoods, with a head aching as though it would burst. I realized I was afoot and I'd have to walk to the Terrapin. I started and sometime later fainted. There seem to have been periods when I was completely unconscious; others when things seemed fairly clear. I can remember stumbling and getting up again, though I've no recollection how long I stayed down. I remember once that my boots had started to pinch. I sat down and passed out again. The sun was lower when I resumed walking. Another time I awakened to find myself resting against a tree, and I was conscious of a terrific thirst along with my dizziness. I had hallucinations. I commenced to see lakes and streams. I can't believe they were the result of a mirage."

"Delirium," Quist suggested quietly.

Tracy laughed shortly. "Delirium is the word for it. I'd pass out and have dreams of Rick or Cody or Tom coming on a horse to find me. Once I regained consciousness, or thought I did, and found myself sprawling in long grass, and I thought I heard hoof-beats and I looked up and saw Dad riding past. It was so real that I called out to him, before I realized I'd been out of my head. It was nearly dark then, but I could still imagine I heard those pounding hoofbeats. I rose and kept going. I don't know how long. I don't even remember reaching the Terrapin. All at once I was suddenly on the gallery. And next I was inside the house."

"You certainly had a hazy time of it."

"A few incidents stand out fairly well." Tracy frowned. "I have a memory of a big blaze in the fireplace, and there was Nash thrashing around on the floor, and I knew he was having another of his attacks." The girl shuddered, her face white and drawn at the thought of that night. "Greg, it was— was horrible, the way he was throwing his body about. You couldn't believe the human form could contort itself in such grotesque positions. Once—once,"—the girl's voice faltered and a quiver rippled through her slim form—"his body jerked suddenly into a sort of bow-form, his head twisted back, resting on the floor, and his feet also touching the floor, but with nothing under to support the weight. His eyes bulged from his head, his face was almost purple and his arms were flinging about . . ."

The girl's voice was rising and she was breathing fast, when Quist spoke sharply, "Tracy! Take it easy." She stopped talking and some of the horror died from her face. Quist continued, low-voiced, quiet, "You don't have to re-live all that again, Tracy. Steady, now."

Tracy swallowed hard. "I'm all right, Greg. It was just pretty awful, that's all. . . . And then I heard a shot——"

"From what direction did it come?"

"I don't know. The next thing that comes to mind was that Nash's actions weren't quite so violent and there was blood on him. And then—then I remember looking down and seeing the gun in my hand."

"You're certain it wasn't your own gun?"

"I wasn't wearing a gun that day. I rarely carry one."

"Try to remember, Tracy. Where did you get that gun?"

The girl pondered, shook her head. "I can't remember, Greg. I can't, I can't, I tell you. I've tried so often." Her voice sounded a tone of desperation.

"You've got to remember," Quist persisted. "Did someone enter behind you and put the gun in your hand? Think! Did you cross the room and get it off the mantel or a table? Could you have gone to that back hall and got it from the hook where it always hung? Think, Tracy, think!"

Tracy shook her head. "No—n-no—I—Greg, wait, there is something. I remember now that I reached down to put my hand on it to stop the spinning——"

"Spinning?"

Tracy nodded, still looking half-questioningly at Quist as though he held the answer. "Yes, it was spinning 'round and 'round with the light from the fireplace glittering on it, and it made me dizzy to watch——" The girl broke off, her eyes wide. "Greg! I never remembered that before. That gun was spinning as though someone had thrown it at my feet." Her forehead was creased in thought and she continued slowly, "I seem to have a vague memory of picking it up. Did I? Greg! What does it mean?" Her face was frightened, drawn.

"It means we've talked enough about it," Quist said calmly. "If you picked it up, you did only what most people would do."

"I can't remember anything more. Rick said I fainted just as he came in. I was ill a long time. Doctor Sturven said I had suffered a slight concussion when I was knocked from my pony. By the time I was able to be up, the trial was over——"

Quist broke in, "If we're going to visit your dad today, we'd best get started." He retrieved the bandanna from the ground, rose and, taking her hand, pulled her to her feet. We'll forget the business for the present, Tracy. A while back I saw you smile. It didn't hurt your appearance any. Let's see you do it again. Don't let this trouble get you down—ever. We'll lick it yet!"

Tracy forced a rather wan smile. They went to the horses and tightened cinches, climbed into saddles. The ponies

splashed across the shallow stream and climbed the opposite
bank. A touch of spurs sent them into a swift lope. After a
time, the color returned to Tracy's face.

Chapter XVI : THE OLD WOLFER

Quist and the girl pushed the ponies steadily and talked very
little. The ride to the Circle-H was made in about an hour
and a half. When they arrived, Chris Hamilton and Brasadero
Banning were seated on the gallery. Hamilton, as usual, had
his lower body swathed in blankets. Rick came around the
corner of the house just as Quist and Tracy were stepping
down from saddles. Tracy kissed her dad, spoke to Rick and
Banning. Banning said he'd take the horses and water them.
Something was said about staying to supper, but Tracy said
she wanted to get back to the Terrapin before too long. Chris
eyed his daughter and Quist with some curiosity. "Thought
you two'd be at each other's throats by this time," he growled.
" 'Stead, it appears you must be getting friendly. Something's
come over you, Tracy. I don't know when I've seen so much
sparkle in your eyes."

Tracy colored. "It's the ride does that. How you feeling,
Dad?"

"Good as a half-dead man ever feels," he grunted. Tracy
started a protest, but old Chris cut her off and turned to Quist.
"When I heard what them damn' fools, Fox and Currie, done,
I calculated you'd be coming here to get at *my* throat."

Quist laughed. "I knew you had nothing to do with that,
Mr. Hamilton."

"Maybe you have good sense, after all," Chris chuckled
through his beard. "Under some circumstances, I'm bettin'
you and me could be friends."

"I'm willing if you are," Quist said.

Hamilton scowled. "You go on back to El Paso, and I'll
give it a mite of thought. 'Course, you won't do that, but
maybe you'll accept the Circle-H's apologies." Quist said
apologies weren't necessary. Hamilton went on, "They brought
Brose Fox back to the ranch a spell ago. He's down in his
bunk now, cussin' his busted shoulder. There wasn't much I
could say to Brose and Jake Currie. They tried to do their
bests for my interests as they saw it. The other boys have
been hoorawin' 'em plenty, though, for the mess they made
of things. . . . You know, I can't understand where Homer

Pritchett got the idea of stopping you. Why should he care
if you're here?"

Quist shrugged. "You tell me and I'll tell you."

Rick cut in with, "Greg, you mentioned in town something about a gun contraption with a string tied from the
trigger to an object that, when moved, would set off the gun."
Quist nodded. Rick asked, "Did Cody Thatcher put that into
your head?" Quist nodded again. "I thought so," Rick
laughed. "I'd clean forgotten at the time you spoke of it, but
one time I was fixing up a contraption like that in the hope of
shooting a lobo wolf that had been pestering our stock. We'd
located the lobo's den, but he avoided all our traps——"

"Did your six-shooter contraption get him?" Quist asked.

"Naw," Rick said disgustedly, "I should have known better
than to have tried. I had a nice thick steak tied around a bottle
of water to give it weight, standing right on the edge of
a ledge. All it needed was a slight touch to knock it over and
explode the gun, but that lobo was too wily. He wouldn't go
near the bait. Old Morg Jenkins trapped the wolf eventually,
though, and we paid the usual bounty. You ought to meet
Tom's father sometime. He's an interesting old codger."

Tracy said, "I thought we might drop in on Morg on our
way back. Tom's always glad to hear how his father is getting
along, when he doesn't get a chance to visit regularly."

The three men and the girl talked on the gallery for a time,
then Rick and Quist went down to the bunkhouse, meeting, on
their way, Brasadero Banning who was just returning with
Quist's and Tracy's ponies. Quist dropped into the bunkhouse
where he found Currie and Fox, the latter stretched out in a
bunk, nursing his wounded shoulder. Both men looked a trifle
shamefaced at seeing Quist, but he quickly put them at their
ease, showing he harbored no resentment. Fox hoped he was
going to stay to supper. Quist said he'd stay some other time.

"Maybe it's just as well," Currie said. "The other boys will
be in then, and with you here, they really would lay into
Brose and me. The joshin' I had to take was something terrific,
and they haven't had a chance at Brose yet. Old Chris, he laid
me out too. Made me quit ridin' for a spell, and Banning's
thinking up all the disagreeable jobs he can find for me."

Quist laughed, said he'd see them again soon, he hoped,
and he and Rick left the bunkhouse. Soggy Hannan stuck his
long-nosed, bald head out of the cookhouse when they passed
and hailed Quist in a loud voice that was lacking in its former
hostility. Quist guessed that while he still wasn't too welcome
in the Gunsight country, he had, at least, gained a certain
respect in Circle-H quarters. Rick stopped at the corral to

saddle his pony, with the remark that so long as Quist and Tracy weren't staying for supper, he reckoned he'd lope into town for a spell. Quist dropped a comment regarding the Bon-Ton Shop and Rick's face got red, when he admitted that was where he was heading. "Give Miss Peters my regards," Quist chuckled, "and tell her I'm aiming to drop in and visit her someday, if I can ever find her without company."

Twenty minutes later Quist and Tracy were again mounted and taking a slightly northwesterly course in the direction of Morg Jenkins' place, which was located in the foothills of the Gunsight Mountains. The grazing lands thinned out as the horses climbed mounting ground or circled low hills. Outcroppings of limestone appeared. The mesquite grew more numerous, though not so high as on the lower slopes. There were considerable live oak and blackjack trees to be seen through the hills. Before long, Quist spotted Jenkins' cabin which Tracy pointed out to him, nestling between two low hills with live oaks on either side making shade. The cabin appeared to be a combination of limestone slabs, 'dobe brick and cedar logs. A sagging porch fronted the building, and there'd been some clearing done in front, though here and there the ever-present clumps of prickly pear raised spiny heads. At the rear of the cabin, Quist could see a corral with a pair of horses standing head to tail, busily engaged in switching at flies. As Quist and the girl neared the house a dog of mixed breeds—mostly hound—ran barking to meet them. Tracy spoke to the dog which immediately commenced wagging its tail and hurried on to the house, ahead of the horses, with its canine announcement of visitors.

The door of the house opened, before Tracy and Quist arrived, and a tall, spare old man, with a back of proverbial ramrod straightness, stepped out. His hair and beard were thick and white; his features were hawk-like in their sharpness, a quality that was immediately softened by the kindly dark brown eyes. He was dressed in flat-heeled boots, denim shirt and faded, patched overalls. Morg Jenkins turned to speak to the dog, "Quit yer yappin', King!" then raised his voice, "Tracy, m'girl, yo're a sight for old eyes. How ye been?"

Tracy and Quist stepped down from the horses' backs, dropping reins over the animals' heads. Quist paused to loosen saddle girths, then followed Tracy up on the porch, where at Tracy's introduction, he grasped Morg Jenkins' gnarled hand. The dog was leaping about, tail switching right and left. Jenkins again spoke to it, then to Quist, "Time was when I owned a hull pack like King when I used to kill cougars, but them big cats has mostly left these parts, so I got rid of m'dawgs. Sorter kept King on fer company. Ain't so many loafer wolves 'round like there used t'be, nuther. Kentry's gittin' too plumb settled, I reckon. . . . Tracy, how's Tom?" Tracy said Tom was all right; that he'd been busy following a trip into Sanchez County. Jenkins nodded. "Ain't seen him for nigh onto ten days, now."

"Morg," Tracy said, "both Tom and I have told you numerous times you should come and make your home at the Terrapin. You'd be welcome."

"Ain't a doubt in m'mind on thet score, Tracy," the old man responded, "but I been here too long to move, I reckon. Tom was borned in this cabin. His mother's headstone is up on that shady slope yonderly. Nope; I'll stay on here, thankee. This is my home—but come on in and rest yoreselves." He held the cabin door for them to pass. The dog was again reprimanded as he tried to dart in with the others, but was finally excluded.

The cabin had but a single, neatly-swept room, with a floor of scrubbed planks. There were a round oaken table covered with oilcloth and a kitchen range with stovepipe running through the slanting roof. Two neatly-made bunks stood against one wall and nearby hung a calendar with a gun company's advertisement. On the wall back of the stove were three shelves holding a slab of bacon, flour and a variety of canned goods. Next to a sack of beans stood a large square container bearing a label which displayed, in red, a skull and crossbones and the word *Poison*. Quist realized at once the poison was intended for use in preparing baits for coyotes and wolves, but the thought of keeping it on the shelf with foodstuffs seemed incongruous. There were further evidences of the professional wolfer's craft in the cabin: sharp-toothed steel traps of various size and design hung on the walls; many had heavy chains with drive pins attached. More chains and coiled ropes hung from pegs. A Winchester rifle and heavy-gauge shotgun were bracketed on one wall, and there was a cartridge belt and holstered six-shooter hung on the back of one of two straight-backed chairs. A rocking chair stood near a partly opened window. There were two more windows, a closed door at the rear wall of the cabin led outside.

Jenkins offered to make coffee, but Quist and the girl refused. Tracy gave the old wolfer such news as she had. After the conversation commenced to lag, Tracy said she guessed she'd take a walk with the dog. Jenkins laughed when she had departed. "I know where she's headed. There's a big live oak, five or six rods back of this cabin. Time was, when she was little, I hung a swing fer her there. Nowadays, when the weather's purty, she gene'ally hies herself out there and catches a nap."

They could hear the hound's gradually diminishing yelps as it accompanied the girl from the cabin. Jenkins stuffed a smelly brier full of shag-cut; Quist rolled a cigarette, and asked politely regarding the wolfing business. The old man replied, "Like I said, there ain't so many loafer wolves no more. Coyotes is as thick as ever. Them yappin' little varmints seem to breed like flies. If they ain't kept down, they can ruin a man's herds. I'm 'bout due to pick up m'traps, fix some pizen baits an' git busy agin." He changed the subject abruptly, "Made any progress in yore detectin' yit?"

"Not much," Quist evaded. "Where'd you hear about that?"

"Passin' riders brings news. A Circle-H puncher passed through here this mornin', and he sorter brung me up to date. Ye shore played hell with Pritchett and them two Circle-H hands, didn't ye? Not to mention Webb Bascom. Y'know, I don't figger ye'll git no place huntin' fer Canfield's killer. Folks is glad he's gone, and they won't help ye none. Canfield was no good, anyway ye jedge him. I got more respect for a measly, sneakin' coyote, than I had for thet Canfield."

"What did he ever do to you?" Quist asked.

"Me? Haw!" Morg Jenkins short laugh held no humor. "Never done nuthin' ter me, 'cause I never give him no chance ter. I didn't trust that bustard from the first. I was right 'bout him. He nigh ruint Tracy's life." The old man sighed. "Time was when I figgered she'd marry my boy Tom, but it didn't pan out thet way. I still think he'd make her a good husband, but I reckon them two don't think the same way."

"Maybe not," Quist said. "You don't know anything that happened the day Canfield was killed, I suppose."

"Nothin' thet'd help ye. I saw Canfield thet day in Hyperion; I happened to be in town fer supplies. Gawd! he was drunk." Jenkins shook his head in disgust. "Jest a mess! All sprawled out on the bank steps, with flies chasin' the snores in and outer his mouth. They was a crowd standin' around, laughin' fit to kill. Folks hated thet dirty son so much they enjoyed seein' him disgrace hisself. Then Cody Thatcher sort of cradles a bottle of Old Crow bourbon in his arms and announces thet Canfield is posin' fer a pitcher of father and child, but thet th' child has sorter got outten control. With thet, the crowd whoops and laughs some more, and a couple fellers lopes off to git the feller from the photygraph parlor to come take a pitcher. But before the feller could get there with his camery, my boy Tom got Canfield headed for the Terrapin. Then I started for my cabin. Next I hears, Canfield has been

rubbed out with a slug of lead, and good riddance to bad rubbish, I thinks. So ye see, I can't help ye none."

"Thatcher has a sort of cruel sense of humor."

Morg Jenkins nodded. "Yep, but Cody's got his good
p'ints too. Somethin' over a year ago, I got took bad with my
rheumatics, and could scarce make to git around. Cody happened to come ridin' this way, lookin' fer strays, and he found
me in muh bunk. Well, he give me a good rub with pepper-
mint ile and he come back three times thet same week and
sorter nursed me. He even cleaned up some of my traps thet
needed preparin' and set out some baits too. I allus felt sorter
obligated to Cody fer thet. I wanted he should send for Tom,
but him and Tom wa'n't too friendly――――" Jenkins paused.
"I suppose ye know Cody wanted to marry Tracy too, one
time." Quist nodded. Jenkins continued, "I reckon they was a
sort of jealous feelin' between Cody and Tom. Anyway, Cody
allowed he could take care of me. I allus felt grateful fer thet,
particular as Cody's paw and me had been good friends afore
he died. It's too dang bad one of them two boys couldn't
have hitched up with Tracy, 'stead of th' louse she caught."

"I guess it is," Quist said. "She sure had a tough time of it,
with Canfield. I got to talking to her today about him, and I
guess she went through a pretty bad business just before he
was shot. He was having one of his wild spells――――"

"I never seed one of them, but I understand the doc warned
him to quit drinkin'. Jest like a wild man, Canfield would git,
and throw hisself around like he'd been bit by a hydrophoby
skunk."

"I guess it was all of that. Tracy said when she went in he
was thrashing about on the floor――――"

"I didn't know he was still alive when she got there. She
was too sick to testify at th' trial, but I understood he was already dead when she come in――――"

"Tracy got to remembering a few things today. The shot
came shortly after she entered, but he was still alive and
throwing himself around when she first saw him. I guess Canfield got in some awful positions. Tracy said once he twisted
his body into a bow-like curve, with only his head and heels
supporting his weight. Did you ever hear anything to equal
it?"

Morg Jenkins frowned and made *Tch! Tch!* sounds with his
teeth. "It must have been a turrible sight for a young woman
to witness――――" He broke off, as though at a loss for words,
pondered a moment, then, "But she didn't have no idea where
the bullet come from?"

"Not a one." There were more *tch*-ing sounds. Quist went

on: "You mentioned a minute back that Cody Thatcher had his good points. Well, he's got some mighty bad ones, too, Mr. Jenkins. Tracy tells me Thatcher has been 'sleepering' her stock for some time now."

"T'hell ye say!" Jenkins exclaimed, an angry scowl furrowing his grizzled features. "I can't believe thet of Cody." Quist repeated the story Tracy had told, adding that Thatcher was probably stealing from other outfits as well. The old man wagged his head. "Now, I don't take kindly to thet idea, at all. And Cody's paw wouldn't like it, nuther, was he alive. If Tracy says so, it's so, and I reckon I'll jest have ter put a bug in thet young feller's ear, and warn him to halt his thievin'——"

"Look here, Mr. Jenkins," Quist protested, "Tracy especially doesn't want Thatcher to learn she knows about it. She feels that Thatcher was done out of a decent price for his land, and if he takes enough stock, it will go a long way toward squaring matters."

"Two wrongs don't make a right." Jenkins bristled. "Cody was brung up by decent people, and he should know better. Don't ye worry. I'll not mention Tracy's name, but I'll tell Cody I spied on him, my ownself, and seed what he was up ter. I could talk sense inter him when he was a younker, and I reckon I'm still man enough t'make thet young gaffer listen to reason. You leave it ter me. I'll tell him."

The setting sun was red on the window panes by now. Jenkins went on, "First chance I git ter talk to Cody, I'll tell him how his paw wouldn't a' stood for sech behaviour, and I don't intend to, nuther. He's jest got off'n th' wrong track fer a spell. I got to git him lined out level again."

The hound's paws pounded heavily on the porch beyond the door. Tracy came in, hands above her shoulders, doing things to her hair of pale gold. "I had the loveliest sleep," she said, showing her even white teeth in a half-concealed yawn. "Now tell me you've missed me."

Morg Jenkins chuckled. "I knowed where ye was, Tracy. I already told Mr. Quist I betten ye was snoozin' under thet oak tree."

"I've heard of beauty sleeps," Quist laughed. "I'm commencing to believe in them, now." He eyed the girl admiringly.

There was some further conversation, then Quist and the girl got into saddles and started for the Terrapin, Quist promising Morg Jenkins that he'd be out to visit again soon. Cody Thatcher's name hadn't been mentioned in the girl's presence.

It was almost dark by the time Quist and the girl splashed

their mounts across the Gunsight River, and once on the opposite bank they put spurs to the ponies and urged them on their way. Once, Tracy said, "You'd better plan to stay at the Terrapin tonight." Quist said he wasn't sure how the bunkhouse would welcome him. Tracy answered, "If you don't stay, Tom Jenkins will feel duty-bound to ride to town with you as a bodyguard. And I wouldn't worry about the other men. I think they feel a little differently about you than that first day you were here. For that matter——" She broke off and changed the subject: "You'll be safer at the Terrapin than any place else I can think of. I wouldn't relish hearing you'd been shot at again on your way to town."

Quist said, "I'd certainly hate to have Tom make that ride just on my account. Maybe I'll accept the Terrapin's hospitality for the night." Tracy nodded, and they rode in comparative silence the remainder of the distance to the ranch.

By the time they'd arrived, the moon was commencing to lift above the eastern horizon. Lights shone from the bunkhouse. Seeing a lamp in the window of the ranch house, Quist wondered if Tracy had guests waiting for her return. The girl shook her head. "If I'm away, Tom or Trunkfoot generally lights up for me." They pulled the horses to a halt before the long gallery. Quist dismounted and opened the door for the girl. She glanced within. "No, nobody there." Before entering, she half closed the door, detaining Quist. "Tell Tom we stopped at his father's cabin. He'll be glad to hear the old man is all right."

"I'll do that," Quist said. "I've enjoyed our ride. *Hasta mañana.*"

Tracy caught at his sleeve. "There's something else, Greg." He could see her eyes, a bit misty, shining in the light from the window. "Two days ago, Greg, I hated you. I thought you'd come here to stir up trouble. I didn't know you then. I feel now I've known you for years. What's happened today— the things you've said and made me say—has made a big difference. It's as though a great load had been lifted from my shoulders. There's a lot of thanks owing to you . . ."

She paused, breathless, and her face lifted to his. One arm stole softly about his neck, drawing him near. And then he was holding her close, feeling her heart beat against his, her lips warm beneath his own. His arms tightened. After a time they relaxed and he stepped back. Tracy caught her breath in a long, indrawn sigh, and found her voice, saying one word, "Understand?"

"I understand, Tracy," Quist replied gravely. As he stepped from the gallery, he heard the door close behind him. Picking up the horses' reins he started down toward the corral. As he rounded the corner of the house he saw a dark figure hurrying away through the gloom. After a moment he realized it was Tom Jenkins. He called to him and Jenkins turned, waiting for Quist to come up. Quist wondered if he had witnessed the scene at Tracy's doorway.

Quist came even with him, and Tom growled, "What you want?"

"Came up to get the horses, didn't you? Tracy has suggested that I stay at the Terrapin overnight."

"I heard you when you rode in. Sure, stay if you like. There're plenty bunks. It's nothing to me whether you go or stay."

Quist knew then that Jenkins had seen him and Tracy at the doorway. He said, "We saw your dad today, Tom. He's a great old fellow. I like him a lot."

Jenkins snapped, "Is that supposed to make me like you?"

"Not necessarily," Quist said quietly. He waited a moment while they walked toward the corral, the horses coming behind, then said, "Tom, don't get any wrong ideas."

Jenkins said sullenly, "I don't know what you're talking about."

"Yes, you do, Tom. You've got to distinguish between love and gratitude before you start making any sure-fire bets."

Jenkins didn't speak again until they'd started unsaddling at the corral. Suddenly he said, "I sure acted like a bustard, didn't I?"

"You sure did," Quist said cheerfully. "You needed time to mull things over. All right, now, is it?"

"I can't say that it is," Jenkins said frankly, "but if you're the man for her, that's all right with me too."

"A man with my life hasn't any business getting tangled with a woman, Tom."

"I'll believe that when I see it." In the light from the bunkhouse windows, Quist saw Jenkins' face darken suddenly. "Quist, if you hurt her in any way, I'll kill you."

Quist nodded. "When that happens I'll be waiting for you to try."

Jenkins fumbled with a cinch buckle on one of the saddles. He said, finally, "Hell! I'm flying off the handle again. Let's get these ponies shoved into the corral. There's hot coffee and some grub waiting for you."

"How are your men going to accept me?"

"Didn't I tell you fodder was waiting? They know who it's waiting for. It hasn't seemed to fret 'em any. Maybe we're all commencing to recognize a man when we see one."

Chapter XVII : CLUES?

Several days passed with nothing of great importance to Quist's endeavours occurring. The morning following his ride with Tracy, Quist had returned to Hyperion, accompanied by Tom Jenkins, both of whom were needed to appear at the inquests held over the bodies of Webb Bascom and Homer Pritchett, and both were exonerated of all guilt in the deaths. The two dead men were buried the same day, Pritchett's interment being attended by a number of his friends, among whom were Cody Thatcher and the Wagon-Wheel crew. After the funeral, when Quist passed Thatcher and his men on Huisache Street, Thatcher nodded coolly but had nothing to say. The Wagon-Wheel punchers directed various ominous glares in Quist's direction, but they, too, said nothing, this a direct contradiction of the threats they were rumored to have uttered previous to the funeral. Whether Thatcher had warned his men not to start trouble, or whether they were just "blowing off steam" and had no intention of avenging the death of their foreman, Quist had no way of knowing, nor did he greatly care, one way or the other. He did notice, however, that not a day passed, from then on, that didn't find Thatcher in Hyperion, rather than at his ranch where it would be expected he'd spend the greater part of his time. Quist wondered if the man were waiting in his vicinity with the intention of starting trouble, when the right time came, or if he were merely staying close as possible to Quist's movements in the hope of learning Quist's intentions.

Quist hadn't returned to the Terrapin with Jenkins, after the inquests and funerals, but had remained in town. For three days he was continually on the move, visiting saloons and other gathering places, where he might encounter people who had known Canfield and could give him any facts pertinent to the man's death. So far, the quest had produced but little beyond the facts Quist already possessed. By this time certain suspicions had jelled in his mind, but of proof he had none. "And suspicions alone are mighty bad for a man," Quist told himself. "They can lead him clear off the track and then drop him flat when he finds he has nothing to base them on."

One morning he rose from his bed at the Hyperion House and after having breakfast in the dining room, headed toward the sheriff's office. Nixon was standing at the edge of the sidewalk, leaning idly against one of the uprights that supported the wooden awning jutting from his building. The sun was bright along the street; the sky cloudless. Already a number of horse-drawn vehicles had arrived in town and were waiting at hitchracks before general stores ard other business places.

Nixon spat a thin stream of tobacco juice into the dusty road when he saw Quist coming up to him. Quist said good morning and the sheriff said, "Still bloodhoundin'?"

Quist nodded. "I'm not doing any barking yet, though." Nixon commented sourly that a barking dog never bites. Quist said, "Maybe that's one reason to watch out for me then, Bard."

"Me, personal?" Nixon asked cautiously.

"I didn't say that."

The sheriff looked somewhat relieved. "I note you been right busy sniffin' tracks through town. Last night when I stuck my head into the Elite Dance and Chance Hall, I spied you buzzin' one of them dancing girls. Learn anything?"

Quist shrugged noncommittally. "Most of the girls seem to have known Canfield pretty well."

Nixon snorted. "Hell's bells! Anybody in Hyperion could have told you that." Quist pointed out that nobody had. The sheriff grunted shortly. "You'll probably find all your trails lead up blind alleys. I'll bet, so far, you ain't yet found one solid clue to go on."

"Clues? Well, now," Quist stated with grave deliberation, "I wouldn't go so far as to say that. I understand there's some man in town who was once done out of a pile of money when Canfield unloaded a lot of worthless mining stock on him. Now, right there's a motive for murder. If I can find out who that man is——"

"Mining stock?" Nixon asked warily. "What kind of mining stock?"

"Red Gila Company. You've probably heard of that stock a gang of crooked promoters sold to the public."

Nixon's jaw sagged. He closed his mouth with an effort and swallowed hard. "Now—now look here, Greg Quist, you ain't sayin' that—why—why——" His long, sun-bleached mustaches drooped despairingly. "Look here, I bought some of that stock from Canfield one time, but that ain't no sign I killed him——"

"You were so busy telling me about everybody else's business that you forgot to tell me anything about yourself, weren't you?"

Nixon smiled sheepishly. "Yeah, Greg, I reckon I was. I didn't see no need for stickin' my head in a noose, when I knew it wa'n't me that killed Canfield. You see, you might have suspected me."

"Maybe I do, now."

"Aw, hell, Greg, you should know I wouldn't do anything like——"

"All right. Forget it. I'll admit I haven't any proof you killed Canfield."

"Who spilled the story about me getting stuck with that no-good stock of Canfield's?"

Quist smiled. "Ask me no questions and I'll tell you no lies. But you should know, by this time, it doesn't pay to keep information from me."

Nixon mopped perspiration from his head. "I sure as hell do," he confessed fervently. "I swear there ain't another solitary thing I can tell you, though. I should have told you about that mining stock, but it's been a sort of touchy subject with me. No man likes to admit he's been played for a sucker."

Deputy Sheriff Joe Menzell emerged from Calydon's Saloon across the street and came walking toward Quist and the sheriff, his booted feet scuffing up small puffs of dust. He nodded genially to Quist. Nixon said, "Is the beer cold, Joe?"

"Not too cold," Menzell said. "Want I should get at those expense accounts now, Bard?" Nixon said that was a good idea, and Menzell disappeared within the sheriff's office.

Nixon said, "Greg, come on over to Calydon's and I'll buy you a drink."

Quist nodded acceptance. "Speaking of drinking," he said, detaining the sheriff a minute, "is it true that Canfield was the drinker everybody tells me he was? I mean, could he hold a lot, or did he just get drunk quick?"

"Canfield could hold plenty. Hell, there wa'n't a week passed that he didn't buy at least one case of Kentucky Cream bourbon for home use. On top of that, there was all his drinkin' in town, and he came to town frequent. He could really pour the stuff down, though it affected him plenty, mentally and physically. Doc Sturven warned him to stop drinkin' before he killed himself, warned him more'n once. Sometimes, he'd get took right bad and act up like a crazy man."

"I've heard of those spells. Nearly everybody's told me about Sturven's warnings."

"It's all true. Doc was called out to the Terrapin, more'n once, to treat Canfield. I remember Doc tellin' me, one time when he'd been there, that there wa'n't scarce a room in that house that didn't have an open bottle of whisky standin' ready to hand. Others have told me the same thing. You know, at Rick's trial, the defense lawyer brought that out. The lawyer put forth the idea that Canfield had committed suicide while under the influence of liquor."

"How'd the jury take that?"

"I reckon the jury didn't believe it, but it did bring into the testimony what a sot Canfield was, and it helped their judgment in declarin' Rick not guilty. That defense lawyer put on a right good show. Along with Canfield's gun, marked Exhibit A, he also had Exhibit B, an empty Kentucky Cream bottle, and Exhibit C, a partly full bottle of Old Crow whisky. The attorney tried to stress the idea that them two bottles, plus what Canfield had drunk in town, made him irresponsible."

"What became of the exhibits?"

"They were turned over to me after the trial. The gun is still kicking around my office some place, I reckon——"

"And I suppose you drank the whisky," Quist laughed.

"No, by Gawd, I didn't," Nixon said virtuously. "I threw the empty Kentucky Cream bottle away——"

"I'm still trying to learn what happened to the Old Crow," Quist persisted, his topaz eyes twinkling.

Nixon laughed sheepishly. "T'tell the truth," he admitted, "I did sort of figure to keep that Old Crow for desk drinkin', but somebody must have had similar ideas, 'cause the same night the trial ended somebody busted into my office and stole that whisky."

"Steal any money or guns or anything else?"

Nixon shook his head. "Just somebody got thirsty and was afeared that liquor would go to waste, I reckon. A lot of good it done 'em though, 'cause the bottle was dropped and broke in their hurry to get away. I found the broken chunks of glass just at the edge of my porch there"—jerking one thumb over his shoulder—"and the lock on my door busted, when I come to the office the next mornin'."

Quist seemed to have forgotten what they were talking about. "Let's go get that drink you mentioned," he suggested.

Nixon agreed and they started across the street. Pushing through the swinging doors of the saloon, Quist saw Cody Thatcher and Doctor Sturven standing at the bar talking to John Calydon. Thatcher turned, saw who had entered, hastily swallowed his drink and started out. He gave Quist and Nixon a cool nod as he passed. Sturven, frowning, looked after him.

"I wonder what got into Cody?" the doctor said. "He seemed in a rush to leave, all of a sudden."

"I reckon he don't like Greg," Nixon said. "He's still feeling right put out about Homer Pritchett, though he admitted, frank, to me that on the evidence Pritchett was in the wrong.

He acts, though, like somebody's concealin' the whole story from him."

John Calydon leaned his portly middle against the bar and grunted, "You don't ever know how to take Cody. Sometimes he's moody as hell. At others, he's everybody's friend. What you having to drink, gentlemen?"

Quist and Nixon took beer. The doctor poured a neat two fingers of bourbon into a glass. There weren't any other customers in the saloon. Conversation was desultory, though Quist noted that Sturven seemed more friendly than he had on their first meeting. Nixon said finally, "Doc, Greg was asking me a spell back what sort of a drinker Canfield was? You tell him."

A frown tinged with disgust passed over the doctor's bony meatures. "If you want it bluntly," he said, "Canfield was a hog. He liked to wallow in liquor. And he was the type that should never have taken a drink. A constitution like his was never meant to absorb whisky—not in the amounts he swilled. It broke him up physically, and it's my opinion it was affecting his mind as well. In time he would have gone insane, I think. He'd drink until his system rebelled and then, like as not, he'd turn into a wild man. More than once it's taken a hypodermic to stop his twitching. Twitching wasn't always the word for it. I've seen him throw regular convulsions. I warned him, more than once, to stop drinking. He'd straighten up for a spell, then the first thing you knew he was off on one of his bats again."

"Well, that's one way for a man to ruin his health," Quist said.

"Ruin his health is no name for it," Sturven snorted. "Hell, a healthy man could have recovered, with proper medical attention, from the shot that killed Canfield."

"You mean the wound wasn't necessarily fatal?" Quist asked.

"I doubt it. I've saved men who were hit worse. The bullet entered Canfield's right side, broke a rib, passed through the lower part of the lung, missed his spine and lodged, on the left side, in the fleshy part of his back. I might have saved him, if I'd been there at the time. But the impact of a .45 slug throws a terrific shock into a man. That shock, plus loss of blood, plus Canfield's already debilitated condition, is what killed him."

"One on the house coming up, gents," John Calydon announced, and served two beers and a whisky for Sturven. This time the doctor merely splashed a few drops of bourbon in the bottom of his glass.

Quist said, "I was out to the Circle-H yesterday. Doctor, do you think Chris Hamilton will ever recover the use of his legs?"

Sturven shook his head. "Don't tell him I said so, though. But I'm afraid the age of miracles has passed. He got sort of peeved at me, lost faith in me, I guess, and insisted I bring specialists in. When they came, they confirmed my diagnosis. I could probably collect a lot of money from Chris for making calls and prescribing some sort of belly-wash, but I won't do it. There's not one damn' thing I can do for him, so I keep away. If he ever decides he needs me for anything else, he knows how to get me."

"What was your diagnosis?" Quist asked.

The doctor rattled off some scientific technical terms that meant very little to Quist, concluding, ". . . in plain language, an injury like that can't be operated on. Too delicate a job, and we doctors don't know enough, yet. I've seen such cases before. Sometimes they recover; sometimes not. All you can do is let Nature take care of it and hope for the best. The specialists agreed with me, that Chris would either recover entirely during the first year following the injury, or he'd never recover. Well, it's over two years now since Chris was hurt. You've got to take into consideration that Chris is past sixty. Old bodies don't mend like those of men in the prime of life."

The talk veered to other subjects. Sturven said he had some calls to make. A few customers entered the saloon. Nixon and Quist finished their beer and took their departure. On the street, Nixon said, "Well, you're off to sniffing at more trails, I suppose."

"Unless you've something better to propose." Nixon said he hadn't. Quist continued, "I had a notion I might drift down to the county house and read the records covering the Canfield murder trial."

"Wait a minute. We'll go over to my office and get my deputy. He can go with you and make it legal, in case some snippy clerk objects to you snoopin' in the records."

"Now that's what I call co-operation," Quist stated.

"Maybe it's about time," the sheriff said heavily. "I didn't like the look in your eye when you brought up that Red Gila stock deal. From now on, so help me Hanner! you get anything I got to give."

Most of the remainder of that day, Quist spent going over the account of the trial and reading the testimony that had been offered by the various witnesses. By the time he had concluded he was thoroughly convinced, if he hadn't known it before, that the Hamilton name carried a great deal of weight in the Gunsight country: the prosecution had been feeble, at best; the judge had been biased in Rick's favor and given his counsel all the breaks; witnesses were reluctant to speak, and

the whole trial had been rushed through in a surprisingly short
time. Later, as Quist sauntered down the street, he mused,
"Nope, Rick never was in any danger of being convicted.".

By this time the sun was low, sending long slanting shadows
along Huisache Street. Buckboards and other wagons had
commenced to draw away from the hitchracks and leave town.
Quist strolled east on Huisache, until he'd reached the Bon-
Ton millinery shop. Peering through one window, he saw
Camilla Peters within. Ascertaining first that she had no customers, he opened the door and stepped inside. Camilla greeted
him, smiling. "Mr. Quist! I wondered when you'd be in to see
me."

"I've been thinking of buying a hat," Quist chuckled, "or
has Rick bought up all your stock? Or maybe he doesn't come
here for hats."

Camilla dimpled. "I imagine you're looking for something
in a cap model with a feather in it."

"Lady, I could certainly use something along those lines,"
Quist laughed. "Rick been in today?"

"He left for the Circle-H about an hour ago," Camilla said.
She indicated a chair and took a seat not far from Quist. Quist
removed his hat. Camilla went on more soberly, "I've been
expecting you in to ask me a lot of questions. What can I tell
you?"

"Anything you might know that would lead to a solution of
who killed Nash Canfield. Where were you at the time he was
murdered?"

"Right here in Hyperion," Camilla said promptly, "though
I don't know of any way I can prove that at this late date."
Before Quist could speak she shook her head. "I'm afraid I
know nothing to help you."

"You do know something, though, concerning Canfield."

The girl's form stiffened. "You mean that he loaned me
money to open this shop? That loan was repaid long ago, Mr.
Quist."

"So I understand. And with interest. Also, you were once
engaged to Nash Canfield."

Camilla surveyed him with cool eyes. "That's true. I can
only say, now, I'm glad I never married him. Maybe I've more
sense than I had in those days. I'll admit, he was a pretty interesting man when I first met him. For that matter, lots of people
change their minds. I happen to be one of them. It was I who
broke off that engagement, if it interests you. Later he became
engaged to Tracy Hamilton, who, in turn, had first been
engaged to Tom Jenkins and Cody Thatcher."

"And now you're practically engaged to Rick Hamilton," Quist chuckled. "It sure looks like a re-shuffling of the deck."

"Doesn't it?" Camilla said coolly.

"What's your opinion of Tracy Canfield?"

"We're good friends. She's the squarest person I know. She says she'll be glad when Rick and I are married."

"Just how do you figure she went about killing Canfield?"

Camilla shook her head. "It's no go, Mr. Quist," she smiled. "I don't figure she killed Nash Canfield."

"Who did? Rick?"

"I can't swallow that either. Rick's no murderer—though he's got some silly idea that the matter has to be cleared up before he and I can get married. If it makes him any happier, I'm willing to wait that long." Quist asked who, in her opinion, had killed Canfield. Camilla said, "I've not the least idea. It's a complete mystery to me."

Quist nodded carelessly. "I suppose." His next question came with disarming nonchalance, "Perhaps you care to tell me why Canfield was seen leaving here around three in the morning, a couple of days before he was killed."

All the color abruptly left Camilla's face. She asked swiftly, "Does Rick know that?"

Quist shook his head. "Is there any reason why he shouldn't?"

"I'd just as soon he didn't, Mr. Quist. People might misunderstand, and say Rick had a good reason for killing Canfield. I wouldn't want that. It might make things look bad for Rick. He's so anxious to get this business cleared up." Camilla paused. "Where did you hear that Canfield had visited me that night—morning, rather."

"I was talking to one of the girls, Irma Cardiff, at the Elite Dance Hall, trying to learn if she knew anything pertinent concerning Canfield." Camilla frowned, stated that she didn't know Irma Cardiff personally, but had heard of her; she added that most of the girls at the Elite probably had known Canfield. Quist continued, "One of Irma's masculine friends, a puncher from the Rocking-B, resented my questioning Irma. In his anger, he suggested that I should question you, instead, inasmuch as he had seen Canfield leaving here around three o'clock on the morning in question."

Camilla drew a deep breath, her chin came up defiantly. "It just goes to show," she said in a cool voice, "that you never know who's spying on you. All right, go to Rick! Tell him what you've learned. I've an idea Rick may——"

Quist cut in quietly, "Who said I was going to Rick? What you do is your own business. I will admit I'm curious though."

Camilla looked quizzically at Quist. "I'm not to be condemned unheard then?" Quist said certainly not. Certain hard lights that had appeared in Camilla's deep violet eyes commenced to fade. "There really wasn't much to it, Mr. Quist. You already know that Canfield loaned me the money to open this millinery shop. Well, on the night, or rather the morning, Canfield came here, I'd been in bed for some hours. A knock on the door awakened me. I didn't recognize the voice; I threw on a wrapper and called through the door to ask what was wanted. The reply said something about a telegram having come for me. Like a silly fool I opened the door and Nash Canfield pushed in, laughing at the joke he had played on me, but insisting he did have something important to tell. He was very drunk. Eventually I learned that he wanted to loan me more money to expand my business—and he wasn't demanding interest this time."

Quist asked, "What was he demanding?"

Camilla looked steadily at him a moment, color rising in her cheeks. "Maybe we'd better not go into that," she said quietly. "I got rid of Canfield as soon as I could. I practically pushed him out the door. I never told Rick for fear it would make more trouble than was already brewing. That's all there was to it. Of course, you don't believe me."

Quist said, "On the contrary, Miss Peters. I know of no reason why I shouldn't believe you." He brushed aside the girl's words of thanks, asking, "Do you know of anything else concerning Canfield, or anybody connected with him—the Hamiltons, Cody Thatcher, Tom Jenkins, Pritchett, or anybody else?"

Camilla shook her head and said she didn't. Suddenly she checked herself. "Wait! Maybe it doesn't amount to anything, but do you know Tom Jenkins' father?"

"Old Morg Jenkins?" Quist nodded. "What about him?"

"This afternoon," Camilla explained, "I was sitting in the shop here. It was rather close and I let the door stand open a little. I heard voices and, looking through the window, I saw Morg Jenkins and Cody Thatcher standing out in front. They appeared to be quarreling."

"What about?"

"I haven't the least idea, Mr. Quist. I could hear the voices but I couldn't distinguish the words, except something Mr. Jenkins said, just before they parted."

"What was that?"

"Morg Jenkins said, 'Cody, I'm giving you your chance. Either sell your outfit and get out of this country, or I'm going to go to Sheriff Nixon and spill what I know.' "

Quist said, "What did Jenkins mean?"

"I don't know. I could see that Cody was terribly angry at first. Finally he nodded his head and seemed to agree with whatever it was Mr. Jenkins wanted. Before they parted, Mr. Jenkins smiled and patted Cody on the shoulder, as though they were friends again. Does it mean anything to you?"

"I don't know," Quist said thoughtfully, and again, "I don't know, Miss Peters. But it might."

Later, when Quist was once more on the street, he mulled the matter over in his mind. "I think," he decided finally, "I'll have to go see Morg Jenkins and learn what Thatcher had to say."

Chapter XVIII : RIFLE FIRE!

The following morning, directly after breakfast, Greg Quist had the black gelding saddled at the Hyperion Livery and took the road west out of town. He had crossed the Gunsight River by eight-thirty and was making his way along the rutted trail that curved between low hills, dotted with live oak, mesquite and opuntia. Overhead, fleecy white clouds chased each other across a turquoise sky. A fresh breeze blew down from the Gunsights, ruffling the tops of the buffalo grass and stirring old leaves from their bed beneath the live oaks. Now and then a paisano bird or jack rabbit darted across Quist's path. Golden dust motes swam in the air in the wake of his pony's pounding hoofs.

Quist was three quarters of the way to the Circle-H when, topping a rise of land, he spied a rider, moving fast, some distance ahead on the trail. An instant later the man and horse had dipped from view in a hollow and were lost to Quist's sight. The man had been too far off for Quist's recognition and at the moment he thought nothing of the matter, but kept his pony at the same even lope. When next Quist topped a rise he saw the rider still farther ahead, the flying hoofs of his mount kicking up huge clouds of dust, as the man urged the horse rapidly across the terrain. Abruptly, a bend in the trail blotted the rider from view. Quist mused, "Whoever that hombre is, he's sure traveling fast."

Twenty minutes later, Quist was approaching the Circle-H ranch house. As usual, old Chris Hamilton, his lower limbs swathed in blankets, was seated on the gallery of the house. A rifle rested against the arm of his chair. There was no one else in sight. The old man raised one arm in greeting, as Quist pulled the black gelding to a stop at the edge of the gallery. "How you doing this morning, Mr. Hamilton?" Quist asked.

"No better than can be expected," Hamilton replied sourly. Then, in a slightly more cordial tone, "Light and rest your saddle."

"I'll ride down and water this pony first, then come back."

"Hell, no. Get down and sit. Brasadero's around some place. He'll be here in a minute and can take care of your bronc."

Quist laughed and started to move the pony away from the gallery. "If Brasadero has to take care of my horse every time I come here, I'll be wearing out my welcome." Hamilton protested further, but Quist kept going, reining his gelding around the corner of the house and on down toward the corrals and bunkhouse. He had nearly reached the watering trough when he saw Brasadero Banning. Banning spoke genially, adding, "Get down and I'll water that pony for you."

Quist said, "Thanks," and climbed down from the saddle, handing the reins to Banning. He continued, "I'm going to drop into the bunkhouse and see Brose Fox. I suppose he's in there?"

"Sure enough," Banning nodded. "He's on the mend. Jake Currie ain't here though. I sent him and Rick out to a spot south of here to build up a water tank. Much against their inclinations, y'understand." Banning chuckled. "These cowhands sure hate to use a shovel. You saw Chris on the gallery, I suppose." Quist said he had. Banning sobered. "The old man's not feelin' so good this mornin'. The inactivity makes him grouchy. He's got his rifle, hopin' another gopher will decide to dig within range."

"This time he can do his own shooting," Quist laughed.

"Aw, you don't want to pay no 'tention to him when he gets those pettish streaks. He's the same with me, lots of times. Put yourself in his place and see how it would be."

"I reckon you can't blame him," Quist agreed. He left his pony with Banning and strode on toward the bunkhouse, passing on his way the saddlers' corral. Glancing through the bars he noticed that one of the ponies, a big rangy bay, showed evidence of having been ridden hard recently. Its hide was streaked darkly with sweat. Foam flecks were drying on the animal's withers. A saddle and blanket rested across one of the top bars. Quist would have liked to have placed his hand on the blanket to learn if it, too, was sweat-dampened, but glancing back, he saw Banning watching him, and continued on to the bunkhouse.

Brose Fox was seated in a chair, his wounded shoulder still

swathed in bandages, when Quist entered. He put down the pink-covered periodical he'd been reading and greeted Quist in friendly fashion. Quist asked how the shoulder was, and Fox said it was just fine. A minute later, Soggy Hannan joined them from his cookhouse and the three men talked on trivial subjects for a time. Finally, Quist started to depart, after refusing Hannan's invitation to eat dinner with the Circle-H.

Outside once more, Quist got his pony from Banning and started back toward the house. Banning called after him, "You aiming to visit a spell with Chris?" Quist said he was. Banning said, "I've got a few things to occupy me here, then. Tell Chris I'll be with him by the time you leave."

Quist delivered the message and took the chair at Chris Hamilton's right. "No gophers yet?"

Hamilton glanced at the rifle resting against his chair arm and said no. "Reckon you must have killed th' last one in the pack," he commented. "Either that, or word of your shooting must have got around to all the gopher villages and they're shyin' clear of Circle-H holdings. Come the right season, I might take to pickin' off a few dove or some blue quail. Still, I sort of like birds; I don't relish shooting anything tame as birds."

"It must get right monotonous, sitting here, day after day."

"You don't know the half of it," Chris Hamilton growled. "Still, I make to get to town, about once a month." Quist looked surprised. Hamilton explained. "They carry me out and lash me to the seat of a buckboad so's I can't fall out. Then Brasadero drives to town. We stop in front of Calydon's and drinks are brought out to me." His voice sounded bitter. "Ain't that a hell of a life for a man?"

"I imagine it's right unpleasant at times," Quist said sympathetically. "Still, you must find some enjoyment in getting out."

"Hell's bells! I do. But it ain't like saddling your own bronc and forkin' him where you want to go."

"No, I guess it wouldn't be," Quist replied. "Were you able to travel to Hyperion to attend Rick's trial last year?"

Hamilton scowled. "No. I was feeling right poorly about that time. Of course, I had one of the boys bring me daily reports, so I kept up on the news that way. The Hyperion *Gazette* carried a good summing-up of the killing and trial. Brasadero got me a transcript of the trial proceedings. All in all, I know pretty much what went on."

"But you're certain there's nothing you can think of that might put me on the trail of Canfield's killer?" Quist asked.

He saw Hamilton's heavy beard bristle with anger. The old

man glowered at him from beneath bushy, iron-gray eyebrows. "Damn it! I already told you I don't know anything beyond what I've read and what Rick and some others told me about the business."

"Just the same I'd be glad to have your version of it."

Hamilton ripped out an oath; his flinty eyes seemed to emit sparks. "What in Gawd's name can I tell you?" he demanded furiously. "You've already heard the kind of buzzard Canfield was, and how Tracy got him out of bed that morning, early, and started him to town for the payroll money. And how he made a fool of himself when he got to Hyperion, getting drunk all over again and bein' nasty with Rick. And a lot of laughin' fools hootin' and yellin' around him. Tom Jenkins got him started for the Terrapin, but finally left him to get home alone. Trunkfoot Wagner saw him arrive drunk. I suppose he continued drinkin' when he went in the house. He always kept plenty liquor at the Terrapin, and somebody in town had give him a bottle. He finished one bottle and had a couple of drinks out of another. Those bottles were brought into the trial as evidence. Maybe the killer was already in the house when Canfield arrived. There must have been a struggle; the room was messed up plenty. Likely Canfield was too drunk to defend himself——" Hamilton paused abruptly at sound of a slight metallic noise, then moved one hand quickly to his rifle and placed it in a more upright position.

"This gallery floor must be sagging," he grumbled. "My Winchester gets to sliding along the arm of this chair, every so often."

Quist had been listening in silence, his eyes fixed on the leafy branches of the live oak trees surrounding the house. He glanced toward the rifle, then said, "Yes, the killer could have been waiting until Canfield arrived home, or he might have come in later, or maybe he wasn't there at all——"

"You hinting that Canfield committed suicide?" Hamilton demanded.

"What do you think?" Quist countered. "After all, the shooting was done with Canfield's own gun."

Hamilton's forehead furrowed with thought. "In the first place," he said finally, "I don't think Canfield had nerve enough to shoot himself. As for his own gun being used, I reckon everybody knew it hung on a hook in that hall, all the time, so a killer would know where to find it."

"Who do you mean by everybody?"

"Anybody that ever entered that house, or at least passed through it. I saw it hangin' there before I had my accident. It was kind of a joke, around, how Canfield was afraid to wear

his gun for fear of it getting him into some trouble. What a
few people know, others soon learn. 'Course, I wouldn't state
positive he didn't commit suicide. Like I say, there's very little
I can tell you, Mr. Quist." He added, "I've said before you
might just as well pick up your traps and go back to El Paso.
You ain't going to learn much hereabouts."

"It's commencing to look that way," Quist smiled. The talk
turned to other subjects, and finally Quist rose to depart. As
he got to his feet he put out one hand to the rifle barrel.
Hamilton looked at him questioningly. Quist said, "I thought
your gun had started to slip again. Maybe I was mistaken."
He strode out to his horse, tightened the cinch and climbed
up. Hamilton told him to call again and Quist said he hoped
to. It wasn't until Quist was some distance from the house
that he remembered he hadn't seen Brasadero Banning again,
before he left.

Quist gave this matter some thought as he headed his pony
in the direction of Morg Jenkins' cabin in the Gunsight foothills. "Banning probably had a hunch," Quist concluded, "that
this was my day for asking questions, and that he'd best stay
out of my vicinity."

As the horse loped across the range, Quist commenced to
wish he'd accepted Soggy Hannan's invitation to dinner. The
sun was high now, its torrid rays baking the soil and sending
heat waves quivering from the occasional outcroppings of
limestone passed. Mesquite appeared to droop in the noonday
warmth, and it was difficult to resist the shade offered by live
oak trees growing on hilly slopes. For an hour, Quist rode
steadily, the hot breeze blowing down from the Gunsight
Mountains lifting and sweeping away the small puffs of gritty
dust kicked up by his pony's loping hoofs.

Horse and man were mounting a gradually-rising terrain, as
they climbed deeper into the foothills. Quist knew it couldn't
be much farther to the old wolfer's cabin, now, and he reined
the black gelding to a slower pace. Suddenly, he stiffened,
jerking his pony to a halt. The wind blowing down from the
mountains had carried with it sharp cracking sounds resem-
bling rifle detonations. He thought he had heard two shots, but
couldn't be certain. At present his alert ears caught nothing
except the soughing of the wind through the mesquite and the
soft rustling of bunch grass. For five full minutes he waited,
then went on again, this time with every sense tensed for
further sounds, or signs of movements.

Before long, rounding the shoulder of a hill, he spied Morg
Jenkins' cabin, nestled between two hills some distance beyond. There was no sign of life about the cabin, though Quist

was still too far away to feel certain on that score. As he pushed his pony forward at a walk, he was forced to swerve, now and then, to avoid tall clumps of prickly pear which obstructed his vision.

And then, when once more his view of the cabin was clear, the black gelding suddenly faltered, swayed a moment and went to its knees. Even before the savage crack of the rifle reached his ears, Quist had seen the spurt of white flame dart from the cabin porch and the sudden puff of black powder smoke as it was swept away on the breeze!

Chapter XIX : KILLER LEAD

As the black gelding crashed to the earth, Quist loosened his feet from stirrups, jerked his .44 from the shoulder holster and leaped to earth, firing as he moved. Simultaneously with the report of his gun, he heard the rifle crack again and caught the vicious whine of angry flying lead as it tore through the air overhead. In an instant he had thrown himself flat behind a clump of opuntia. The .44 bucked in his hand and the heavy detonation of the shot rolled through the hills.

He swore softly in some irritation, knowing the range to be too great for the .44 for accurate shooting, particularly when the shadow of the porch made it difficult to discern clearly his adversary. The two shots Quist had fired were intended, more than anything else, to keep the enemy dodging while an opportunity to consider the situation was made. "This is one time," Quist grunted, "when I should be carrying more than this .44. What wouldn't I give for a rifle, right now?"

He peered cautiously between the spiny pads of the opuntia, but could make out no movement on the cabin porch. He realized quite suddenly he hadn't even caught a good look at the hidden rifleman.

"I wonder who the devil he is," Quist pondered. "Surely old Morg Jenkins wouldn't . . ." He paused. Where was Morg Jenkins? Quist raised his voice, calling, "Mor-rg-g! Mr. Jenki-i-ins! It's me, Quist-t-t! Are you there-e-e?"

There was no answer. Quist eyed the house steadily for a moment, but was unable to detect the slightest sign of movement. He raised his gun and fired two more, widely-spaced shots toward the cabin, hoping to draw further fire from the enemy. The effort brought no answering shots; all was as silent as before.

"I can't believe that was Morg Jenkins fired on me," Quist told himself, grimly. "Either he's not there—or he's dead." He added hopefully, "He might be only wounded."

The situation looked ominous. Quist twisted around from his prone position on stomach and glanced toward the gelding. The horse showed no sign of movement. Blood seeped from a black hole almost in the middle of its forehead. Quist swore with some feeling. "A damn' good little horse, too. A mite higher and that slug would have got me."

He turned his attention back to the house, considering the situation, then shoved fresh cartridges into his gun. He gazed about on the earth until he'd found a short dead branch of mesquite. After trimming this off, he thrust one end into his sombrero and cautiously shoved the hat around the edge of the opuntia clump. In his right hand he held his gun, ready to shoot if the bait were taken. A minute passed, two, five. No further shots came from the cabin's vicinity.

Ruefully, Quist withdrew his hat and placed it on his head. "I reckon that hombre knows the old hat trick," he told himself. "I'm just wasting my time."

He waited another five minutes. Once he thought he heard sounds from the horses in Morg Jenkins' corral, but he couldn't be sure. Nor could he see the corral which stood back of the cabin and was partly obscured by high clumps of prickly pear cactus. He cast another look at his dead pony, his face darkening, and pondered the situation some more.

"I reckon there's nothing else to do," he told himself. "I'm set afoot, and I've got to get one of those horses in Jenkins' corral. That means I have to approach the cabin. The sooner I start, the better."

Gun in hand, he commenced the long journey toward the house, his muscular form bent nearly double, taking advantage of every clump of grass or mesquite brush that offered the slightest concealment. He was moving in a wide half-circle, so as to approach the cabin from one side. At times, he was almost flat on his stomach; now and then, when tall brush offered shelter, he scurried across the earth in a stooping position, expecting every instant to hear again the bark of the rifle. In this manner, after a half hour had passed, he had progressed within twenty-five yards of the house and halted behind a high stand of prickly pear cactus to consider his next move.

"I've got to chance it," Quist told himself. "There's only one way to get to that cabin without wasting more time, and that's to stand up and make a rush for it." He hesitated a moment longer, suddenly remembering that nothing had been heard from Morg Jenkins' dog. If King were in the vicinity it was queer he'd heard no barking, or at least seen it running about. The whole situation was appearing more strange every minute.

Quist finally formulated his plan. "Well, here goes," he muttered. Clutching the six-shooter in his right hand, he suddenly rose and leaped into the open, running a zigzagging course toward the cabin and expecting his move would bring a prompt reaction from the enemy. But nothing happened.

Almost before he realized it, Quist had covered the intervening yards to the cabin, leaped to the porch and flattened himself against the front wall, between a window and the closed door. Again he waited, straining his ears for the slightest movement within the cabin. There wasn't a sound to be heard.

A thought flashed through Quist's mind: the lousy buzzard who shot at me is holding his fire, waiting for me to enter. He listened for another five minutes, then decided to move. Stepping quickly to the closed door, he raised one booted foot and gave it a violent kick. There came a sharp splintering sound as the door catch gave way. The door crashed back to bang against the inner wall. At the same instant, Quist leaped swiftly to one side, his gun lifted to answer the shots he expected would come thundering through the opening.

The shots failed to eventuate. Gradually, a long pent-up breath whistled through Quist's lips. Flattened against the outer front wall, close to the door, Quist waited. From within the cabin, he could hear the buzzing of myriad flies. Nothing more.

Again he moved suddenly, his leap carrying him within the house. Here he stopped short and slowly lowered his gun. There wasn't a living soul in sight. The cabin interior looked as Quist had last seen it, except that the rear door stood open, and lying on the floor were the lifeless bodies of the old wolfer and his dog King.

Quist caught the whole picture in an instant: the dark crimson stains slowly congealing on the scrubbed floor planks. The silent forms of the old man and his dog. Flies buzzed angrily through the room. Quist crossed the floor in quick, lithe strides, paused but a second before emerging from the rear doorway of the cabin, then pulled up short at sight of the empty corral with its wide-open gate.

"Out-foxed, by God!" Quist swore bitterly. "What a fool I am! Quist, if your brains were dynamite, they couldn't produce enough force to jolt your hat off your head. You, a detective? Oh, hell! That bustard didn't wait after he fired on me. While you wasted time sneaking up on the house, he slipped out by the rear, and, keeping the house between you and him, released the ponies in the corral, then forked his own pony, likely walking the animals soft and easy, until he'd reached the cover of the trees. Oh, you utter damn' fool, you!"

Seething with self-denunciation, Quist reluctantly reholstered his .44 and sent his gaze darting up the slopes of the surrounding hills. Only tall brush and live oaks, mesquite and blackjack, blowing in the strong breeze, met his eyes. "You simple jughead," he swore wrathfully at himself, "why did you have to watch that cabin so close? If you'd taken a glance at the hills, you might have spied him getting away. Even if you were afoot, you'd known what direction he took."

Quist again ran his gaze around the horizon, and this time was rewarded: there, skylighted on a high ridge to the south, a rider was urging two horses before him at breakneck speed. The man was too far distant for recognition, and the next moment had vanished from view beyond the opposite side of the ridge.

Quist swore in angry frustration. "That murdering vulture is driving those ponies far enough off so they won't drift back home for a long spell. Damn his hide!"

He returned to the house, closing the rear door behind him. The body of the old wolfer lay huddled on its side, one knee drawn up. Without touching the body, Quist was able to make a fairly good inspection of the wounds. One bullet had entered just below Jenkins' left shoulder blade. Quist muttered, "Judging from the way that slug ploughed in, I'll bet it was fired from some point higher than Jenkins was standing." He moved around to the front of the body and saw that a second bullet had torn its way through the pit of Jenkins' stomach. In Quist's judgment, either wound could have proved fatal.

The dog lay nearer the open front doorway, its head resting in a sticky coagulation of darkening blood from its mouth. The back of its head had been nearly blown away. Apparently the killer's lead had entered the dog's open mouth and crashed through the rear of the skull. Quist glanced around the floor; the bullet might be somewhere about.

He didn't see the bullet, but a metallic gleam caught his eye and he picked up an exploded rifle shell. He saw at once it was a .38-55. A moment later, he picked up a second shell of the same caliber. Two shots had been fired from close-up, within the cabin. Quist glanced around the cabin once more. None of the old wolfer's equipment seemed to have been disturbed. After a moment he secured a pair of blankets from one of the bunks and covered the still forms of man and dog.

Quist moved slowly out to the porch, drawing the door

closed behind him. The broken lock refused to catch, but the door stayed shut. On the porch he found two more exploded shells, both of the same caliber as those he'd picked up within the cabin. "These are the ones the dirty son fired at me," Quist grunted.

He saw also drops of blood on the porch, and for a moment hoped he had winged his adversary, but the idea was quickly dispelled when he saw more blood on the porch steps. This had gone unnoticed before, when he was approaching the porch in his hurry. Beyond the porch steps was another damp-ish brown stain. Quist moved out from the house a way, pro-ceeding in a stooping position as he scrutinized the earth and read "sign."

At the end of ten minutes, his experienced eyes and mind had constructed a fairly accurate picture of what had hap-pened. The earth was scuffed in places; here and there faint impressions of the dog's paws were left on the hard soil, but Quist had no idea how long ago they had been made. Of the rest of the "sign" he read on the earth, he felt more certain.

He finally straightened to his feet, "It looks to me," Quist told himself, speaking half aloud, "as though Morg Jenkins had come out of his house and walked to about where I'm standing, now. Probably he was just looking around, or some-thing may have drawn him out here. I don't know about that." His gaze shifted to a tree-and-brush-covered slope rising some distance away. "The killer was hid up there, waiting for a chance at Jenkins. When Jenkins' back presented a good target, the killer pulled trigger and Jenkins dropped. I reckon I was still too far off to hear that shot when it was fired."

Quist summarized some more: "But he wasn't killed instant-ly. I don't know how long he lay here, but eventually he started to crawl toward the cabin. It was a long hard trail. Those bloodstains are large enough to prove he had to stop and rest, every so often. Meantime, the killer, seeing him move, must have started down the hillside to finish the job from up close. He probably arrived shortly after Jenkins got into the house. Likely the dog put up some sort of defense, or the killer woudn't have shot him, then he shot Jenkins again. Or he might have shot Jenkins first. I don't know. All I know is that Jenkins never had a chance. His rifle and shotgun were still on the wall; he didn't have his six-gun on. Probably lacked even the strength to reach it, once he'd made the house. It's a dirty cold-blooded murder if I ever saw one."

Quist glanced over the surrounding country again, then moved around to the back of the house. Here, near the corral, the eath was harder packed and sun-baked. He found a few signs, but nothing distinguishing about them, showing where the killer had come down from the hillslope and left his horse, while he went around to the front of the cabin to complete his murderous task. Both hoof and boot prints were faint. Quist considered ascending the slope to look over the ground, but gave up that idea as being scarcely worthwhile and unlikely to add anything to the information he'd already gained. He saw to it that both front and rear doors of the cabin were closed, then paused but a moment longer, trying to decide whether or not to strip the saddle from the dead pony laying off in the brush.

"I reckon not," he said at last. "I've got enough of a walk ahead without being weighed down by nigh forty pounds of rig. The sheriff or whoever comes out can get it for me."

He waited but an instant more, then started out in the direction of the Circle-H, walking with long even strides. Before he had gone far he realized more than ever how hot the day was. "Anyway," he told himself with some satisfaction, "it's mostly downgrade to the Hamilton outfit." He considered a moment as to whether the Terrapin might be closer, and finally decided it wasn't.

He went on, but hadn't progressed far when he stopped to remove the spurs from his boots. These he stuck in the side-pockets of his coat, removed the coat and slung it over his shoulder and once more struck out. By the time he had progressed three miles across the sandy, limestone-encrusted soil and dodged various trees and other plant growths, a blister had commenced to form on his right foot. Another mile brought a blister to his left heel. He tried walking without boots for a time, but embedded bits of rock had a fiendish custom of bruising the soles of his feet, and his boots were again drawn on.

"I think I can realize now," Quist mused, "exactly how Homer Pritchett felt that day, limping around El Paso. I sure wish it was him making this walk, instead of me, though on second thought I wouldn't want to change places with him. It's probably hotter down there where he is, or I miss my guess."

Gritting his teeth, he lengthened his stride and pushed on.

It was very late that night when Quist came limping into the Circle-H. The ranch house was dark, but lights still burned in the bunkhouse. Passing the saddlers' corral, in the bright moonlight, Quist thought he had never seen such a beautiful sight as the horses standing within the enclosure. He approached the bunkhouse, knocked, then pushed open the door and entered.

A group of surprised faces greeted his arrival. Rick, Brose Fox, and Jake Currie were engaged in a three-handed game of seven-up. Soggy Hannan was already snoring in his bunk. Tim Baird, Gus Diehl, and Nick Logan were in bunks, but not yet asleep, having been pleading with the cardplayers to "for cripes' sake douse that overhead light." Brasadero Banning was seated at a rough board desk in one corner, going over a tally book by the light from a kerosene lamp. A suspicious frown crossed his face at Quist's entry. Rick exclaimed, "Greg! What are you——?"

"Damned if you don't move quiet," Brose Fox said, looking up across the cards held in his free hand, and wincing a little as his sudden movement brought a twinge of pain to his bandaged shoulder. "I didn't hear your hawss arrivin'."

"I come on foot," Quist said.

The men in the bunks swung their legs to the floor. Soggy Hannan rubbed his eyes, grumbling something about "idjits" that never learn the night was made for sleeping. Gus Diehl dropped a sarcastic remark about it being a beautiful night for a walk. Quist snapped, "Yes, it is, especially on the upgrades. It brings out all the water in a man's blisters——"

"Look here, Quist," Banning said heavily, "what's the idea of you snooping on foot around here?" Instantly the other men sobered.

"Get it through your head I'm not snooping," Quist said tersely. "I'd hoped to get a horse here. I've walked from Morg Jenkins' cabin where I was set afoot. Some back-shooting, son-of-a-leech killed Jenkins and his dog. Now if you'll lend me a mount I'll get on my way to the sheriff's office, so you won't have to worry about any snooping——"

A chorus of protests broke out. Shamefaced, Banning said he was sorry he'd spoken that way and asked for details. Quist told the story, leaving out only mention of finding the empty cartridge shells, and again asked if he could borrow a mount. The room was full of angry exclamations. Morg Jenkins had been well-liked throughout the Gunsight country. A couple of the men asked Quist if he had picked up any clues. Quist evaded the question with the reply that it was difficult to speak with any certainty until he'd mulled over the matter a little longer. He turned back to Banning, "Now if you'll let me have a pony and rig, I'll get going."

Banning had opened his mouth to speak, when Soggy Hannan broke in, "No, goddammit, you can't have no pony—yet. Let one of these other sway-backed, good-for-nothin' waddies make that ride to Hyperion. You've covered enough ground for one day, Mr. Quist, and you ain't had no supper yet. I aim to remedy that *pronto*." Turning, he hurried through the door leading to his cookhouse. A moment later they could hear him shoving kindling into the stove.

"Soggy's got the right idea," Banning agreed. "I should have thought of that myself." He said to Jake Currie: "You ride in and tell Bard Nixon what's happened. You'll have to stop at the undertaker's and have him hitch up too. Hurry up, now!" He swung back to Quist. "The sheriff will stop here on his way through, anyway. He can hear your story then."

Quist nodded, abruptly aware that he was very weary. "Somebody should ride to the Terrapin too," he suggested, "and let Tom know about it. His father's death will likely hit him right hard."

"No doubt on that score," Banning said. His gaze swept the punchers in the bunkhouse. Before he could speak, Gus Diehl said:

"I'll make that ride to the Terrapin, Brasadero. I've knowed Tom Jenkins since he was a button."

"I was just about to suggest that you go, Gus," Banning replied. "Break it easy-like if possible."

"It's one of those things that can't be broke easy," Diehl growled, "but I'll do my best."

By this time, Jake Currie had left the bunkhouse. Gus Diehl wasn't far behind him. Within a few moments the drumming of their horses' hoofs was heard leaving the Circle-H.

"I reckon," Banning said, "I'd better go up to the house. Chris will hear them ponies and wonder what's up. They're sure to wake him. I'm bettin' a pretty it will throw him into a rage not bein' able to get out and find that murderer. He thought a heap of old Morg."

"Maybe he'll want to hear the story from me, direct," Quist suggested.

"Maybe he will," Banning said. "If so, you can give it to him tomorrow. You've done enough for one day. If he has to have it tonight, a couple of us can carry him down here in his chair."

"Want me to go up and tell Dad?" Rick asked.

Banning paused. "No, I reckon I better be the one, Rick. I can handle his mads better than you can, and he sure gets mad when somethin' catches him helpless this way." Banning put on his sombrero and stepped out, closing the door behind him.

The men asked further questions of Quist, which he answered as well as possible. Soggy Hannan commenced to make trips from his kitchen, each time bringing platters of food, to set on the table before Quist. The sight of the big coffeepot decided the others to have cups. Before Quest was half through the meal, Soggy appeared once more with a huge dishpan of hot water. "I got bakin' sody in this," he stated. "There ain't nothin' like bakin' sody and hot water to fix blisters. Strip off them boots and socks and you can be soakin' your feet while you eat."

Quist was too weary to protest. He did as ordered, sitting with both feet in the pan under the table. He commented on the excellence of the food. " 'Course it's good chow," Soggy said. "Between you and me, it's too blasted good for the loafers around this outfit. With you, it's different. You got appreciation for fine food."

"Fine food, hah!" Brose Fox snorted sarcastically. "Trouble with you, cookie, Mr. Quist is so fagged out that he imagines your lumpy sourdough and embalmed beef is food. And this coffee! It's so weak it keeps fallin' down in my cup."

"A lot you know about coffee, Brose," the cook retorted. "I floated my six-shooter in it like always. If the hawg-laig don't float, the coffee's no good. Trouble with you, your palate is so pickled in rotgut whisky, it requires a slug of sheep-dip to start your taste to workin'."

"It's not the whisky"—Fox winked at Quist—"it's the chow you dish up that's petrified my taste buds."

"Your what?" Soggy asked suspiciously.

"My taste buds. You probably don't know what they are."

"If it's anythin' for a growin' appetite," the cook growled, "you sure got 'em. Only the way you stow away food, they ain't buds no longer. They've plumb bloomed, if you ask me!"

Tim Baird and Nick Logan rushed to Fox's defense. The joking at Soggy's expense went on for some time, with the cook more than capable of defending his culinary abilities. There wasn't a man in the bunkhouse who hadn't been hard hit by the news of Morg Jenkins' murder; this joshing was merely their method of concealing their real feelings.

"When you get ready, Greg," Rick said, "drop into a bunk. I'll wake you when Bard Nixon gets here."

It was nearly daylight by the time the sheriff arrived and heard Quist's story. He, too, asked if Quist had discovered any rifle shells lying around. Quist said evasively, "To tell the truth, Bard, I didn't search around as much as I could've. With that long walk staring me in the face . . ." He let his voice drift into silence.

Nixon drew his own inference: "Probably too smart a bustard not to pick up ejected ca'tridges. He'll cover his trail well, and it's going to be one hell of a job to lay hands on him."

He left the bunkhouse and again climbed into the saddle.

The sun was up before the undertaker drove his wagon through, on the way to the same grim destination. By this time, Quist was again sound asleep in one of the bunks.

Chapter XX : SHOWDOWN

Quist learned from Nixon the following evening, in Hyperion, that Tom Jenkins had reached the old wolfer's cabin before the sheriff. The two men were standing talking, in John Calydon's saloon, at one end of the bar. Quist asked, "How was he taking it, Bard?"

"Outwardly calm. He's hit pretty hard, of course, but it don't show on his face. But I've known Tom a long time, and you can bet he's smoldering inside, and pretty well broke up inside too. I'd hate to be that murderer if Tom ever gets a chance at him."

"Did Tom look over the ground any?"

The sheriff nodded. "His sign readin' agreed with your story. Matter of fact, goin' over the ground with him, saved me some time too." The sheriff added after a moment, "Tom and I buried the dawg while we were waitin' for the undertaker to show up."

Quist asked, "You didn't see anything of the two horses the murderer drove off, did you?"

"They came wanderin' in just before we left," Nixon said. "I turned 'em over to Tom to take back to the Terrapin with him. . . . Greg, who do you think done it?"

"I wouldn't say."

"Wouldn't, or couldn't?"

Quist smiled thinly. "You're not accusing me of holding out on you, are you, Bard?"

"T'tell the truth I'm never sure what to think about you. You know, I could use some of your detectin' ability on this case. Why don't you lend a hand?"

"I've no authority in Castaneda County, Bard. This is your problem. Remember, I was brought here to work on the Canfield case."

Nixon swore. "T'hell with that. You're not making any progress, there. You might as well forget it, and help me. I'll give you all the authority you want."

"Plus getting me further leave of absence from the T.N. & A.S., I suppose. And an appropriation from the county to handle my expenses?"

"The first I wouldn't know how to get. The second the county officials wouldn't stand for—dammit!" He scowled. "I should be gettin' on that murderin' skunk's trail right this minute, but dam'd if I know where to start."

"When does Doc Sturven plan to hold his inquest?"

"Day after tomorrow, at ten in the morning. Doc plans to probe the slugs out of Morg's body tomorrow and reach such decision as possible. He's already got his jury lined up and they'll view the corpse tomorrow night. Then, the following morning the inquest can get goin'. By the way, Chris Hamilton told me he was going to have the boys bring him in so he can attend. Chris is right worked up about the killin'."

"I can imagine. They were old friends, I guess."

The sheriff suddenly remembered something. "Oh, yes, Doc Sturven told me to ask you to draw a sort of sketch of the cabin where you found the body—y'know, just an interior plan with marks to show where the body was laying' and so on. He'll want it for his jury."

Quist nodded. "I'll see Doc tomorrow and give him what he wants."

"Good. You know, maybe this will get folks' minds off'n the Canfield killing for a spell, and the ruckuses you've been havin' since you got here. It's certain Morg's murder had nothing to do with the Canfield affair."

"Maybe so," Quist nodded carelessly. "I wouldn't be sure though."

"Got anything to go on?"

"I didn't say that either," Quist replied. "Well, I'm going to push along to my hotel. I've got a couple of blisters I want to nurse. I'll see you tomorrow."

The sheriff said *Adios,* and Quist left the barroom.

A wave of indignation had swept through the Gunsight country when news of Morg Jenkins' murder became known. The old wolfer had been well thought of, and the usual hue and cry of inefficient law enforcement commenced to be heard. Many people had appeared at Bard Nixon's office, demanding that he apprehend the murderer within "a damned reasonable time"—as one outraged citizen had put it—or not expect to be returned to office when next election time rolled around. The sheriff was at his wit's end, trying to placate his aroused constituents, and making promises of prompt action which he wasn't at all sure he could fulfill. A certain faction looked on Gregory Quist with some suspicion: he could have killed Morg Jenkins. After all, he was a stranger in Gunsight; the sheriff had only Quist's word for what had happened.

However, it bothered Quist but little and he dismissed the matter from his mind.

With the inquest open to the public, small wonder that the morning of the inquiry saw people from all points of the compass riding to town. Long before the hour appointed for the inquest, Huisache Street was lined with vehicles and saddled ponies, and people were streaming along the plank sidewalks in the direction of the two-story brick county building on Huisache, just east of Fanning Street, where on the lower floor (generally used for trials) the inquest was due to open. Chris Hamilton had arrived early, lashed to the seat of a buckboard driven by Brasadero Banning. Hamilton's own armchair had been brought along, and seated in this he had been carried within the hall by Rick and Banning, with some assistance from Deputy Joe Menzell.

Tracy Canfield had come riding in with Tom Jenkins a few moments later, and Cody Thatcher had arrived directly on their heels and followed them inside. The rows of straight-backed chairs filled rapidly, and many people were forced to stand against the wall. Tall windows on either side were opened to allow for ventilation. Hamilton sat in the front row of seats, blankets swathed around his legs. To his right sat Quist and beyond Quist were the sheriff and his deputy. On Hamilton's left sat Banning. Rick was seated next to Banning, then came Tracy and Tom Jenkins. When Cody Thatcher arrived, he started for a chair in the second row, then seeing the chair next to Jenkins vacant, he came around and spoke to him, offering his sympathy, then sat down. The two men talked quietly for a few minutes, but ceased their conversation as doors at the rear opened and Sturven and his six-man jury filed up the aisle and took their positions at the front of the long room. Two of the jury carried with them a large blackboard on which Quist had sketched in chalk a floor plan of the old wolfer's cabin, with crosses indicating the positions in which he had found Jenkins' body and the dead dog; at the rear the corral was shown and roughly drawn circles represented the hills about the cabin. The blackboard was set up where both audience and jury could see it, then Sturven picked up a gavel and rapped for silence on a small table. The buzz of conversation gradually subsided and Sturven commenced to speak.

The doctor mentioned briefly why the inquest was being held and that the testimony to be given would, it was hoped, throw some light on the identity of the man who had murdered Morgan Jenkins. He warned all witnesses that while the

same rules didn't hold as were observed in a court trial, still
witnesses would be under oath to speak the truth, and failure
to do so, if discovered, would lead to prompt prosecution
under the law relating to perjury.

The inquest proper then got under way, Sturven pointing
out the condition of the deceased, and his estimate of the
time of death. He spoke of the two bullets he had removed,
mentioned their caliber and the course they had taken after
entering Jenkins' body: one bullet, in Sturven's estimation,
probably brought instant death; the other while also fatal may
have, if fired first, allowed Jenkins a brief half hour or so of
life.

While the doctor was talking, Quist shifted in his seat a
little and glanced at Tom Jenkins. Jenkins sat, listening to
the doctor, not the slightest sign of emotion on his features;
he was holding his feelings in good check. Quist turned in his
chair and glanced back. Some half dozen rows to the rear sat
Camilla Peters, her gaze fixed on Sturven. There was something of anxiety in her face and Quist supposed she was wondering whether or not her name would be brought up and
thus, connected with that of Cody Thatcher. Quist had not
mentioned to Sturven, or anybody else, the conversation between Thatcher and Morg Jenkins, overheard by Camilla
Peters a few days before. If the subject of the conversation
between the two men had been the "sleepering" of Terrapin
cattle, Quist reasoned there was no use confusing the minds
of the jury with any mention of stock rustling.

"Mr. Gregory Quist!" Sturven called.

Quist realized he was being brought to the stand in his
capacity of witness. He rose, went to the table where a clerk
administered the oath, then launched into his story of the
incidents that had taken place the day he visited Morgan Jenkins' cabin. A silence fell over the big room while he talked,
faces darkened angrily when he mentioned the finding of the
body of Jenkins and that of the dead dog. He concluded with
the story of the long walk to the Circle-H. Banning was the
next witness. He gave the time of Quist's arrival and departure
from the Circle-H the day Morgan was murdered. Somewhat
reluctantly, Sturven called Tom Jenkins to the stand. Jenkins
told how the news had been brought to him at the Terrapin
and how he had immediately set out for his father's cabin. His
findings agreed pretty much with those in the story Quist had
told.

Sheriff Nixon was next called as a witness and spoke of the
news being brought to him by Jake Currie, and related how
he had at once mounted and started for the old wolfer's cabin,

stopping off at the Circle-H to hear Quist's story; on his arrival at Jenkins' cabin, he had found Tom Jenkins already there. Other minor witnesses were called: the undertaker, men who had talked to Morg Jenkins the last time he had been seen alive in Hyperion. No one, it appeared, had heard of any threat to Morg Jenkins' life, nor had the old man mentioned any enemy with whom he expected any sort of trouble.

The foreman of the jury asked a few questions which were relatively unimportant, doing more to establish his self-importance in his position than anything else, then Sturven stated that such evidence as was possessed had all been given, and the jury retired to a small room at the rear to reach its decision. A buzz of conversation once more broke out in the hall, but was silenced when Sturven gaveled for quiet and announced that he had an important announcement to make: Mr. Chris Hamilton, owner of the Circle-H Ranch, was offering a reward of five thousand dollars for information leading to the capture, dead or alive, of the man who had killed Morgan Jenkins.

Voices again filled the hall. No one left his seat. In view of the testimony given and that it was already past dinnertime, the audience felt the jury would not remain out very long. And the audience proved to be correct; within fifteen minutes the jury had returned with its findings: the verdict rendered, stripped of all legal verbiage, was to the effect that Morgan Jenkins had come to his death as a result of rifle bullets being fired into his body by some person unknown. The jury foreman added that Sheriff Bard Nixon be at once advised to take immediate steps toward the apprehension of the murderer. Sturven thanked the jury for its services and the inquest was finished.

Chairs banged through the hall, feet shuffled, while a large share of the audience tried to be first in gaining the outdoors and escaping the confining closeness of the hall. The crowd bunched up at the double-doored exit, and Nixon ordered his deputy to see what he could do about preserving a little more order, before somebody got trampled on. Some of the men in the room were leaving by the open windows in the side walls. The jury members had been first to realize this way of departure and were already, possibly, lined up at some bar discussing the testimony that had been given and speculating on the identity of Jenkins' killer.

Banning and Rick were preparing to lift the chair holding Chris Hamilton and carry it out to the waiting buckboard when Tracy interposed, "Why not wait until this crowd is out of here? It will only be more difficult if you start now."

"That's right, Tracy," Chris growled. "It ain't once a month

I get in to visit with folks, and now Brasadero's in a rush to get me back. Just hold your horses a mite."

The hall gradually emptied. Only Tracy and Chris Hamilton were still seated. The men were on their feet, stretching their legs. Tom Jenkins was pacing back and forth at one side, his face set in the same stolid lines. Cody Thatcher was bending over Tracy's chair, talking in a low voice. Rick rolled a cigarette and passed the "makin's" to Quist. A match was scratched; blue smoke spiraled about their heads. Banning, Hamilton and the sheriff were engaging in futile speculations regarding Morg Jenkins' murderer. Sturven was arranging papers at the small table and making notations with a stub of lead pencil.

Steps sounded at the rear of the hall, which was by now emptied of all except the small group near the front. Nixon looked around and saw his deputy approaching. "Joe," he ordered his deputy, "close them doors. We're visitin' a mite." Joe nodded and said he guessed he'd go get his dinner if the sheriff didn't need him for a while. "Go ahead," Nixon said. "Then you'll be finished by the time I'm ready to eat."

The deputy departed, closing the doors behind him. Sturven approached Nixon, "Well, Bard, you heard the jury's recommendations—take immediate steps to apprehend the murderer."

Nixon glared at the doctor. "Creepin' buzzards! What do you want me to do—pull him outten my Stet hat?"

"It's your problem, Bard. I wish you luck."

"But I ain't the least idea where to start," Nixon pointed out.

"It's not my business to tell you," Sturven said. He turned to Hamilton, "Long spell since I've seen you, Chris. How are the legs these days?"

"Like two lengths of ice, Doc," Chris growled. "What you think I keep 'em wrapped in blankets all the time for?"

"If you can feel the cold, maybe life is returning to 'em."

Chris said, "Bosh! You know better'n that—only you wouldn't tell me the truth." His voice softened somewhat, "Doc, why'n't you ride out and visit with me some day. Ain't no need you keepin' away just because I'm a hopeless case . . ."

What else was said, Quist didn't hear as the sheriff cut in, "Greg, I wish you'd help me a mite on this Jenkins' killing. You heard Chris offer a reward of five thousand dollars. Maybe you can make your stay here pay off after all."

"I came here for the Canfield business," Quist said. "I'd like to get that cleared up, if possible."

"Cripes! Aren't you interested in money?"

"I certainly am," Quist smiled, "but I like to do one job at a time. I was hired to find the Canfield killer. I can't get my pay until I do. Nope, Canfield comes first."

"Canfield!" Chris Hamilton, who had been listening, snapped disdainfully. "You'll never get any place on that, Quist. It's all done and finished with. Take my advice and forget it. If you want to get your teeth into something though, take out after Morg's killer. You'll never catch the man who killed Nash Canfield."

"On the contrary, Mr. Hamilton," Quist said quietly, "I figure there's a showdown due, right *pronto.*"

"You mean to say you've uncovered something?" Nixon demanded.

"I'm quite sure I have."

A trace of belligerence crept into Nixon's voice. "Now don't you go off half-cocked, Greg, with a lot of wild guesses. It's easy for a stranger to make enemies in the Gunsight country."

"I've realized that for quite a spell," Quist said dryly. "I've been bucked at every turn. Everybody I've talked to has concealed something, until I managed to work it out of them, for fear I'd suspect them or their friends. There seems to be a feeling that anyone born with the name of Hamilton is to be protected——"

"We're still waitin' to hear what you've got," Nixon said testily. "Do you want to talk now?"

"If you'd like to hear what I've got to say," Quist nodded.

Cody Thatcher had moved partly away from Tracy. He paused awkwardly, then said, "Do you mind if I stay and listen? I'm no law officer, Quist, and I'm not related to the Hamiltons . . ." He hesitated as though about to add "yet," then said instead, "but I'm as curious as the next man."

Quist appeared to consider a moment, then shrugged his shoulders. "If nobody else has any objection, Cody, I haven't. Eventually, you'll hear it all, anyway. Sure thing, stay if you like."

"Cut out the palaverin'," Chris Hamilton snapped, "and get to your story, Quist." He smiled sourly, "Tell you what I'll do. You heard me offer a reward for the capture of Morg's killer. I'll give you another five thousand if you can name the man who shot Canfield."

Quist's topaz eyes narrowed. "I won't hold you to that offer, Mr. Hamilton. You see, I know you're the man who did that shooting."

Chapter XXI : DEFINITE PROOF

For a minute all they could do was stare in bewilderment at Quist. At the far end of the hall, noises from the street penetrated the thick double doors but faintly. Within the long room no word was spoken until Tracy finally found her voice, "Greg! Do you realize what you're saying? How could Dad——"

Rick said, "Good Lord, Greg! You can't mean Dad——"

Protests from the others drowned out the remarks. Thatcher, Tom Jenkins, Banning, Nixon were all engaged in trying to impress on Quist just how wrong he was, that Chris Hamilton was unable to ride or walk. Sturven said, "You're forgetting, Quist, that Chris is paralyzed, and is unable——"

"Chris Hamilton has fooled a lot of people the past year and more," Quist stated. His words carried so much assurance that the others turned to Hamilton sitting silent in his chair, his bearded face working with angry emotion.

Tracy said, "Dad, you make it clear to Greg that——"

"I'll make it clear, all right," Hamilton growled in a disgusted tone. "Of all the fool talk I ever heard, this takes the jack pot. Quist, you'd better pick up your string of spools and slope back to El Paso where they swallow such guff. It don't go down, here."

"I'll have to force it down, then," Quist said tersely. "I don't bluff easy, and your bluff has run out, where I'm concerned. You can walk—I don't know how well—and you can ride."

Hamilton sneered. "Got proof of that, have you, Mr. Tinpot Detective?"

"Enough to convince me. Sure, I don't doubt you were paralyzed at one time, after your accident, but that paralysis wore off in time. That first day I met you, out to the Circle-H, and saw you sitting wrapped in blankets on your gallery, you had all my sympathy. Remember, there were a great many flies buzzing around that day. One lighted on your right knee and, I saw you unconsciously, move that leg slightly, to chase it away, though you'd stated there was no strength or feeling in your legs——"

"Dam'dest nonsense I ever heard!" Hamilton snarled. The others had fallen silent now.

Quist went on, "A little later I shot a gopher for you. That was an excuse to get your gun and pretend to drop it. You thought I was merely clumsy when I banged you on the knee with the stock, but it hurt like hell, didn't it, Mr. Hamilton? I'm sorry about that, but I had to find out if there was any feeling in your legs. Oh, it hurt all right. You went white, but you covered up well, trying to pretend you were angry because I'd used your gun without permission——"

"Enough of such talk," Hamilton exclaimed furiously. "By God, if I had a gun on me, I'd put a stop to your nonsense——"

"Call it nonsense if you like," Quist cut swiftly in. "You know I'm right. As for riding, four days ago when I started for Morg Jenkins' place, I saw a rider quite some distance ahead of me on the trail to the Circle-H. I figure he must have caught sight of me, because he was sure quirting hell out of his pony when I last saw him. I stopped at your place and talked a spell. You were that rider. There was a bronc in your corral that had been rode hard. While I was talking to you, we both heard a slight metallic sound which you blamed on your rifle—said it was slipping from the arm of the chair. But you'd moved one of your legs again—and I recognized the sound a spur rowel makes when it rolls across a floor. I wasn't fooled then, and you're not going to fool other people any longer. I don't know how many of your outfit is aware of your real condition, but I think Banning knows. The night I made that walk from Jenkins' cabin, Brasadero was in the bunkhouse. He's supposed to act as your nurse and helper, so I reckon he knows you're right capable of taking care of yourself if you have to. How about it, Brasadero?"

Banning could only stare at Quist for a moment. Finally, he said hoarsely, "You're—you're crazy, Quist."

"We'll see," Quist went on. "The evening of the day Canfield was killed, Tracy was making her way home after being knocked from her saddle. She saw her father ride past, but in her half-conscious condition, she laid it to delirium. Mr. Hamilton, it was you who went to the Terrapin and shot Nash Canfield, wasn't it?"

Silence filled the room. Hamilton faced Quist defiantly like an old buffalo bull at bay. The others were speechless, waiting for Hamilton to deny Quist's accusations. Hamilton's chin came up, his eyes hard on Quist's. "You can't prove I went to the Terrapin that night, Quist."

Quist smiled thinly. "You're stubborn. You told me yourself you were there—no, wait it was just a slip of the tongue. Do you remember the day I was questioning you about Canfield's movements that day? Except for a few words, your story was practically the same as the others I've heard. But in speaking of your suppositions, after he got home, you made one bad slip. You said, 'He finished one bottle and had a couple of drinks out of another.' How did you know one bottle wasn't already empty when he reached home? How did you know that he hadn't uncorked the fresh bottle before he got home? But, no, you were very definite in your statement, and you couldn't have been so definite if you hadn't been at the Terrapin, a witness to Canfield's actions."

Hamilton swallowed hard and glared at Quist. His voice shook a little. "The court records of the Canfield trial——"

"I've read those records," Quist cut in swiftly. "They contain nothing that says in what order Canfield drank from those bottles. Only a man who had witnessed that drinking could know that."

Tracy left her chair to drop on her knees before Hamilton. "Dad! It's not true. Make Greg see it isn't true!"

Hamilton gazed fondly at his daughter, his grizzled features working with emotion, then raised his head and glanced around, seeing in the faces of the others their belief in his guilt. When he could control his voice, he said softly to Tracy. "You sit down, girl, and listen to what I got to say." Tracy resumed her seat at his side. Hamilton spoke to Quist, grudging admiration in his eyes. "You're a right smart hombre, Greg Quist. If I had to be licked, and I know I am, I'm glad it took a good man to do it." He cut short Quist's reply, and faced the others. "Yes, I'm able to ride, once I'm in a saddle, and walk, too, though the walking isn't so good since that night. I reckon I'd better make a clean breast of it. It's true. I killed Nash Canfield."

His gnarled fingers fumbled with tobacco and brown cigarette papers while he talked. Quist struck a match for him. "Time was, after my accident," Hamilton said, "when I didn't think I'd ever fork a bronc again. Then, gradual-like, I commenced to get better, but that was after I'd got peeved at Doc Sturven and told him he needn't make any more visits, as he wa'n't doing me any good. Then I began to improve. It seemed too good to be true so I just told Brasadero, at first. I made it up with him to give Tracy and Rick a real surprise some day. I'd practice riding and walking, when they weren't around, and keep at it until I got real good and could sit a saddle like formerly, then I'd spring it on 'em and watch the looks on their faces."

Chris Hamilton smiled ruefully and exhaled a cloud of cigarette smoke from between bearded lips. "Oh, it was to be a prime surprise for my two kids. Tracy was at the Terrapin.

Rick was working out on the range most days, and nights he mostly rode into Hyperion to see Camilla Peters. Sure, the rest of the hands knew what I was doing, and they kept quiet so as to help with the surprise when it was ready. I don't know as they're absolutely certain it was me killed Canfield. They never asked and I never said. But they ain't dumb and they know I was away from the Circle-H that night. They're loyal as hell, though, and they'd do anything to protect me and mine——"

"Dad," Rick protested, "you should have told us."

"Mebbe so, son. Fact remains, I didn't. Well, once I was able to get into a saddle with Brasadero's help, my riding came back fast. Usually I stayed close to the Circle-H buildings in my riding. Brasadero or one of the other boys kept a watch, in case Tracy or Rick was to arrive, so I could be warned before they got there. That applied to other folks as well." He broke off to speak to Quist. "Yes, you nearly caught me the other day. I spied you from a hilltop and sloped fast for home."

"I had an idea it was you," Quist nodded, "particularly when I heard the sound of your spur rowel that day."

Hamilton went on. "Like I say, my riding was improving every day, though it was harder to walk. I could only make to step out short distances. Meanwhile, life for Tracy with Canfield was getting worse all the time." Chris drew a long sigh. "Well, I decided something had to be done about it, and it looked like I was the man for the job. Tracy came here one day and said that Canfield was started on another of his jags and that the men hadn't been paid. I made her promise to get Canfield out of bed early the next morning and insist that he go to Hyperion for the payroll money. I figured once the hands were paid, they'd all head for town. I didn't figure Wagner would remain behind; besides, I didn't have my plan all worked out yet. I asked Tracy to come here when she got Canfield started for town, explaining I wanted her to carry a note to the Rocking-B for me. That morning, Tracy did as requested. After she'd left for the Rocking-B, Rick, who had gone to Hyperion that day, came home and told me he'd met Canfield in town and had a fight with him. Right then, Rick had murder in his mind, and I knew I had to act before he done something rash. I asked Rick where Canfield was. Rick said he had started for the Terrapin."

Hamilton drew a long breath. "It looked like the time was ripe. The Terrapin crew would be away. Tracy would be at the Rocking-B. I figured Rick would go back to Hyperion, and he started for there all right. As soon as he left, I had

Brasadero bring up a horse for me. He wanted to come along, but I convinced him I could manage, then if anything went wrong, he wouldn't be incriminated."

"In short," Sturven put in, "you constituted yourself judge, jury and executioner—took things in your own hands———"

"Canfield deserved death if ever a man did," Hamilton said grimly. "Well, I made the ride to the Terrapin. It wasn't complete dark when I got there. There were no lights. I never dreamed of Wagner being in the bunkhouse. I didn't dare ride right up to the house, though, so I dismounted a short distance off and left my pony under a live oak. Then I walked to the back of the house and entered by the rear, through the wing where the bedrooms are. Did I say 'walked?' It was getting to the house that broke my legs down. They were weaker than I'd figured. I fell down a couple of times, and there was a heap of pain in my spine. I could just about make it and that's all. I sneaked into the hall, opened the door a slit, and peeked into the main room. It still wasn't total dark, and I saw Canfield in the room, finishing off a bottle and talking to himself."

Hamilton paused to collect his thoughts. "Sudden I remembered that Canfield's six-shooter hung in the hall where I was standing, and I got the idea to shoot him with his own gun and then fixing things to make it look like suicide. With my bad legs and the darkness of that hall, it took me a mite of time to locate the gun. When next I looked into that room it was dark, but I could hear Canfield stumbling around and knocking things over. Finally he got a blaze lit in the fireplace, and I saw him get a bottle from the mantel-piece. He held it against the light from the fire and then pulled the cork; he took a couple of drinks from the bottle and sat down again. I waited a spell, hating like the devil to shoot from ambush, like you might say, but still working to convince myself it was the only thing to do. Maybe if my legs had worked better, I'd just walked in and let him have it. Or I might have given him his own gun and an even break."

Hamilton broke off. "No need going into that. About the time I got ready to shoot, Rick arrived, and I thought my plans were spoiled. There's no use repeating what passed between Rick and Canfield—how Canfield flew into a rage and then got took with one of his fits and so on. Then, Rick started for the doctor———"

Cody Thatcher broke in. "I never knew that Rick was there before Canfield was killed."

"He was," Hamilton said shortly, "though that part never come out at the trial. Well, with Rick gone and Canfield throwing himself around on the floor, I'd never have a better chance. I opened the hall door farther, leveled Canfield's six-shooter and pulled the trigger. The only light in the room was from the fireplace, and with all his lurching and jerking around on the floor, he made a bad target, but I got him with my first shot. I'd intended to go in and place the gun in his hand, but I sudden discovered my legs were too weak to chance getting there. So I give the weapon a quick toss into the room, figuring to have it land close to his body."

Hamilton paused and drew a long breath. "I still hate to think of the next few moments. That's when I really got a shock. Oh, the gun landed near his body all right. I watched it spinning around, with the firelight gleaming on the metal. Then there was a movement and a hand stretched down to the gun. I raised my eyes and saw—Tracy." The words ended in something like a groan. "I'd been so occupied with watching Canfield twisting around on the floor and trying to get a good shot at him, that I never noticed Tracy come in. But there she was, with the door open behind her, and I heard hoofbeats and realized Rick was returning. Figuring he'd take care of her, I worked my way back into the bedroom wing of the house, just as Trunkfoot entered by the other rear door. Still hoping they'd think it was suicide and that Tracy would explain about picking up the gun, I sneaked out of the house and made my way back to the horse, though I had to crawl part of that distance. My legs wouldn't support me no more. Once I'd hauled myself up into the saddle, I walked my pony quiet until I was well out of earshot, then I lit out for the Circle-H."

He looked resentfully at Quist. "And then you had to come and heat up a cold trail. Oh, yes, I can ride and the use of my legs is again coming back fast, too. There ain't any doubt"— with mocking grimness—"that I'll be able to walk to the gallows when the time comes."

Cody Thatcher moved quickly over to Chris Hamilton, reaching for his hand. "Chris, regardless what anybody says, you did the right thing. I'll stand by you, and I'll bet my life the whole Gunsight country will do the same. You'll never go to the gallows for the Canfield killing."

Chapter XXII : CONCLUSION

Chris Hamilton took Thatcher's hand and thanked him. Others voiced similar sentiments. Tracy's eyes looked misty. Hamilton patted her knee and said, "Don't you worry, girl. At least, I won't have to keep up this hypocrisy no longer." With some irritation he yanked the blankets from his legs and bundled them into his lap, displaying his trousered legs and booted feet. "I won't have to keep my pins wropped up no longer, either." He shot a quick glance at Quist. "Well, Mr. Railroad Dick, you got your killer——"

"Wait a minute," Quist protested, assuming a surprised look, "who said anything about killing? I haven't claimed you murdered Canfield. I only said you shot him."

"Don't that amount to the same thing?" Nixon demanded.

Quist shook his head. "That shot wasn't fatal. I'll leave it to Doc Sturven. Doc, what did you tell me, the other day?"

Sturven frowned. "We-ell, it's true that shot wasn't fatal in itself. It was the shot plus Canfield's poor physical condition. Had I been there at the time, I might have saved his life even then."

"Cripes!" Nixon growled, while Hamilton listened in surprise. "It amounts to the same thing. It was the shot brought on death. Chris, I hate like hell to do it, but there's my duty——"

"Hold your horses a minute, Bard," Quist interrupted. "That shot didn't bring on death."

The sheriff snorted in irritation. "Now, you're talking in riddles, Greg. Try and make sense, will you? If that bullet didn't kill Canfield, maybe you can tell me what did."

"Sure I can," Quist said quietly. "Canfield was poisoned."

Surprised exclamations left his listeners' lips. "Poisoned!" Thatcher said incredulously. "How do you know?"

Quist explained. "For some time I went along on the theory that Canfield had been killed with a gun bullet. People had told me how he had those convulsions from too much drinking, so I didn't think anything about that. Then, Tracy put me on the right trail. She was telling me about arriving at her house the night of Canfield's death, and seeing him throwing himself about on the floor. She thought it was from drinking, but when she mentioned that Canfield had once jerked himself into a sort of bow form, his back arched and

168

his body supported only on his head and heels, it gave me a clue——"

"What poison was it," Sturven demanded excitedly, "strychnine?"

"Strychnine," Quist nodded. "I'd once seen a man die who had taken strychnine by mistake. His body assumed that same bow-like form during his convulsions, so I figured——"

"Opisthotonos," Sturven said, abruptly.

Quist paused. "What was that?"

"It's a medical term," Sturven said, "to describe the spasm which forces a human body into that arched position. It's one of the symptoms of strychnine poisoning. Also of certain forms of extreme hysteria. Blast my soul!" he went on in self-condemnation. "If I hadn't been blind I'd have seen something in Canfield's body to make me suspect poisoning. But there was the gunshot wound, and I knew his condition. It's not surprising I failed——" He broke off, turning to Chris Hamilton. "You were there when Canfield was undergoing his convulsions. Do you remember, Chris, if his eyes bulged and his face got contorted? Did Canfield act as though he was being suffocated?"

Hamilton's brow knitted in thought. "Near as I can remember, considering the light in that room, that's about it. I thought he was having one of his drunken attacks——"

"Look here," Cody Thatcher proposed suddenly, "an inquiry in the stores around town might tell who bought strychnine a short time previous to Canfield's death. 'Course, the storekeepers can't be expected to remember, but there's a chance——"

"That won't be necessary," Quist cut in. "I know where the poison came from." Instantly he was deluged with questions. "The first day I visited Morg Jenkins' cabin, I saw a can of it on a shelf with his foodstuffs——"

"Sure enough!" Banning exclaimed. 'Wolfers always keep strychnine on hand for fixing their poison baits. But why should Morg have killed Canfield——?"

The words were scarcely out of his mouth when Tom Jenkins rushed at Banning, seizing him by the throat. For a few moments, Jenkins' speech was chaotic with anger, then, ". . . you know almighty well Banning, that my dad never killed——"

Immediately he and Banning were the center of a seething group of men, as Quist, Thatcher, Nixon and Rick fought to separate the two men. Finally, Banning stood back gasping. Jenkins immediately rushed at Quist one fist swinging. Quist caught the man's wrist in his left hand, gave it a sudden twist that threw Jenkins off balance, then caught his other wrist in a vise-like grip that Jenkins couldn't break, struggle as he might.

"Take it easy, Tom, take it easy," Quist said sharply. "It's one thing to show loyalty to your father's memory, and I can admire that but it's not going to do any good for you to go off half-cocked until you know what's what."

Quist continued in this strain for a few moments and finally Jenkins subsided. He cast an apologetic glance toward Tracy who hadn't moved from the seat next to her father's through all the tumult, and mumbled something about being sorry. Quist released him and he moved off to one side, his dark eyes smoldering.

There was an instant's silence before Cody Thatcher spoke, "If Morg Jenkins didn't feed Canfield that poison, I'm craving to know who did."

A thin smile crossed Quist's lips. "Thatcher, you should know better than ask a thing like that, when you already know."

"What do you mean?" Thatcher demanded.

"It was you who gave Canfield that strychnine." Startled comments followed that statement, as every face swung toward Thatcher.

"Me?" Thatcher stiffened. "You're crazy as a loon, Quist! What reason would I have for killing Nash Canfield?"

"He cheated you on the deal for Terrapin land. You held a grudge on that account. He married the girl you had hoped to marry. You thought if you could get rid of Canfield you'd still have a chance of not only getting the girl and your land back, but you'd come in for a share of the money Canfield left——"

"That's the most idiotic thing I ever heard." Thatcher's face went white, then red with anger. He commenced to stammer denials. Abruptly, Sheriff Nixon reached over and jerked the six-shooter from Thatcher's holster. Thatcher turned on the sheriff. "What's the idea of that, Bard?"

"If Greg makes his accusation stick," the sheriff said, thrusting the gun in his trousers waistband, "you're under arrest, Cody. I just ain't takin' any chances."

Thatcher started to mouth a furious protest, then paused. With an effort he gained control of his feelings and managed a cool, contemptuous shrug of his shoulders. "Have it that way, if you like. But just remember that Quist hasn't yet produced any proof of what he charges. It's nothing but surmise, guesswork. He's cooked up the whole business in his mind, figuring the rest of you people will believe him, because he proved himself correct where Chris was concerned. Actually, he knows he's licked on what he came here to do. Isn't that right, Quist?"

"You're dead wrong, Thatcher. Remember, I could have let Chris stand charged with murder had I wanted to. . . . Let's go back a way. Thatcher, you didn't welcome my arrival in this country, did you?"

"Not for one minute," Thatcher snapped. "Nobody else——"

"Why?" Quist interrupted.

Thatcher cast a quick glance toward Tracy. "Well"—the words came a bit awkwardly—"to tell the truth, I'd suspected that Tracy—or Rick—killed Canfield. I was afraid you might learn that——"

"You were so anxious to keep me away from the Gunsight country that you sent Homer Pritchett to El Paso to scare me into staying there."

"That's a lie!" Thatcher said quickly.

"Is it?" Quist's voice was scornful. "Suppose I told you that Pritchett had a few minutes to talk before he died, and that he had stated that you loaned him your rifle to take to El Paso? He was to locate me and do his best to throw a scare into me. Later, when that didn't work, you had Pritchett hire Webb Bascom to kill me."

Thatcher's eyes shifted nervously. "I—I——" Then with sudden decision and a certain amount of bravado, "All right, I'll admit it. There's not much you can do to me, though. I was only trying to protect Tracy and Rick. Pritchett's dead. You've no proof of his confession."

"I didn't say definitely he'd confessed to anything. I merely stated a supposition, and you jumped to conclusions," Quist said. Thatcher crimsoned, as he realized his blunder. Quist continued, "You say you were trying to protect Tracy. You weren't afraid I might stumble on evidence of your 'sleepering' Terrapin calves, were you?"

"That's more of your lying!" Thatcher charged furiously.

Quist shook his head. "Not this time. We've got proof. Tracy has been spying on you and your men for quite a spell. I think one of the first things the sheriff had better do is round up your crew, and learn what's what. I'd not be surprised if other outfits had lost stock too."

"I'll do just that, by Hanner!" Nixon snapped. "Thatcher, you——"

Thatcher interrupted, "All right, it's true." He cast a shame-faced glance toward Tracy, shrugged his shoulders and tried to brazen it out. "I only planned to take enough stock to square up for what Canfield did to me on that land deal. You can't blame me too much for that. . . . But all this is not the point. Quist, you're beating around the bush." He managed a confident, sneering smile. "You've not yet offered one bit of proof that I poisoned Canfield. I defy you to state how I could have contrived to give him the poison."

Quist laughed shortly. "In the first place, Thatcher, you didn't dare buy strychnine in town, for fear some storekeeper would remember your getting it. You dropped in on Morg Jenkins one day and saw that he had a good supply of those deadly little crystals. There was your chance. Morg was sick, and under pretense of caring for him, you watched your chance and stole what strychnine you needed. Next you put the poison in a bottle of whisky and waited for the opportunity to give it to Canfield. Your chance came that day when he was drunk in Hyperion. He took the bottle home, drank from it and died. Chris's shooting of Canfield was something you hadn't foreseen; that merely made things safer for you——"

"You're making up a pack of lies!" Thatcher charged furiously.

"Just a minute, Quist." Doc Sturven frowned. "Strychnine is bitter to the taste. Don't you think Canfield would have detected that bitterness when he drank the whisky?"

"Certainly he would," Thatcher grasped at another straw. "Your whole case falls to pieces, Quist."

Quist ignored the man and turned to Sturven. "Doc, do you think Canfield, drunk as he was, would notice that bitter taste, when he was already so steeped in liquor? His wits were completely addled."

The doctor nodded and remained silent.

Quist continued, "Later, Thatcher, when you saw your chance you stole what was left of that poisoned whisky from the sheriff's office, and broke the bottle. That, just in case somebody remembered you giving Canfield that bottle, that day in Hyperion. With Canfield shot and the poisoned whisky gone, you thought you'd covered your tracks——"

"God! I never heard such a made-up story in my life," Thatcher sneered. "All right, let's take it into court and see how your story stands up with a jury. I'd never be convicted —not for a minute—because, Quist, you haven't one shred of proof to back up your wild yarn. It's all one hundred per cent imagination."

"If he hasn't got proof, that's right smart guesswork," Chris Hamilton growled.

"It's guesswork," Quist admitted quietly.

A wave of relief swept across Thatcher's face, but before he could speak, Quist continued, "Of course, we could have Canfield's body disinterred and examined. I'd stake anything I have that an analysis would produce traces of strychnine. But of course that might not convict Thatcher either, and I don't think it's going to be necessary."

He paused a moment. "You know, if a man is to be hung for murder, I don't think it makes much difference which murder he is hung for."

"What in the devil are you talking about, Greg?" Nixon demanded.

Quist smiled, "Don't rush me and I'll explain. The day I first met Morg Jenkins I was telling him about the way Canfield died—the way his body contorted into that bow-like shape, and so on. I don't think it registered on Morg right then, but later he probably got to thinking about it. He knew the effect strychnine poisoning produces, I imagine. After I'd left he probably got to thinking about the time Thatcher had stayed with him. One thing led to another, and he deduced that Thatcher had poisoned Canfield——"

"More of your damnable lies!" Thatcher violently pounded one fist into the palm of his other hand.

"And so," Quist went on, ignoring the interruption, "Morg decided to do something about it. To himself he likely admitted that Canfield's death was a good thing for all concerned. At the same time he figured Thatcher shouldn't go scot free, though he was willing to give him another chance. He warned Thatcher to pull up stakes and get out—incidentally, Thatcher, I have proof on that point. Thatcher promised to leave the country, but at the first opportunity he went up to Morg Jenkins' cabin and shot the old man to death."

Thatcher swallowed hard. His face was ashen white. "That —that's another lie you can't prove," he said hoarsely.

Tom Jenkins took a quick step toward him, then hesitated uncertainly, glancing toward Quist. Quist said, "I think I can prove it, Thatcher." Then to the others, "It is well-known that the firing pin of a gun leaves its own distinctive marking on a ca'tridge. Some firing pins make deeper dents than others, some are a trifle off-center, and so on. But no two firing pins leave identical markings on shells. I've already talked this over with your local gunsmith; he'll back up what I say."

Quist thrust one hand into his coat pocket and drew out five exploded shells. "One of these shells has an identifying scratch on it, made by me. It came from the gun that fired on

me in El Paso. The other four shells I picked up at Morg
Jenkins' cabin. All five came from the same gun—Cody
Thatcher's .38-55 Winchester rifle." In the stunned silence
that followed the words, Quist added softly, "I don't think
you need further proof that Thatcher murdered Morg Jenkins."

The others jerked their heads around to look at Thatcher
whose guilt was now written plainly on his ashen features.
Sheriff Nixon bellowed indignantly, "Greg! You never told
me you found them shells——"

For just an instant Nixon was off-guard, and Thatcher
seized desperately the chance offered. The murderer's right
hand darted to the gun in Nixon's waistband, and the next
instant he had the room covered, the muzzle of the six-shooter
swinging in a wide arc to bear on all present.

"Up with 'em!" Thatcher snarled. "I'll plug the first man
who tries to draw!"

Arms darted into the air, Quist's with the rest, Quist saying sternly, "You can't get away with it, Thatcher. You'd
best give up."

"I'll get away with it all right." Thatcher's short laugh was
harsh, ominous. "My horse is out front. I'm leaving. You'll
all stay right where you are—if you want Tracy to stay alive.
Try to rush me, and I'll plug her first."

Tom Jenkins hadn't heard the last words. Through the insane red fury that had suddenly enveloped his senses, but
one fact stood clear: his father's killer was about to escape.
Throwing caution to the wind, Tom lowered his arms and
reached for his six-shooter.

Despite his threat to shoot Tracy first, Thatcher's reaction
was involuntary. White fire spurted from his weapon. With
his gun only half-drawn from holster, Tom gave an agonized
cry and pitched to the floor where a small pool of blood commenced to gather beneath his head.

Swiftly, Thatcher's six-shooter swept back to bear on Quist,
but in that same instant, old Chris Hamilton, with a quick
flip of one sinewy wrist, had grabbed the gathered blanket
from his lap and sent the unwieldly missile flying through the
air toward Thatcher. The blanket fell far short of reaching
its goal, but it brought a momentary distraction, causing
Thatcher to miss his shot.

Quist had already thrown himself to one side, drawing
from his shoulder holster and firing as he moved. Three
times, flame and black powdersmoke thundered from his
Colt's .44, while Thatcher's shot was smashing into the
plastered wall at Quist's rear.

Thatcher staggered in mid-stride, the impact of Quist's savage fire jerking him off balance before knocking him from his feet. As he crashed down, reflex action sent a final bullet flying harmlessly from his weapon, before his nerveless grasp opened and the gun clattered to the plank floor.

Smoke haze swirled through the room, stinging eyes and nostrils. The echoes of the heavy detonations died to silence, though some dust still sifted down from the shaken rafters overhead. Quist glanced quickly around. Tracy had already left her chair and was kneeling at Jenkins' side. Rick, Banning, and Nixon stood as though frozen, arms at their sides holding half-lifted six-shooters. Quist spoke terse, grim words, "You can holster those guns. Thatcher's finished. *I know.*"

Chris Hamilton was standing a bit unsteadily, one hand bracing himself on chair arm. "Fastest shooting I ever saw," he growled. "I reckon it's a good thing you were here, Greg Quist." A trifle weakly, he lowered himself to his seat.

"I'm not forgetting that you helped a lot, Chris," Quist said.

Nixon had started to apologize for his carelessness in allowing Thatcher to get the gun, when a pounding came at the closed doors. Excited voices were heard from the street. "I'd better go see that crowd doesn't get in here," Nixon said, and hurried down the hall.

Sturven had already joined Tracy, at Tom Jenkins' side. Followed by Banning and Rick, Quist went to Thatcher and examined the still, limp form. The man was quite dead. The space of a handsbreadth could have covered the place over Thatcher's heart where Quist's .44 slugs had ripped in. Quist's voice sounded weary as he said to Rick, "Well, son, the job's finished." He didn't mention Camilla's name, but Rick knew what he meant when he added, "You're free to do what you wanted to now."

He brushed away Rick's thanks and crossed to Tracy who was standing alone, against one wall, a short distance from Jenkins' unconscious form being attended by Doctor Sturven. Quist said, "How bad is Tom hurt, Tracy?"

The girl's voice shook a little. "He was pretty lucky. The bullet just ploughed a ragged furrow through the flesh above one ear. Doc Sturven says he'll be all right, before long." Quist said that that was good news, and for a minute silence fell between them. Tracy said finally, "Well, Greg, you've done what you came here to do. You'll never realize how much we're indebted to you." Quist told her a trifle roughly to "forget it." Tracy said, "There are some things I can never forget . . . But, now what?"

There was something wistful in Quist's smile. "From here

on out, I reckon Tom will be able to take care of you—or
you, him——"

"I mean, what will you do?"

"I'm needed in El Paso. There'll be other work . . ."

"But you'll come back here again some day," the girl insisted. "At least for a visit." Her velvety brown eyes, beneath
the hair of pale gold, held his gaze, almost against his will,
and one of her hands came out to touch his wrist.

Quist drew a deep breath and his voice wasn't quite steady
when he replied, "Tracy, I don't think there's anything in this
world that could keep me from returning here, some day——"

And then the doors of the hall opened and a crowd from
the street, overcoming Nixon's objections, flowed into the big
room. Men pushed excitedly between Quist and Tracy, and as
he stepped back, Quist realized he was being forced farther
away from the girl with every instant that passed.